Caffeine Nig

Shadow of the Beast

Michael Fowler

Fiction aimed at the heart
and the head...

Published by Caffeine Nights Publishing 2016

Copyright © Michael Fowler 2016

Michael Fowler has asserted his right under the Copyright, Designs and Patents Act 1998 to be identified as the author of this work.

CONDITIONS OF SALE
All rights reserved. No part of this publication may be reproduced, stored in a retrieval system, or transmitted in any form or by any means, electronic, mechanical, photocopying, scanning, recording or otherwise, without the prior permission of the publisher.

This book has been sold subject to the condition that it shall not, by way of trade or otherwise, be lent, resold, hired out, or otherwise circulated without the publisher's prior consent in any form of binding or cover other than that in which it is published and without a similar condition including this condition being imposed on the subsequent purchaser.

All characters in this publication are fictitious and any resemblance to real persons, living or dead is purely coincidental.

Published in Great Britain by
Caffeine Nights Publishing
4 Eton Close
Walderslade
Chatham
Kent
ME5 9AT

www.caffeinenights.com

British Library Cataloguing in Publication Data.
A CIP catalogue record for this book is available from the British Library

ISBN: 978-1-910720-63-9

Also available as an eBook

Cover design by
Mark (Wills) Williams

Everything else by
Default, Luck and Accident

Michael Fowler was born and brought up in the Dearne Valley area of Yorkshire where he still lives with his wife.

At the age of 16 he left school with the ambition of going to art college but his parents' financial circumstances meant he had to find work and so he joined the police.

He has never regretted that decision, serving as a police officer for thirty-two years, both in uniform and in plain clothes, working in CID, and undercover in Vice Squad and Drug Squad, he retired as an Inspector in charge of a busy CID in 2006.

Since leaving, Michael has embarked on two careers: he is an established author with two crime series to his name, DS Hunter Kerr and DS Scarlett Macey. and has also co-written a true crime story.

He is a member of the Crime Writers Association and International Thriller Writers.

Michael has also found considerable success as an artist, receiving numerous artistic accolades. Currently, his work can be found in the galleries of Spencer Coleman Fine Arts at Lincoln and Stamford.

Find out more at www.mjfowler.co.uk

Also Like Michael on Facebook.

THE DS HUNTER KERR TITLES

HEART OF THE DEMON
COLD DEATH
SECRETS OF THE DEAD
COMING, READY OR NOT
BLACK & BLUE (e-book novella)
REAP WHAT YOU SOW (short story)

THE SCARLETT MACEY SERIES

SCREAM, YOU DIE

OTHER NOVELS

CHASING GHOSTS (short book)

NON-FICTION

SAFECRACKER (The true story of Britain's most infamous safe blower)

To Liz, my best friend, my shoulder to lean on, my one and only.

Shadow of the Beast

To Dorothy, with very best wishes

Michael Fowler

CHAPTER ONE

September 2009

Not that they would ever find anything here, nevertheless, he always went through his safety checks with precision before entering his home; listening before turning the key in the lock, cracking the door just a fraction to see if the cotton had been broken between the bottom of the door and the jamb, before opening it fully. Today was no different.

Once inside his small kitchen-diner he trained his eyes over the scrupulously clean kitchen surfaces and floor looking for the telltale marks of uninvited guests. Through the open door he could see into the lounge and he scoured the room to see if anything was out of place. Only when satisfied that no one had visited him would he let the knife rest back in his pocket and set his shopping down on the table. He knew some would say this was paranoia but carelessness gets you caught. And he'd already been caught once. The final part of his sequence was checking his house phone. There had been three calls while he'd been out – all of them from the same number. On the last call a message had been left and he dialled to retrieve it.

"Can you ring me please?' That's all the man had said before hanging up, but it had been delivered in such hurried fashion that it gave away the anxiousness in his voice. Breathing deeply, he deleted the call and then rang the number. It was picked up on the second ring.

"Have you seen this week's Chronicle?'

The voice was low yet forced and he guessed the man wasn't alone in the office. He could just visualise him sat at his desk, sweat starting to form on his brow, chewing on the quick of his index finger, like he always did when he was stressed.

"I have," he steadily replied. He was conscious of the still sluggish drawl in his voice even after all the years of therapy. It was a lasting reminder of his stroke; that and the slight limp to his right leg.

'They've started digging up the estate.'

'I know.'

'So what if they find them?'

'They won't.'

'I fucking hope not, or we're screwed.'

He couldn't miss the raised note in the man's voice now and sensed he was starting to panic. Catching his own racing heart, he replied 'Don't worry, they won't.' Then, with commanding tone he said, 'Don't do anything rash. Remember what I've always told you. Just carry on as normal and don't draw attention to yourself. We meet at the same place like we normally do—okay?'

There was a couple of seconds silence down the line before the man replied with a sigh, 'Yes, fine.'

'Good. And don't ring me unless it's absolutely urgent.'

Cutting the call and replacing the handset he took a long look in the mirror. As usual, saliva had trickled from the right side of his mouth onto his chin. Once upon a time it would have formed in his beard, but these days he had kept himself clean shaven; he had removed his beard before his release to add to his disguise. He wiped the dribble away with the back of his hand, canting his head and pursing his lips as he took another look at himself. He couldn't help but notice that the bags beneath his eyes had darkened this past week – a sign of the restless nights. He thought about the conversation he'd just ended and about what they had done together all those years ago. More important, he tried to recall how deep they had buried the bodies.

CHAPTER TWO

In her stocking-feet Dawn Leggate faced the long mirror in the hall. She checked herself, stepping up on tiptoes, turning slightly, tightening her tummy. She liked what she saw. She thought that the new white blouse was the ideal choice for her knee-length skirt and, although it was more than she usually paid for a work top, she had to admit it certainly gave her the look she was after. Pressing close to the mirror, Dawn finger-brushed back her auburn-tinted hair, and following a few seconds of further scrutiny finally decided she was happy with her appearance and made her way to the kitchen, beating a path to the kettle. She needed a coffee. Last night's garlic from the Italian still clung to her taste buds despite two swills of mouthwash. Grabbing the kettle, she shook it to check it held enough water and switched it on. Spooning coffee into a mug she looked at her watch. Seven twenty-five a.m. – in an hour and a half's time she had to be at Ecclesfield Police Station – she was carrying out a review of a murder investigation – a shooting on one of Sheffield's most notorious estates. The victim, Noel 'Sonny' Johnson, had been a well-known drug dealer, who had been ambushed outside his home six months ago and it bore all the hallmarks of an assassination by rival gang members. Dawn already knew from her pre-read material that the team investigating was pretty confident who had carried out the killing, but so far had been unable to get the hard evidence to put the perpetrators before court. Sure, arrests had been made, but everyone who had been nicked had kept tight-lipped, and the only evidence they had came from anonymous sources or informants and couldn't be used in court. It also hadn't helped that many of the significant witnesses were either scared of repercussions, or were anti-police and refusing to cooperate. The enquiry had put the Detective Superintendent running the investigation, together with the Force, under intense media scrutiny, as the spate of stories arising from the murder had likened the shooting to those occurring across the border in Manchester.

There had been pro-active work orchestrated in an effort to defend the Force's reputation; Crime Manager, Michael Robshaw, her live-in partner, had organised several press conferences, repeatedly stating 'that although shootings on the streets of Sheffield weren't new, they certainly shouldn't draw comparisons with the problems in Manchester', but it had done nothing to prevent damaging headlines, many of which centred on the inability of the police to get to grips with the upsurge of gang-related violence linked to drugs.

These last few months Dawn had seen him casting aside the evening paper with disgust and witnessed the pressure building up; his sleep pattern had become more and more restless. His tossing and turning frequently disturbed her, keeping her awake– worrying. Dawn had wanted to help him, and even though she had her own pressing work schedule, because of her previous experience of conducting reviews, she had suggested to Michael that she go through the mass of information collected and conduct an assessment of the enquiry to ensure every angle had been covered and feed that back to the press to encourage more positive stories. Although she knew she would be putting herself under the spotlight as well, she felt it would be worth it if it got Michael back to being his usual self again.

Opening the fridge for the milk she switched on the small TV beside it. She wanted to catch the local news to see if there were any traffic snarl-ups that would delay her journey. The last thing she wanted was to be late. Punctuality was one of her idiosyncrasies. As she added milk to her coffee she momentarily diverted her gaze to a free-standing mirror on the work surface, she checked her make-up. She needed to ensure that she'd hidden the crow's feet that had crept up on her this past year, while making sure she didn't look too brassy. As a Detective Superintendent she had a professional role-playing image to maintain. She had seen too many women in the job be the brunt of alpha-male banter because they'd put too much slap on their face, and she was buggered if she was going to be one of those women. Cocking her head, she checked that her eye shadow and lipstick were not too dark and then returned to making her coffee. This is when she thought about having a cigarette, even though it had been two years and almost nine months since her last one.

There had been many times since then when she had been tempted, especially following the ending of her marriage to that prick Jack. He had caused her all sorts of problems during their ensuing divorce but thanks to Michael's support she had resisted. The nearest she'd come to hitting the fags again had been five months ago. That night still haunted her. She and Michael had caught Jack stalking her, believing him to be the hooded serial killer she was chasing at the time. Not only scaring the wits out of her, it had made her the brunt of Force headquarters gossip for weeks and she still hadn't got over the pain of embarrassment he had heaped upon her professionally.

Suddenly her phone beeped: it was an incoming text. She scooped up her BlackBerry, detached it from its charger and activated the screen. It was Michael. At work. She read his text.

'Have you seen the news?'

She flicked her attention to the soundless TV. The picture showed a skinny male reporter standing in front of wire-mesh fencing. There was a large yellow security sign fastened to one of the gates and she recognised it as the entranceway to the construction site at Chapel Meadows; a supermarket giant was building a new distribution centre there. Dawn was aware that its construction should have gone ahead eighteen months ago but had met local controversy and there had been a public enquiry. Judgment had gone in the supermarket group's favour and three weeks ago the construction company had moved onto the land and begun clearing the site. This last week, driving past the place on her way to work, she had seen the landscape transformed, though not pleasing to the eye. There had been daily demolition of the derelict Victorian terracing taking place, and now they were starting on the old chapel, a large Gothic building, which, once upon a time, had been the hub of that community. Having frequently passed the boarded up, ugly fire-blackened building, she had to admit its demise wouldn't be a sad thing.

She picked up the TV remote and turned up the sound.

'We have some breaking news,' the young reporter began, 'I am here at the proposed multi-million-pound distribution centre that has caused much controversy here in Barnwell over the last eighteen months. Twenty minutes ago work stopped at this site after construction workers found human remains in the ruins of the old chapel behind me. It is not clear how long the remains have been there and the police have been contacted.'

For several seconds Dawn's eyes remained glued to the TV, even after the broadcaster announced that there would be an update later and that he was now returning you back to the studio.

Human remains! Why on earth haven't I been rung?

Setting down the TV remote, she speed-dialled a contact on her BlackBerry.

CHAPTER THREE

Surrounded by scum-topped puddles, shoulders hunched, hands tucked deep in his overcoat pockets, Detective Sergeant Hunter Kerr stood in the doorway of a Portakabin sheltering from the rain, staring out across an area the size of half a dozen football pitches which presently resembled a bomb-site. Among broken brickwork, roof tiles and trusses from demolished Victorian terracing stood a single white tent upon which he centred his bright blue eyes. Inside, forensic anthropologist Dr Anna Wilson was carrying out an examination of a human skull uncovered three hours ago by a JCB driver. The digger that had unearthed the remains hadn't been moved since the find and loomed over the tent, its open jawed bucket frozen in mid-air. As Hunter eyed it he couldn't help but think it looked like a mechanical dinosaur protecting its young.

Except for the driving rain, the scene before him was still. All work on the site had been halted three-and-a-half hours ago following the discovery of the skull. When he'd arrived he had found the demolition crew hovering around the human remains pestering Doctor Wilson and he'd had to order them to the cabin where he was now standing sentry until the forensic anthropologist's investigation was over. Now the workmen were seated around trestle-tables supping hot drinks, making the most of their time-out by telling not-so-politically-correct jokes that kept breaking into Hunter's concentration. On more than one occasion over the last couple of hours he'd had to fight back the urge to laugh and when he had been unable to resist a smirk he had ensured he'd kept his back to them in order to maintain a professional bearing. In between the jokes he'd been asked half a dozen times by the site foreman, 'How long are you going to be here? You do realise it's costing the firm money. 'All he'd been able to respond with was a shrug of the shoulders and the unhelpful response of, 'Until the doc's finished her examination nothing on this site moves.' He couldn't think of anything else to say. This wasn't what he was used to. In fact, he couldn't understand why he'd been called out to attend; not to oversee the excavation of ancient bones. As far as he was concerned this was a uniform job. Why Dawn Leggate had singled him out for babysitting an anthropologist playing at being Howard Carter, he'd no idea. Besides that, he had other jobs to do he was half way through sorting his desk and boxing up his old files in preparation for next month's move; he was presiding over the department's transfer to a state-of-the-art facility on the edge of Barnwell which would host the Force Training Department and the Major Investigation Team, of which he was a member. Purpose built for handling serious crime it was going to be a big departure for the squad. He had already viewed the huge air-conditioned room earmarked for the team and he couldn't wait to get in there. It was a far cry from their present accommodation in the outdated old sub-divisional headquarters that was always cold during the winter months and baking hot in summer.

A sharp pain in his toes brought back his thoughts – the cold had started to bite through his soles. It felt more like winter than the beginning of autumn he chuntered to himself as he began stamping his feet. Staring down at his shoes he cursed. He'd freshly cleaned them last night, buffed the toes until he caught his reflection – and now look at them – covered in mud. His day was getting shittier by the minute.

A sudden cry of 'Detective' made him jump and he shot a glance in the direction of the forensic tent. Dr Wilson's head was poking out through the opening flap. Her ruddy round face displayed a wry smile.

'I think you need to come and have a look at this,' she said.

* * *

Following his viewing of Doctor Wilson's discovery, Hunter had immediately told the foreman he was sequestering the Portakabin as a temporary incident room and that he wanted everyone to leave. The crew weren't happy about that, and not all of them were happy that they had to give their details and it had taken more than gentle persuasion to get them to comply. Now he was following them to the exit, his thoughts going through action points from his crime scene training; he had already telephoned the communications room, updated the Incident Manager and requested the attendance of a Senior Investigating Officer, plus Crime Scene Investigators and also asked for members of his Major Investigation Team to join him.

The site foreman was the last person to leave, upon which, Hunter heaved the metal gate to, leaving just enough space for someone to squeeze through and began unwinding a roll of blue and white crime scene tape to seal the place off to Joe Public. The driving rain had stopped, but a biting wind was making the job difficult and he was still battling with the tape when the first of those he had requested appeared.

Hunter watched his team's unmarked car approach, rocking on its chassis, throwing up brown slush as its wheels dipped in and out of the deep ruts that made up the track to the site.

It parked up a few yards away in front of the barricade of heavy mesh panels, which protected the compound, and Hunter watched three of the doors opening, trying his best to suppress a grin because he knew what was coming.

His working partner, DC Grace Marshall, her trim figure dressed in dark trousers and Barbour jacket, was the first to emerge. Opening the front passenger door, she planted her feet down heavily, and he observed her tawny face screw into a grimace as her ballet-style pumps disappeared into soaking clay with a squelch. For a second Grace stood there, up to her ankles in mud. Momentarily she looked down at her feet and then lifted her gaze and threw him a daggers look.

Biting his lip, he called out, 'I hope you've brought wellingtons with you, you'll need them.' Then he added, 'You'll need your protective suits as well.'

DC Tony Bullars slammed shut the driver's door, his chiselled features wearing a not too impressive look as he lifted a sludge-caked shoe, stared at it for a second before switching his gaze towards his Sergeant. 'Bloody hell Hunter, you could have warned us.' Returning his soggy foot to the mud he added, 'Anyway, what's this about? I've had to leave tea and toast and a nice warm office behind. I hope it's worth it?'

Hunter nodded as he saw the final member of his team, DC Mike Sampson, push open the rear door and swing out a leg. He replied, 'You guys should know me by now. One thing I don't do is bring you out on a wild goose chase. Believe me, this is worth it!'

* * *

While briefing Grace, Tony and Mike, as to the forensic anthropologist's find, Hunter got a phone call from Dawn Leggate. In her Scottish burr she informed him that she was on her way back from Sheffield and ordered him to 'sit on things' until she got there.

The four of them kitted themselves out in protective suits, and then set down reinforced plates from the gated entrance to the Portakabin and across to the white tent. Today they served a dual purpose, not only did they provide a mud-free route to where the bones had been found, and thus not further forensically contaminate the locale, but also serve to keep everyone's feet dry.

They were about to return to the Portakabin when Hunter spotted the slim figure of SIO Dawn Leggate plodding towards them. She was wearing a waterproof jacket with the hood up and designer wellingtons. Glancing at the labelled woollen socks covering the tops of her boots Hunter fought back a smile. Since the Detective Superintendent's arrival a year ago there had been constant office competition in the fashion stakes between his working partner Grace and his boss. It had been the subject of much conversation between the men as to who should turn up looking the best. They had even occasionally bet a first round of drinks on it

At least, unlike his partner, she was dressed for the weather, Hunter thought as he watched her approach.

A sudden cry of 'Detective Superintendent' brought her march to a halt.

Hunter swung his gaze sideways and clapped eyes on three people foot-slogging towards the SIO. One of them had a TV camera on his shoulder. He recognised another as the local Chronicle reporter. *Shit!* He had completely forgotten about them. They must have been in their cars sheltering from the rain. This was not good. He switched back to his boss, whose face, until this instance, had borne her 'down to business' appearance. Now he could see it had taken on a look of anguish. But it was only momentary. With true professionalism, she turned to face the media and pasted on a faux smile.

Holding up a hand she said, 'Guys you can see I've only just got here. As soon as I have something I'll make a statement.' With that she carried on towards Hunter fixing him with a stare.

He mouthed the words 'sorry' as she neared. He was about to speak when she brokered his silence with a raised hand.

Dawn Leggate said, 'Warn me next time, Hunter,' adding, 'and get uniform down here pronto, I don't want the press trampling all over my crime scene.' Then, taking a deep breath she continued, 'Okay now tell me what we've got.'

Swallowing hurt pride and composing himself Hunter answered, 'As you already know this past week they have been demolishing the old chapel estate and at just after seven o'clock this morning one of the JCB drivers had started to clear away the remains of the old chapel when he unearthed a skull. He stopped work immediately and the site foreman called us. Uniform came down here, confirmed it was a human skull, spoke with the Incident Inspector back in communications, who then called out the forensic anthropologist and you asked me to attend to oversee the excavation. Just over an hour ago now Dr Wilson discovered...' Hunter paused. '...well I think you're going to love this. This is the weirdest thing I've ever seen.' At that moment over his boss's shoulder he saw the forensic van drawing up and recognised the driver. 'Tell you what boss, Duncan Wroe's here now. You can get suited up, I'll have a quick word with Duncan and we'll all take a look and see.'

* * *

Huddled together, almost scrum-like inside the tent, amongst broken scorched timbers, fire-ravaged sandstone bricks and rubble, Hunter, SIO Dawn Leggate, Crime Scene Manager Duncan Wroe and Dr Anna Wilson stood around a shallow sludgy grave in which lay the remains Dr Wilson had uncovered; spread-eagled before them was the strangest looking, partially clothed, human corpse Hunter had ever seen. Parts of the brown-stained skeleton were covered by a thick sticky, soapy white substance, some of which had mould growth and, although his mind was telling him it was flesh, it certainly didn't look like it. Even stranger was the bony structure lying across the corpse's chest.

CSM Duncan Wroe leaned in and started taking photographs.

Dawn Leggate couldn't take her eyes off the aberration. Shaking her head, she said, 'Jesus, what's that on its chest? It looks like an alien!'

Dr Wilson turned and answered. 'I'd love it to be! Now that would be a first. But sadly it's not alien, it's animal. What you're looking at is the skull of a cow.'

Dawn Leggate traded eye contact with Hunter and they both said 'Cow?' at the same time.

The SIO took back her gaze and fixed the anthropologist. 'You're telling me that a cow's head has been placed on the chest of a dead body. In some kind of ritual or what?'

The doctor shrugged. 'I've never come across anything like this before.' Anna re-covered her mouth and nose with a face-mask and crouched down at the edge of the grave. Slowly rotating a trowel over the skull, its toothy grimace staring back mockingly, she said, 'When I got here only the skull had been exposed by the digger, so before I started work on the excavation I spoke with your sergeant, and the foreman, about the history of this place, so that I could get a sense of what I might be examining.' She glanced up, 'You know, to get an indication as to likely age of the skeleton. I was presuming that given that the burial of the skeleton was beneath where the wooden altar used to be that the body here was more than likely the benefactor who had provided the funds to have this place built and been given a worshipful burial, but the more I exposed, the more I realised this skeleton is not as old as I expected, hence the reason you're all here.'

Staring at the body with a mixture of disbelief and morbid curiosity Hunter said, 'The clothes?'

The doctor fixed Hunter's gaze. Only her dark brown eyes were showing. They twinkled. The rest of her face was covered by the hood of her Tyvek suit and face mask. She replied, 'Exactly. Dead giveaway eh?' She dipped her trowel back over the remains, working her way around the cow's skull she picked out the dirty pair of pleated, pastel-pink, trousers encasing bony legs and a soil-stained white, woollen, cap-sleeve jumper that had ridden up towards the neck. 'I'm no fashion expert but those clothes look like what someone would have worn in the 1980s, and their style suggests to me that this body is female.'

Dawn Leggate said, 'So we're looking at a female who's been buried here sometime in the nineteen-eighties?'

'My initial examination indicates that, though I'll know a lot better when I get the body back to the mortuary and do a post mortem.'

'And can I ask you about the cow's skull Anna? I can see tufts sticking to it. Was it already a skull when it was placed over the body or was it a full cow's head?'

'Oh I'm fairly confident it would have been a full cow's head when it was put here with the body. The state of decomposition looks to be the same.' She glanced up from her crouched position. 'Bizarre eh? But thankfully that's not my job to find out the reason behind why it was put here. That's yours.'

Hunter eyes were glued to the discovery. Arrowing a finger towards the cadaver he said, 'Sorry to interrupt you Doctor but can I just ask what that slimy stuff on the body is? Is it flesh?'

'It is flesh. We anthros call it "grave wax". Its real title is adipocere formation. It's when the fattest parts of the body turn to a slimy substance. And it occurs because of the damp soil. In this case, the temperature inside the chapel has been temperate. The foundations of any old building are always damp. It could have done us a favour, especially when I do the post mortem. Although it looks messy it's actually preserved some of the flesh, which could help with identifying the body and it may also give us a clue as to how this person met their death. I'll be able to do a more thorough investigation once we get this body to the mortuary.'

Just before turning to leave Hunter took one last glimpse at the repulsive looking corpse and the cow's skull covering its chest. A chill travelled down his spine. His head was trying to make sense of it all. He just knew that this was going to be a case like no other.

CHAPTER FOUR
DAY ONE OF THE INVESTIGATION

In the MIT office, hair fastened up, dressed pin-neat in dark blue slacks and a white cotton blouse, and looking fresh, Detective Superintendent Dawn Leggate stuck an A4 photograph of a brown-stained skeleton onto a white board, adding to the two crime scene photos already there. This image depicted a series of mud-encrusted bones laid out in anatomical position on a metal gurney; it was a shot taken in the Medico-Legal centre prior to its post mortem examination. Next to it the SIO wrote in capital letters VICTIM and added a question mark.

Slapping a hand over the image and turning to face her team, she opened with, 'Yesterday's photograph of our victim excavated from its grave, taken just before Doctor Anna Wilson carried out her examination.' Pausing, checking she had everyone's attention she continued, 'As you all know, originally what we had was a skull unearthed by the driver of a JCB yesterday morning from beneath the wooden altar of the old chapel at Chapel Meadows, and it was initially thought to be the body of someone from the Victorian era who was buried there when the chapel was built. What we discovered when Doctor Wilson uncovered the rest of the skeleton was anything but. Yesterday afternoon Doctor Wilson carried out a post mortem on the remains and has confirmed that this female was killed and buried there a lot more recently, most probably in the nineteen-eighties. She has a few more tests to carry out before she can nail anything down as to a year.' She flicked her head back at the photographs. 'What we have here is a female, and the doc has been able to narrow down her age to between late teens and early twenties. She was white, between five feet six inches and five feet eight inches tall, with light brown hair at the time of her death. From examination and x-rays she's found that our victim has suffered a fractured right wrist, which had healed, though the injury occurred only a few years prior to her death, and she had also suffered fractures to two lower ribs on her right side. The doc believes that these fractures occurred around the same time as one another and are consistent with a violent physical assault.' Dawn Leggate paused. 'This information will be very significant when it comes to the tasks I'll be allocating.' Pausing again she continued, 'What the doc has also found is that the victim had a broken jaw, a fracture to her right cheekbone and she had two fractured fingers on her right hand. Unlike the other fractures these were caused very close to her death. She had also been strangled. Her hyoid bone had been fractured. That was likely to be her cause of death.' She took a deep breath and tapped one of the crime scene photographs. 'And this bizarre discovery will not have gone unnoticed by you all.' She stuck a finger over the large skull laid across the corpse's chest. 'Doctor Wilson has confirmed that this is the skull of a cow, that it was crudely severed from its body and that it was more than likely as fresh as our victim when they were buried together.' Placing her hands on her hips she continued, 'I've dealt with a lot of murders in my time, but this is the first time I've ever come across anything like this and it's certainly raised a number of questions, which I'll come on to in a minute.' Waiting for a second for what she had said to sink in, she picked up another photo and fixed it to the board. This was a shot of soiled pink trousers, a dirty white woollen top, and a dirty white bra and pants. 'First, more evidence. This is the clothing our victim was wearing. It's all UK size twelve. The label on the jumper is Richard Shops, a fashion store which no longer exists but was popular in the seventies and eighties. I will be putting out an enquiry to see if we can narrow down this particular style and year of manufacture.' With a smile she added, 'The doc told me this is very similar to clothing she wore in her teens, during the eighties, so I'm going with that era at the moment. What is interesting is that her bra was found beneath the body with the clasp broken, which would suggest that it been forcibly removed. It also has stains, which forensic believe might be blood stains, mainly around the right cup, suggesting she had suffered some form of injury to her right breast.' She momentary studied the faces of her team, 'And we also have this,' The SIO put up another photo, this one depicted a heavily soiled oblong piece of patterned carpet. The specific design, made up of red, green and brown, could not be picked out because of the ingrained dirt. 'This piece of carpet was found during the unearthing of the skeleton. She was lying on top of it with the lower part wrapped around her legs.

Duncan Wroe has done an initial examination, and believes that given its size, and how it's been cut in places, that once upon a time this was made to go in the back of a van.' She jabbed a finger over a portion of the photograph. 'See here, there are a couple of identical sections cut out opposite one another where Duncan believes it would have fitted around the wheel arches. Apparently he has come across something like this before in another job and so he's pretty confident about his suggestion. With that job he was able to find the van and make the fit. However, in this case we may have our work cut out. The van this carpet came from has more than likely been scrapped years ago, but at least it's a start.' Staring into the room she said, 'Given this information, the possibility is that the chapel is not the primary site where our victim was killed. The likelihood is that she was killed elsewhere – that could be in the back of a van, or she was put into a van after she was killed, and then transported to the chapel where she was carried in this carpet and then buried.' Facing the room and rubbing her hands together she said, 'That's the evidence guys. Now the enquiries. Following my conversation with Doctor Wilson and the Crime Scene Manager the likelihood is that our victim was sexually assaulted, given that her bra has been snapped and removed, and at some stage she has put up a struggle, resulting in the fractures to her cheekbone and fingers. She was killed when her attacker, or attackers, strangled her. Until further tests are carried out we aren't sure whether she was raped or not, but given that her trousers and pants were still in place it's not believed that is the case.' She bounced her gaze around the room, 'And as you all know we have this find thrown into the mix, which has baffled me, but will feature in our enquiries.' She threw a glance over her shoulder to the crime scene photo of the cow's skull lying across the chest of the corpse. 'Dr Wilson states that when this was laid across the chest of our victim it will have been a full cow's head.' Her face formed an incredulous look. 'The placing of the cow's head on the body before she was buried is obviously significant to the killer or killers but to us, at this moment in time, it's a mystery. Whether it was done as part of some satanic ritual is anyone's guess. I'm hoping that once we find out who this unfortunate woman is we might get an answer.' Lifting her hands to her face, forming them prayer-like in front of her mouth and tapping her bottom lip she momentary observed her team. After several seconds of silence, she dropped her hands and said, 'Right everyone, lines of enquiry. Who is our victim? We already have the old injuries – the broken wrist and ribs – which might assist in identifying her. She must have at least had her fractured wrist treated and therefore there should be medical records somewhere. And secondly, dental records. Our victim has had a number of fillings carried out. The doc's recorded them and I want that enquiry doing. The doc's also gone some way to providing a brief physical description and we have her clothing. I want checks done of all local missing persons from the eighties. The press already have the heads up on this find so I'm doing a press conference later today which will be going out on this evening's news. I'm going to give them the description of our victim and photographs of the clothing to run with and see what comes back. I am not going to disclose how our victim met her death and I am certainly not going to mention the cow's head. I am also going to hold back on the carpet evidence.' Her voice trailed off as she glanced once more at the faces of her team. 'With regard to the piece of carpet she was found partially wrapped in, as I've already said, we are more than likely looking at the nineteen-eighties when this happened. Forensics are going to work on a section of the carpet to see if they can come up with a design. They certainly will be able to get its composition and from that I will be putting out an enquiry to identify the manufacturer and determine local outlets. Duncan is going to work with the forensic service to see if we can narrow down the make, or makes of van, it could fit. As to the time-frame of this murder the doc thinks she might be able to tighten this up to within a specific year or two, but she's going to have to carry out some more tests of the bones and those results will not be with us for a good few days. Until then we work with what we've got.'

Many of them displayed signs of concentration – just what she expected at first briefing. It meant that they were already focussed on the work ahead. Taking a deep breath, she moved on. 'There is still some work to do at the scene. Forensics are looking to see if anything has been left at the scene, tool-wise, by the perpetrators, which would indicate how she was buried. Except for her clothing, we haven't found her shoes or any other personal effects, such as jewellery, handbag, purse, etcetera, which you would expect to find, so they are also looking to see if there is anything in the grave which might help us identify her.' She clasped her hands and interlocked her fingers, 'One last thing I want to raise and I want following up. I've passed this location over the past twelve months on almost a daily basis and, before it was knocked down, the chapel looked to me as though it had been set on fire at some stage. I want to know when that was. I know the building's been derelict a long time so it might just be kids who did it, but now we've found this body it could also have been started to cover up the crime. I also want to know a lot more about that area, what kind of community it was and the people who lived there. Especially anyone of significance who we might want to look at as a suspect. And also, are there any reports of satanic or ritualistic events ever taking place there?' She unlocked her hands. 'Okay everyone there's a lot to do. The DI will allocate you your tasks.' She gave a last look around the room, hopping her gaze from detective to detective. 'We have a female who was murdered some thirty odd years ago, buried in extraordinary circumstances and so far very little to go on. We also have a crime scene that has been severely compromised because of the digging, so our work is really cut out. Let's make every enquiry count. We owe it to our victim.'

CHAPTER FIVE
DAY TWO

Hunter had just got off the phone and was gazing around the office tapping the handset against his chin. There was lots of frantic activity. Many of the detectives had phones pressed close to their ears, deep in conversation, and he knew they would be making appointments with potential witnesses or following up enquiries they had been allocated the previous day. A couple were hammering away at their keyboards. Hunter's thoughts drifted to yesterday's discovery. He still couldn't get the vision of the cow's skull covering the corpse out of his head. It had stayed with him all of last night, even lodging in his brain into sleep. Then it had strangely interspersed with images from *The Blair-witch Project,* resulting in a sleepless night. Now he was knackered and he still had at least another twelve hours of work ahead. The sudden movement of Detective Inspector Gerald Scaife roving into his sightline brought back his focus. The office manager was going from desk to desk with a handful of papers. He watched him place a couple of sheets in front of a detective and then move on. Hunter knew that each of these would be a Line of Enquiry. He had already received his LOE when he'd been first through the door that morning. He brought back his gaze. It was always like this during the early stages of a case and especially after morning briefing. In another half an hour the office would be empty as detectives chased up their assignments. He and his partner, Grace Marshall, would be among them. Last night's television appeal had brought over two dozen new enquiries. Though typically there had been the usual crackpots amongst them – callers declaring they were psychics or clairvoyants, who had received a vision of the killing and would like to help – many of the callers had phoned in because they thought they knew who the victim might be. Although well intentioned he knew from experience that the majority of the calls would be fruitless. Nevertheless, they all had to be followed up.

The job he'd been tasked with was to get as much detail he could about the community, especially how the location looked during the 1980s. Not an easy assignment given the time-span, but he did have a head start. In his teenage years the fields, woods, and canal around that area had been somewhere he had regularly roamed and played with his mates, and even though he had never strayed directly into the streets around Chapel Lane, as it was seen as a place to be avoided for fear of getting a good hiding, he did have an impression in his head of what that neighbourhood once looked like and some of the people who lived there. He had tried to remember what his recollections had been of the place when he had joined the police eighteen years ago. It had been an area he had patrolled frequently, but only to chase away vandals or search for the occasional Missing from Home, because by then the commune was virtually derelict, the majority of the terraced houses boarded up, with its inhabitants moved to council homes in the Wood Estate less than a mile away. He had also been given the job of looking into whether the chapel had been used at any time by any cult or sect practising non-conformist religion. Immediately after briefing he had started his assignments and, thanks to his contacts, he had managed to track down the secretary of Barnwell Heritage Group. He had just got off the phone with him, having had to spend the first twenty minutes listening to him moaning on about the local councillors who he felt had been derelict in their duties with regards the protection of Barnwell's industrial history, even suggesting that some of them were in the pockets of the builders and that is was nothing to do with regeneration. Some of what he had said had prompted a flash-back. He recalled that the local media had headlined the campaigns and demonstrations the Heritage Group had been involved in over the past eighteen months. And there had been a public enquiry – the secretary refreshed his memory that the Ombudsman had ruled in favour of the supermarket chain, much to his disgust. Although he'd had to suffer the man droning on, he did have sympathy for him, despite the fact he hadn't the same passion about the destruction of the estate. To Hunter it had been run-down for as long as he could remember and as a police officer he had only seen the estate as a magnet for thieves and vandals. Toward the end of their phone call he had placated him frequently, reinforcing how vitally important it was to their enquiry they should meet, so he could pick his brains about the estate – to get on record what he knew about the neighbourhood and its inhabitants and give their murder investigation a sense of place. Hunter's words had eventually struck a chord and he had managed to persuade him to meet that afternoon at the construction site.

Returning the handset, he glanced across to his partner sat at her desk opposite. He saw that Grace was talking on her BlackBerry, twisting loose strands of her hair around a finger. Hunter noticed that she'd got rid of the blonde highlights in her shoulder length tight curls, returning it back to its natural black colour. He thought it looked better. The vision of her spiralled him back to when he'd first set eyes on her at training school in 1991. Back then she had been fresh faced and, like him, had stood out because of her youthfulness. He and Grace were the youngest probationers of that intake and within days found themselves teaming up. Hunter quickly latched onto how quick on the uptake she was and it set in motion a healthy competitiveness between them to be the best, which, whilst challenging, was also fun. At the end of the course she outperformed him in the final exam earning her the accolade of Best Recruit much to his consternation. She still ribbed him about it, particularly when she felt he needed putting in his place. Upon completing the 14 week course they had been posted to the same division, albeit at different stations, and he'd come across her regularly. They had done their CID aide-ship at the same time and worked together on some enquiries. It was during those investigations he had witnessed first-hand that in spite of her turning up for work looking as if she was ready for a night on the town, she was not afraid to roll up her sleeves and muck-in. Since then she'd had two career breaks to raise her two daughters, though that had not dented her enthusiasm and passion for the job. In fact, just the opposite, and her effectiveness in detecting crime had helped her beat a path to the door of CID. When he had been appointed Detective Sergeant in the newly formed MIT unit two-and-a-half years back, and been asked to form his team, he hadn't hesitated in contacting Grace. Since then they had forged a formidable partnership, wrapping up a number of murder enquiries between them.

She glanced across, meeting his gaze.

In exaggerated fashion Hunter tapped his watch, and she responded by holding up a finger and mouthing that she would be one minute. He scribbled the name and phone number of the heritage group secretary onto a piece of paper and dragged his coat off the back of his chair.

Grace ended her call with a heavy sigh and pushed back her seat.

'All done and sorted?' enquired Hunter. He knew she had been allocated the task of finding out when the chapel had been set afire and to see if anyone had been arrested.

Shaking her head, Grace picked up her bag, dumped her phone in it and slung it onto her shoulder. 'Not a chance. I've been passed from Communications to the Crime Bureau and they're both telling me the same thing. That it's too long ago. The paperwork will have been destroyed, and one supervisor, who's a retired cop, told me that it might not have even been recorded anywhere given the era. It would more than likely have been a message on a slip of paper given to the community Bobby. And because the chapel was derelict it wouldn't have been recorded formally unless it had been detected to keep the crime figures down. And after all that, even if someone had been arrested for it I can only link it if I know the name of the offender and then I can run their name through PNC.' Letting out a huff she finished indignantly, 'My only chance, I'm told, is to contact the Chronicle newspaper and see if it's in their archives. Can you believe that?'

Hunter smiled, 'I can actually.' Then, he said, 'I've been giving it some thought this morning because I used to play around that area in the mid-eighties when I was a teenager. From what I remember of the place it was a real rough-hole. A lot of the homes were boarded and empty and even back then I can recall seeing the chapel after it had been set on fire, but to be honest Grace it's such a long time back I can't pinpoint exactly when that was. I've got a feeling I would've been roughly fourteen or fifteen, so you're looking at nineteen-eighty-six or seven if that's any help.'

She pulled her overcoat off her chair and draped it over her arm. 'I've been given a right monkey with this enquiry. Come on I need a decent coffee.'

* * *

They had almost an hour to kill before they met with the secretary of Barnwell Heritage Group and so they called off at a coffee place and got two lattes. Over the milky drinks, after sharing their current domestic situations, which usually got around to how the job impacted on their lives, they made a natural transition of switching the conversation to the investigation.

Continuing on a low-note, checking no one was in ear-shot, Grace said, 'Not our usual blood and guts murder is it? This is one of the weirdest I've been involved in. It must have been a right shock for the digger driver. Just imagine, one minute there you are thinking about what you've got for lunch and the next there's this skull grinning up at you.'

'I have to confess I was really cursing the boss yesterday when I was freezing my bollocks off and getting piss wet through, thinking it was a waste of time, and that the pile of bones was some old fart who'd been buried there as a thank you for stumping up the money to pay for the chapel. I couldn't believe it when the doc showed me that body. Especially with the cow's head and the eighties clothes. I never expected that. The cheeky bugger eh? Burying a body beneath the floor of an old chapel? If it hadn't been demolished, we might never have found her.'

'It reminds me a bit of that case last year. Remember? The skeleton we dug up in the woods? She was murdered and buried in the eighties.'

Hunter did remember. They had almost lost their colleague Mike Chapman on that case. He had been stabbed while staking out the killer. He shook away the memory. 'I'll give you the skeleton in the shallow grave bit Grace, but she was different. We knew she'd been murdered and buried, we just didn't know where her body had been put. This person, and the job itself, is a puzzle. We have no idea who she is, or why she was killed and left like that.'

'Not at the moment we don't but once we start checking the mispers we might get lucky as to who she is and what's behind her murder.'

'Fingers crossed,' Hunter replied, finishing the dregs of his latte. Putting down his cup he snatched up the car keys, 'Come on we've got a local historian to see.'

* * *

Hunter pulled off the main road onto the rutted dirt track leading to the construction site. There were still a few puddles in places but the going was nowhere near as bad as yesterday. Within a couple of seconds, he spotted the grey estate car he'd been told to look out for. It was parked in front of the entranceway. As Hunter pulled up behind it the driver's door opened and a portly, squat man wearing a blue quilted coat alighted. Ratcheting the handbrake and killing the engine Hunter thought that the dishevelled looking historian with the straggly grey hair and beard ambling towards them looked to be in his late sixties. Hunter got out and greeted him with, 'David Simmons?'

The man nodded, held out a hand and shook Hunter's. His grip was firm. Hunter introduced Grace, then said, 'Thank you for agreeing to meet.'

'Only too glad to be of help. I've bought you quite a bit of stuff.' David replied and turned back to his car. He opened the back door.

Hunter joined him and shot a glimpse inside the historian's car. He couldn't help but think that it was as untidy as its owner as he set his eyes on dozens of yellowing newspapers, bundles of stapled and ribbon bound documents, plus at least six rolled up maps scattered across the back seats. As he brought back his gaze he prayed he wasn't going to have to stand around going through all this lot, having his ears bent again. All he wanted was a short account of how the Chapel Lane community used to be during the 70s and 80s, view a few old photographs and then be on his way.

Releasing Hunter's hand and shaking Grace's, David Simmons beamed them a broad smile. Facing Hunter, he said, 'You said on the phone you're local and you know this place?'

'I know it, but not that well. I used to play around here as a kid and I did patrol it from time to time when I was in uniform but I only remember it as a bit of a dump. I can remember some of my older colleagues talking about what this place used to be like, especially some of the people who lived here. Some real hard cases by all accounts.'

David Simmons let out a short laugh. 'An understatement. If the place was still thriving today I think it would be labelled a no-go zone! This was a hellish place to live. It was originally built to house the hundreds of destitute Irish who came across to work down the mines and build the canal. Very quickly the houses were crammed beyond capacity and many of the families were living in squalid conditions. There were no bathrooms and only outside toilets. Sometimes there were up to twenty people living in one house. Can you just imagine what it must have been like – all those people living on top of one another? Stereotypical of an area like this making many of the men hardened drinkers. Squabbles and fights broke out. In fact, there were a couple of murders back in Victorian times through family feuds, and a police officer was killed by two brothers during the eighteen-nineties. After that it was seen as a place with a reputation. No one with any sense chose to live here. You were bottom of the pile if you had to.' Grinning he added, 'Even the police used to avoid this place – only came when they had to. Though there was one policeman I recall who could hold his own here – Bobby Scot they used to call him. Have you heard of him? He was the community bobby around here in the sixties and seventies. He might have even been here in the eighties. He was a six-foot-seven ex-Scots Guardsman who was hard as nails. I'm guessing he was hand-picked for this area. I know nobody messed him about, or woe betide them.'

Something triggered Hunter's thoughts. 'Do you know I have heard him mentioned in the past, but I think he'd retired by the time I became a cop. I certainly don't remember him being at Barnwell nick when I joined. You don't recall his full name by any chance?'

David lifted his eyes skywards for a couple of seconds deep in thought. Returning them he answered, 'Jennings! That was his name, PC Jennings. I don't ever recall hearing his first name. They called him Bobby Scot because he was Scottish. I can vaguely remember him.' He cracked a grin. 'Not that I had any dealings with him, mind you.'

'You wouldn't know if he's still alive by any chance?'

'I've got a feeling that he's still around, though he must be in his seventies at least. I can't remember seeing in the local obituary that he's died. If he is alive he'll be able to tell you far more about this place than I can. Especially about the folk who lived here. Which brings me around to your investigation. I don't want to pry or anything but all I know is what was on the news last night – that workers here have found a skeleton. I'm guessing from your contacting me and asking about what this place was like in the eighties, that it's not that old.'

Hunter nodded. 'We think she was killed and buried in the old chapel during the nineteen-eighties. I can't say much more than that I'm afraid at the moment. There's going to be a press conference this afternoon, so you should see some more about it on this evening's news.'

'She! You know who it is?'

Hunter shook his head. 'Other than the gender – not a clue at the moment. Still too early in the enquiry. That's why I contacted you. One of the things I'm after is a list of the people who lived here during the eighties. An old voter's list or whatever from back then.'

David Simmons screwed up his face. 'I haven't got anything like that I'm afraid. The council might be able to help you there.' Then, he threw Hunter a studious look. 'Do you know, mentioning that the skeleton you've found is a *she* has just triggered something!'

'Oh Yes?'

'Yes. The Beast of Barnwell!'

Grace's eyes widened. 'I've heard that name,' she interjected, swinging her gaze from the historian to Hunter she added, 'Remember when we were working on the Demon case?' She looked at Hunter but didn't wait for a response. 'Me and Mike had the task of checking out the Missing from Homes? All the old files were in the basement at headquarters. I can remember seeing an old box down there with loads of files and photos from that case.' She tapped her bottom lip, 'Now what was his name?'

'Terrence Arthur Braithwaite,' David Simmons interjected.

Hunter screwed up his face, 'What's he got to do with this?'

The historian thumbed back over his shoulder. 'This was where he used to live. Chapel Street. He murdered a young lass back in the early seventies and dumped her in the woods not far from here. Raped a few as well if my memory serves me well. He got life, but I can remember seeing in the local paper that he got released a couple of years ago.'

'What's made you link him with this skeleton we've found?'

'Because I can remember at the time from the newspaper reports after his trial that it was suspected that he'd done more than just that young lass.' He paused and said, 'Check him out. You'll have enough on him. He made lots of headlines. He was a real monster.'

The cogs started whirring inside Hunter's brain. He shot a glance over the historian's head to the construction site where a larger white tent had now been erected over the empty grave. Two forensic officers stood chatting by its entrance. They appeared to be examining something. He brought back his gaze, a surge of excitement engulfing him. Yesterday's image invaded his thoughts again. A beast's head. Had the heritage secretary just given them an early breakthrough?

CHAPTER SIX

Dawn Leggate pulled her car onto the driveway, nosed up to the rear of Michael's parked car, set the handbrake and switched off the engine. Grabbing her bag off the front passenger seat she noticed the house was in darkness and for a moment it threw her. *Where's Michael?* Then she remembered. His curry night. *Damn!* It had completely slipped from her thoughts with everything that had gone on. A sudden twinge of guilt engulfed her. She had promised him a lift to the pub, where he was meeting up with his buddies for pre-drinks before the meal. Opening the car door and looking up at the house she realised that he must have got a taxi. She would wait up for him and apologise, though, she knew she needn't – he would understand – he had been in her position only 18 months ago.

Entering the house, she pulled off her shoes, placed them neatly beneath the radiator, scrunched out the tension from her toes in the softness of the hall carpet and made her way through to the kitchen. There, she slipped off her jacket and dumped it together with her bag and keys onto the work surface, picked out a glass from the cupboard and poured herself a generous measure of wine from the fridge. Taking a mouthful, she savoured the refreshing hints of pear and lemon and felt herself beginning to unwind from her hectic day. She had already decided that she was going to finish this, pour herself another, have a soak in the bath, put on her dressing gown, throw together a ham salad and then watch some mindless television until Michael got home.

She had just drained her glass and was reaching for the wine bottle when her mobile rang.

* * *

Drawing his coat around him Michael Robshaw stepped away from the doorway of the Indian restaurant into the cool night air. He stood for a second, buttoning up and taking in the street. The square to his left that had been busy earlier was now relatively quiet. A couple were locked together, arm in arm, steering a path to the pub four doors up. A man was by the entranceway, leaning against the wall, having a smoke. He was staring skywards and looked to be in his own world.

Momentarily, Michael followed his gaze. The sky was especially clear tonight. He immediately recognised the Big Dipper. It was the only star constellation he could remember from his school science lessons. The sudden blare of a car horn made Michael jump. He spun his head in the direction of the sound. Across the road a silver VW Passat was parked with the engine running. The driver's window lowered and his friend Peter stuck his head out.

'Are you sure you don't want a lift?'

He fastened the last button and shook his head. 'Positive. It's only a twenty-minute walk. I'll have burned off some of the meal by the time I get home.'

'Okay mate, I'll be in touch.' Peter gave him a quick wave, wound up the window and set off up the steep hill, beeping his horn as he left.

Michael watched the brake lights go out of view, hitched up his collar and set off walking. He loved these nights. A few beers and a curry with his friends, though their numbers had diminished over the years. There used to be half a dozen of them meeting up every three months to catch up, and share what was going on in their lives, but one of their number had died last year of a heart attack, and tonight one other couldn't make it, leaving just himself, Peter, Stuart and Keith to meet up at their favourite curry house, where for the last two and a half hours they had talked and laughed, sharing anecdotes about the job they all did and loved. They were cops. He, Peter, Stuart and Keith had been fledgling detectives together and despite all going their separate ways over the years – his because of promotion – they had kept in touch. Michael was now the Force Crime Manager – Detective Chief Superintendent – though not for long; although relatively young at 49, he had already determined that in two years' time he would be opting for his pension and retiring. He had already begun making plans.

He was half way up the hill, catching his breath – telling himself he must get back into his exercise regime – when he heard the slow rev of an engine behind him.

Pete! Larking about. Smiling, he didn't look back.

The car revved again. This time it was more determined.

He took the edge off his pace, and half turned to check no one was around to catch him sticking up two fingers. The car was twenty yards away in between streetlamps. As he fixed his gaze on the front grill the headlights blazed, blinding him. For a couple of seconds stars cascaded before his eyes. As he fought to clear the flashes, he heard the engine purge to a roar, followed by a screech of tyres. The next thing he felt was a powerful blow to his legs and suddenly he was flying upwards. Flashes of bonnet, and windscreen, and a starry sky filled his vision and then everything went black.

He was unconscious by the time the car reversed back over him.

CHAPTER SEVEN
DAY THREE

The alarm woke Hunter at 6.30 a.m. As he climbed out of bed he noticed the heating had kicked in – it must have dropped cold overnight.

Showering quickly, he dressed on the landing so as to not wake Beth and then tiptoed downstairs, avoiding the second from bottom step which always creaked.

In the kitchen he made tea by dunking a teabag in a mug and whilst adding the milk, loaded crumpets into the toaster. Waiting for them to toast he loosely fastened his tie and then, mug in one hand and buttered crumpet in the other, he made his way to the French doors and looked out. He could only see to the bottom of his garden. Beyond that a veil of mist blocked his view into the fields beyond and he realised now why the heating had come on. He brought his gaze back. Everything in his garden was damp and flat and he noted that most of the border plants had lost their blooms. He told himself that he must catch up with some gardening on his next days off.

In spite of this morning's weather he loved this time of day and loved it when the house was in this tranquil state. In another hour he knew it would be anything but. The boys would be up and Beth would be anxiously cajoling them into getting ready for school. Thankfully he wouldn't be around – he struggled to cope with Jonathan and Daniel in the morning. He marvelled at how Beth managed, more so when it was her day to work, and she had to oversee them getting prepared for school, as well as get herself organised within a tight schedule.

He dragged himself out of his ruminations and finished his second crumpet, his thoughts switching to the day ahead. There was nothing Hunter enjoyed more than when a new case started. The first few days he experienced that rush all detectives get when a fresh investigation was underway. There was nothing they wanted more than to catch the killer and yesterday's reveal by David Simmons might just be the lead as to who had murdered their victim.

At 7.10 a.m. Hunter put his mug in the dishwasher and made his way to the hall where, in front of the mirror, he buttoned up the collar of his shirt and secured the knot of his tie. He paused for a moment staring back at his image, checking he was good to go. Then, picking up his car keys he quietly let himself out of the house.

* * *

Bounding up the back stairs Hunter had expected to be entering a highly charged office with everyone in high spirits. However, the atmosphere he encountered as he stepped into the room was anything but. As per normal detectives were making phone calls, or chatting amongst themselves but instead of being buoyant their mood seemed sombre. Puzzled, Hunter made his way across to his desk, slipped off his coat, draped it around the back of his chair and leaning across his desk sought out his partner's attention.

Grace looked up from what she was working on and offered up a weak smile.

He returned a quizzical frown and flicked his head backwards. 'What's up with everyone? Someone died?'

'Haven't you heard?'

Hunter screwed up his face even tighter. 'Heard what?'

'Detective Chief Superintendent Robshaw got knocked down last night! He's in a critical condition!'

Stunned, Hunter slumped into his chair, 'Mike?'

Grace nodded, 'Looks like a hit and run.'

'Christ!' Hunter locked onto Grace's concerned look. Michael Robshaw had been the Investigation Team's SIO until last November, when, following promotion, he had been assigned to headquarters to manage the force's Crime Portfolio. Before that he had forged a very close working relationship with Michael. He had been his DI during his CID days, had supported and encouraged him to get his promotion to sergeant and had recommended him for Drug Squad. When the Major Investigation Teams were being set up across the force it had been Michael Robshaw who had telephoned him at home and given him the 'heads up' to apply for one of the Detective Sergeant's posts.

Hunter was extremely fond of him. He trusted and admired him.

'What happened?'

Grace shrugged her shoulders. 'Not quite sure. All I know, from what I've been told, is that last night he went out with some of his old work mates to *Asian Spices* in the square, and was making his way home when he was hit by a car which didn't stop. He's in intensive care in a really bad way apparently. They don't know if he's going to make it. The gaffer's with him.'

'Morning guys' Detective Inspector Gerald Scaife's announcement lifted everyone's heads.

Hunter followed the DI's slow walk to the front of the room where he stopped by the incident board.

Slim built, but not skinny, in his early forties, with brown, greying hair cut short to the scalp, Gerald Scaife wore a steely expression as he faced the team. 'I'm sure everyone's heard the sad news about Mr Robshaw this morning,' he roamed his gaze around the room but didn't make eye contact with anyone. 'The gaffer's been by his bedside since late last night and doesn't know when she'll be in so she has asked me to hold the fort and take briefing this morning. With regard to the accident, I have briefly chatted with her but she knows very little about how it happened because of Mr Robshaw's condition. There is an ongoing investigation by traffic as we speak, so as soon as I know anything definite I will update you. Regarding Mr Robshaw, he does have some very serious injuries, the most serious of which is a fractured skull, which has caused a bleed in the brain and when I spoke to the gaffer an hour ago he was in theatre being operated on. As soon as I get an update I'll let you all know.' Pausing a second he added, 'I think I speak for us all when I say we wish him our very best.' For a brief moment his glanced at the floor. Then, looking up he continued, 'Now back to our enquiry. Overnight, following the TV appeal, a number of callers have left names of who they believe our victim is. There are at least a dozen and the HOLMES team will be checking them against Missing Persons Index. If we get a match to our profile it will be immediately put out as an action to follow up. At the scene, Doctor Wilson and forensics have almost finished their work around the gravesite. Late yesterday afternoon they recovered a black stiletto shoe, size five, with a broken heel, which we believe is the victim's and also a pair of 9ct gold loop earrings. Pictures of those will be put up on the board during the day. Forensics are going to extend the search but, as you all know, because of the state of the site this is not going to be easy.' Breaking, he focussed on Hunter. 'Enquiries-wise, you and Grace got something after you spoke with the local historian. Do you want to take us through it?'

Hunter looked up from his journal. He had been doodling – a habit of his. Covering his head and shoulders cartoon sketch of the straight-faced DI with his arm, Hunter cleared his throat and responded, 'Yeah, very interesting chat with the secretary of Barnwell heritage group yesterday afternoon. We met him down at the site. He gave us a little bit of history about the area which, though interesting, doesn't help us with regard to the time period we're looking at. He's loaned us a couple of ordnance survey maps and a few black and white photographs that could help us to get a picture of how the area around Chapel Meadows looked before the recent work started. The really interesting thing he did tell us, and it could be something of significance, but requires some following up, is that the killer Terrence Arthur Braithwaite used to live on this estate.' He saw from the faces of some of the team that the name had registered – but not in everyone's. He continued, 'To those who are not familiar with the name, you may be familiar with the nickname he was given in nineteen-seventy-three when he was jailed for life – The Beast of Barnwell.' Now he saw everyone's face light up. 'Not wishing to jump the gun here, but I couldn't help but think that the cow's – as in beast's – head, placed on top of our victim, might just be his signature.' He looked around the room for any reaction. His colleague's faces were deadpan. Shrugging his shoulders, he continued, 'Anyway, Braithwaite's case was well before anyone's time here, but the reason I'm bringing his name into the enquiry is because the heritage secretary told me that, although he was only convicted of killing one girl in nineteen-seventy-two, he said that he was suspected of killing others, but it was never proved. I have to confess I haven't had much time to follow up the latter part of what he told us, but I have pulled off what's recorded on PNC and I can confirm that Terrence Braithwaite lived at 16 Chapel Lane at the time of his arrest – less than fifty yards from the chapel where our victim was discovered. And, I can also confirm that in nineteen-seventy-three he was found guilty of the murder of a seventeen-year-old girl called Glynis Young, plus the rape of four other women and was sentenced to life.' Hunter paused and took a deep breath. 'The heritage secretary told us that a few years ago there was a feature piece in The Chronicle about Braithwaite being released.' He looked at the DI. 'I've got to follow this up as well.' Glancing across to his partner he added, 'I think Grace knows where we can put our hands on information from the original investigation.'

Grace pushed herself back in her chair, 'Yes boss,' she began. 'When we were working on the 'Demon' case, just over a year ago, Mike Chapman and I had the task of checking through all the old Missing from Home files, to see if we could find a couple of his victims. We discovered that those files had all been stored in the basement across at District HQ. Well, whilst we were down there I found this large box full of statements, crime scene photos and the crown court file relating to Braithwaite. At the time I only cherry picked through the stuff in there, more out of curiosity, so didn't get the full picture of what he'd done exactly, but there was so much in that box that I'm pretty sure it's everything to do with the original investigation'.

'Okay, brilliant Grace,' DI Scaife took back the briefing. 'And well done you two. And using your own words Hunter "not to jump the gun here", but he's certainly worth looking at. Get the ordnance map section of the estate blown up and put onto the incident board. Let's identify where Braithwaite's house was in relation to the chapel. And check if that box of files is still in the basement at headquarters, and if it is, get it brought across here. This Braithwaite guy needs some in-depth work.'

* * *

Hunter pulled up outside retired PC Gordon Jennings home and ran his eyes over the 1960s semi. It was an ex-police house, and unlike many of the other ex-police houses on the road which had undergone extensive renovation since they were sold off, Gordon Jennings's still retained its original features – flat fronted, with large windows and a wooden glass panelled door. The front garden was immaculate with a bowling green lawn and neat borders.

Gordon had the front door open before Hunter and Grace were halfway down the path. Despite a stoop, which Hunter guessed was aged related, Gordon filled the doorway. He was a big broad-shouldered man with a thick head of white hair and Hunter couldn't help but admire how well he looked given that he was 74.

Hunter had to look up at him as they shook hands. Gordon's large hand peppered with liver spots enveloped his and the grip was strong. He recalled what David Simmons had said about his reputation and wasn't surprised one bit given the man's present stature. *He must have looked a man-mountain when he was on the beat.*

He showed them through to the kitchen, indicating for Hunter and Grace to sit at a table while he went to the sink and filled up the kettle. Switching it on, and arranging three cups in a line he glanced over his shoulder and said, 'Since you phoned I've been up in the loft and found all my old pockets books.' He nodded at two shoe boxes in the centre of the table. 'I never handed mine in when I retired. I always fancied doing my memoirs one day.' He let out a small chuckle and returned to preparing the drinks.

Hunter noted he still had the hint of a Scottish accent. He remembered what the locals referred to him by when he'd patrolled the streets.

The kettle boiled and Gordon began pouring hot water in the cups. He paused while filling the third cup and looked back, 'Sorry I never asked what you wanted. I've made tea. It's just automatic.'

Hunter looked at Grace. Whereas he loved tea he knew she was a coffee fan. She nodded back and mouthed the words 'fine'. Hunter replied, 'Tea's good.'

The retired Constable stirred the tea cups, adding milk, and set down them down on the table. Then, bringing a plate of biscuits he took a seat with them. Dragging one of the shoe boxes towards him he hooked off the lid. 'These have not seen the light of day since I finished back in nineteen-ninety-four.'

Hunter saw that the box was crammed with police issue notebooks. There must have been at least thirty of them in two neat rows.

Gordon said, 'I saw it on the news last night about the girl's body you've found in the old chapel. Your Detective Super said that you're looking at the possibility that she might have been killed and buried there during the nineteen-eighties.'

'That's right,' Hunter replied.

'So I'm guessing that you wanting to talk to me about the people who lived on the estate around that time – see if I could recollect anyone going missing from around there – that you haven't managed to identify her yet?'

Hunter nodded. 'Other than the clothing that was on the body, we've got nothing else to go on. We've taken DNA but we're only going to get a match if we can locate her family. The thing that's going to complicate this, because it's so long back, is the likelihood that all our Missing from Home reports will have been destroyed. Some of the long term mispers have been entered on our computer system, and we've got some records filed at district headquarters but we don't think they go back that far. We are going to be reliant upon someone telling us who she is.'

Gordon rubbed his chin, 'I've not had time to look through any of my pocket books yet, but I've really racked my brains and I can't remember any girl disappearing from around the Chapel Estate. Not permanently anyhow. There were a couple of girls who were always going missing, but as far as I can recall they always returned home.'

Hunter tutted, 'Never mind Gordon. To be honest it was a long shot.'

'It did get me thinking though and I remember that in the eighties we used to get a lot of women visitors to that area. Many of them from West Yorks.' He looked from Grace to Hunter, tapping his nose. "Ladies of the night" – you know what I mean.'

'You mean street workers?' said Grace.

He nodded and with a note of disdain he replied, 'Aye, that's what they call them now. Label them how you want, but it's just a fancy name for prostitutes. The place was bad enough as it was without them coming and making it worse. I'd see them off the minute I clapped my eyes on them. Send them packing I would.'

'Street workers on the Chapel estate? Why would they come to a place like that, if it was as bad as what they say it was?' responded Hunter.

Gordon gave him a nonplus stare. 'Safety of course.'

'Safety?'

'Yes Laddie, safety. Just think about what was going on back then.'

It was Hunter's turn to issue a confounded stare.

'The Yorkshire Ripper.' He gave off a sigh and said, 'The girls didn't feel safe on the streets of West Yorkshire so they came here.'

Hunter gave a look of understanding. 'Sorry Gordon I wasn't on your wave length. I was only a teenager when Peter Sutcliffe was on his killing spree. It was just news headlines for me I'm afraid.'

'Aye well. The knock on effect for us was immense. Because we were in easy travelling distance of Leeds and Bradford we were inundated with prostitutes. Not just this neck of the woods, but Doncaster and Sheffield got their fair share as well.'

'So what I think you're hinting at Gordon is that there's a possibility that the body we've found buried in the chapel could be a street worker?'

Gordon opened out his hands and canted his head. 'It would make sense. As I've said I can't remember any local lasses disappearing. But if it was one of the street girls, her family, or whatever, might well have reported her missing in West Yorks and the police there more than likely looked in the wrong place for them.'

Hunter glanced across to Grace, 'That would certainly make sense.'

She acknowledged his comment with a nod.

'I soon got to know a couple of the regulars who came here, but likewise they got to know me and as soon as they saw me coming they made a beeline for The Navvi…'

'The Navvi?' interrupted Hunter.

'The Navigation Inn. It was the local. Only pub on the estate, come to that. A real dive, as you can probably imagine. They'd go in there because they knew I wouldn't go in. As big as I was, it was a place I wouldn't go in alone.' His eyes drifted a second and he paused as if reminiscing. Then bringing back his gaze he continued, 'They used the place as a base, especially in winter, and then ply their trade on the back lane that ran beside Chapel Meadow. It was a narrow road back then which was used as a short-cut to the pit and also between us and Mexborough and

Bolton-on-Dearne, so it would get a fair bit of traffic passing through, which was good for the girls' business.'

Inside his head Hunter quickly re-ran what the retired officer had just told them and thinking allowed said, 'So if our victim was a street worker from the West Yorkshire area then no one from her family or friends might be any the wiser that she'd ended her time right here in Barnwell?'

Gordon gave a sharp nod. Hunter could see Grace out of the corner of his eye stroking her lower lip. She appeared deep in thought and he guessed she was also mulling over what the big man had just said, but there was something puzzling him. Before he had time to check back with the retired officer, Gordon picked up the conversation again.

'And I think that leads us on nicely to the other question you asked me on the phone this morning. You said you wanted to pick my brains about Terrence Arthur Braithwaite?'

'Oh Yes.' Hunter flipped open his folder and tested his pen on the corner of a blank sheet. He'd been so engrossed he had forgotten to write anything down. He would have to store to memory what Gordon had just said. He scribbled the words 'Ripper' and 'Street workers' as prompts for later and then said, 'His name cropped up in an enquiry yesterday afternoon. We spoke with the local heritage secretary who told us about Braithwaite killing a seventeen-year-old girl and committing a series of rapes around the estate back in the early seventies and that he used to live on Chapel Lane. In fact, it was him who gave us your name as being the community bobby for that area during Braithwaite's spree.'

Gordon took a quick sip of his tea and said, 'Now that was one weird guy. No cancel that – one evil, weird guy. It was me who gave CID Braithwaite's name after the second rape on the estate. The first one he did wasn't dealt with as a rape because the woman involved had a bit of a background and so her complaint was knocked. I have to say, at the time, because I knew the woman, and I knew she was telling the truth, I was furious, but it didn't get me anywhere – I was just the community bobby – a lazy thick woodentop.' He set down his cup, eyeing Hunter and Grace thoughtfully before continuing. 'I'm being a bit facetious but that's what it felt like. As I said I knew the woman – they didn't, and the bottom line is if they'd had done their job properly, I'm convinced he wouldn't have raped again and Glynis Young would still have been alive.' He seemed to ponder a moment then continued, 'I got myself in a bit of bother over it. I went to the DCI and made my feelings known about the detectives who'd interviewed her but it only resulted in me getting a good and proper dressing down.' He held up his hand and made a sign with his finger and thumb. 'Made me look that small, he did.' He dropped his hand, shaking his head. 'The arsehole!' He took a deep breath. 'The upshot was that the incompetence of a couple of detectives was swept under the carpet and I was sent back to my beat with a flea in my ear.' He paused, glanced between Hunter and Grace and, forcing a smile, added, 'You probably see that I'm not a fan of CID, present company excepted.'

Hunter returned a meek smile, 'I can't talk for officers back then but I'd like to think we do our job properly.'

'As I said present company accepted.'

'There're a lot of questions I want to ask you Gordon, especially the angle involving the street workers, but we'll do them in order. First, from what you've just said about Braithwaite and the rapes, can you tell us what really happened regarding his victims – not what came out in court – so I can see if he fits into our enquiry anywhere?' Hunter got ready to write.

'Yeah okay, I'd love to. I've had to bottle some of this up for years. It would be good to give my side of things after all this time. What the DCI said to me wasn't right. If he hadn't been a gaffer I'd have punched his lights out.'

Hunter studied the man's face and smiled to himself. The big man reminded him so much of his retired CID mentor Barry Newstead, now a civilian investigator with MIT. Similarly, Barry had had a habit of saying what he thought and rubbing the bosses up the wrong way, and he could be handy with his fists. *These two would have worked well together.* Putting the thought to one side he said, 'Tell us about Braithwaite then?'

'Terry Braithwaite was one of those people I was told to keep my eye on by my tutor bobby, who showed me around my beat. He was pointed out to me back in sixty-nine, when I'd started. Braithwaite had just done a stretch in prison for burglary – eighteen months, if my memory serves me right.' He paused, switched his gaze from Hunter and Grace and continued, 'I say burglary, because that was what he was charged with, and convicted of, but there was more to it than that. My tutor told that me he'd actually attacked a fifteen-year-old girl in the house he was burgling. Apparently, the daughter of the couple whose house it was had not gone to school that day because she had flu. Her Mum had called back at lunchtime to see she was all right, and then had left her tucked up in bed, locking up as she left to go back to work, but had left the back window open to let in some fresh air. According to the girl she woke up a couple of hours later to find him in her room and she instantly recognised him because he only lived half a dozen doors away. She told detectives that he'd pinned her down on the bed and covered her mouth with his hand and then he'd started to fondle her, but she managed to bite his hand, and started screaming and he ran off. He was nicked by CID within hours of the job and admitted breaking into to the house but wouldn't have anything to do with fondling the girl. His explanation was that he'd panicked when he'd found her there and that he'd got on top of her to cover her mouth to stop her screaming.' He gave a look of derision. 'I was told that detectives had not been convinced by what he'd told them, but because he also admitted he'd done a couple of other houses on that estate and cleared up half a dozen other jobs, CID were happy with that and didn't press the assault charges on him. When he came out of jail he went back to living with the woman on Chapel Street he'd been with before going down and he returned to his old job at the pit. It caused a bit of a rumpus at the time – him coming back. The family whose home he'd burgled sold up and left, which was really sad.' He paused and said, 'I know what I'd have done to him if that had been my daughter.' Shrugging his shoulders, he picked up his cup again. 'As I say all that was before I started the job. I did try to keep my eye on him, but he kept his head down and we had no more jobs like that round there so I never came into contact with him until a couple of years later. In early nineteen-seventy, we had two attacks on young women on Chapel Lane, both within a short time period of one another. On both occasions the women were approached from behind, dragged to the ground and their breasts were fondled. All we had by way of a description was a man in dark clothing with a scarf covering his face. There was an investigation that lasted a good couple of months. They drafted in CID from all over the district and I got overtime and worked in plain clothes doing observations around the estate. To be honest we never gave Brathwaite a thought because of the MO and the enquiry died a death. And then six months after these two attacks – on Halloween Night – we had the rape of Jessie Appleton. She was walking home from the Navvi when she was grabbed from behind, dragged across the fields, and she told detectives that her attacker had made her remove her tights and knickers and then had sex with her.' Gordon set his eyes on Grace, 'This is the job CID knocked.' He paused again and then said, 'As I've already said Jessie had problems. She was no angel. That night she'd had her usual skinful, and unfortunately she also had a bit of a reputation in the locality amongst some of the men – you get my drift. The fact that she told detectives that *he'd* made *her* remove her own tights and knickers, meant they quite simply didn't believe her story. They put more energy into knocking what she said than investigating the crime. The sad thing is they could have detected it. The man who'd raped her – Terry Braithwaite – had not worn a condom. Of course we didn't know it was him at that time, but he would have been caught earlier if the job had been done right and they'd got a sample from her. They just never bothered and the enquiry was put to bed so to speak. I was disgusted and had a quiet word with the DS first, but the sergeant was on the side of his detectives. They took no account of what I said about her – especially that I believed her. Even when I said she was a snout for me. She used to tell me what was going on in the estate and who was up to what. But it cut no ice and that's when I went to the DCI and got a bollocking. I mean, I know she put it about a bit with other men and she could be a bit of a fire-brand when she'd had a few. Nevertheless, she deserved better than she got. I spoke to her on numerous occasions about what had happened and I can tell you that she was definitely raped.' He broke off.

Hunter stopped note taking and took in the pained expression displayed on the retired officer's face. He was about to say something when Gordon started speaking again.

'And then between Christmas and New Year in nineteen-seventy, we had another rape. A young woman coming home from bingo was making her way along the back lane near Chapel

Meadow when, like Jessie, she was grabbed from behind and dragged into the fields. She told detectives a very similar story – that her attacker told her to remove her own tights and knickers. But this time he held a knife to her throat while he raped her.' He pursed his lips. 'As you can probably imagine CID were in a bit of a flap because of what they'd done with Jessie's rape, and so they investigated this one thoroughly, but it was never detected. A lot of blokes were interviewed from the Chapel estate, but I don't think they had a firm suspect. I certainly can't recall Braithwaite's name being in the frame. Anyway, it went quiet all through the spring, and then in the summer of seventy-one we had the third. The MO was similar to the other two – woman making her way home, dragged from behind, forced to remove her clothing. He held a knife to her throat on this occasion as well, but this time he took things a bit further and bit one of her breasts. It was this job that got him his nickname *The Beast* from the papers. It was also this job where we got a lead.' He paused, glanced at the box containing his pocket books, returned his gaze and continued. 'The woman lived at the end of Chapel Lane and knew Braithwaite by sight, and she told detectives that although her attacker had tried to disguise himself with a scarf she thought that the man bore some resemblance to him – eyes, nose, hair and build. The upshot was that Braithwaite was brought in and interviewed. He said the woman must have been mistaken and provided his wife as his alibi. By then he'd married the girl he'd been living with.' Gordon started tapping his temple. 'I'm trying to remember what his wife was called, but for the life of me I can't. My memories getting shocking.' His face took on a studious look for a few seconds then un-knotting his brow he said, 'I guess it'll come to me, most probably when you've gone. If not, her details will be in one of my pocket books and I can ring you. Anyway it doesn't matter now she's dead.' He shook his head and gave out a long exasperated sigh, 'The result was that she alibied him and so they released him. For me, I felt they didn't push her enough on the alibi she gave and also they didn't search his house. Because of my feelings about what had happened with Jessie I volunteered to help on the enquiry, but the cheeky bastard of a DS who was running the job told me that 'they were experienced in these matters and could handle it'. I was totally peed off with them, I can tell you, but I'd already had one bollocking for expressing my thoughts and didn't want another, so I left it.' He shrugged his shoulders. 'The DS who dealt with the job...it was *him* who got done for perjury last year. Alan Darbyshire.'

Hunter's head shot up. *Alan Darbyshire!* Nine months ago his name had been linked to a cold-case murder they had been investigating. They had uncovered irregularities in the interview of a convicted killer conducted by him in the early nineteen-eighties, and as a result, they had arrested him and charged him with perjury. Six months ago he had been convicted at crown court and was now serving an eighteen-month prison sentence. *Well it's a small world!* The sound of Gordon clearing his throat brought Hunter's thoughts back.

'Braithwaite was taken out of the frame much to my disgust and for months, I have to say, I went on a bit of a crusade to get him. I used to lie in wait for him going to work and pull him up in his van. I did my best to rile him every time I stopped him, just so I could nick him, but he wouldn't play.' A smile lit up his face. 'Good job they hadn't got CCTV around then eh. I'd more than likely have been sacked.'

'And so that's when he went on to rape again?' said Hunter.

Gordon nodded. 'It was almost a year later – autumn, nineteen-seventy-two. Raped an eighteen-year-old. Bit her breast just like the last woman. Braithwaite was immediately listed as a suspect but before they could bring him in for questioning he killed Glynis Young and that's when his luck ran out.'

'How did that come about then?' enquired Grace.

Gordon fixed her with his watery blue eyes. 'It was actually down to a member of the public, certainly not CID. It was a real nasty job. Halloween again. Glynis had had a row with her boyfriend at the youth club and was making her way home on foot. She lived in Mexborough and had to go over the canal bridge on Chapel Lane to get there. It was a case of her being in the wrong place...' He shook his head, fixing Hunter and Grace with a vacant stare and then continued. 'We believe Terrence Braithwaite came across her whilst driving home after his shift at the pit. It was a rotten night and we think that he most probably offered her a lift. The sighting we had of them was just before ten o'clock in the car park at Barnwell Lake. One of the night fishermen was just packing up and was heading back to his car when he heard Glynis scream. The back doors of Terry's van were open and he saw her fighting with Braithwaite. The fisherman went to her aid, and there was a bit of a struggle between them, but Terry got top side and gave him a couple of thumps and knocked him to the ground and managed to drive away with Glynis in the back. The man ran after them and banged on the roof as Terry drove out of the car park and, fortunately for us, he also got part of his reg number. It didn't take us long to trace the van and we went straight round to his house. We found him cleaning his van, and you won't believe this, but it show's you just what kind of man Braithwaite was, he'd also changed the wheels of his van, so the tyre treads wouldn't match those at the scene. He was arrested and his house searched but there was no sign of Glynis. But we did find this weird stuff in the cellar.'

'Weird stuff?' enquired Hunter, his eyebrows knitting together.

'Gordon nodded. 'Occult, Devil-worshipping stuff!' The cellar door was padlocked, so the first thing we thought was that Glynis Young was down there so we busted the door down. She wasn't but what we did find I've only seen the likes of in horror films before. The walls were covered in occult symbols – upside down crosses, pentagrams – that kind of stuff, as well as Devil drawings and paintings. He'd also painted severed women's heads dripping with blood. We thought at first it was real blood but forensics said it was animal blood.' He looked from Hunter to Grace. 'See what I mean when I said weird?' He shook his head. 'Anyway Braithwaite was locked up and interviewed for hours but refused to talk. The next morning Glynis's body was found in the woods just off Chapel Meadow. She'd been stabbed and strangled. Braithwaite denied everything. In the hour it had taken for us to trace his van and get around to his house, as well as changing the wheels, he'd also bleached the inside of the van, sandpapered and bleached the bottom of his shoes and his clothes were being washed in the machine. The thing that sealed his fate was that he'd not thought to clean the top of his van and the fisherman who'd tackled him's handprint was found on the roof. The jury found him guilty of the murder of Glynis Young and also the rape of the woman who had recognised him. The jury couldn't deliver a majority verdict for the other rapes and so they were left on file.

The judge gave him life. That was in nineteen-seventy-three.' Gordon's mouth tightened. 'It was a good job he was caught when he was because I, and many others like me, were convinced he would've gone on to kill again. Terry Braithwaite was an evil nasty piece of work and showed just what he was like during the judge's summing up. While he'd been on remand he'd had this tattoo done on his chest by his cell-mate. He'd had THE BEAST done in capital letters and a face of the devil, and he ripped open his shirt while he was in the dock and started snarling like a demented dog.' He shook his head again. 'I was in court that day and I couldn't believe it. I've never seen anything like it. Me and several others had to drag him out. It took four of us to restrain him. He'd totally gone.' He shook his head again as his voice trailed off.

Hunter rocked his neck, studying Gordon for a moment and mulling over what he had just told them. He said, 'God, what a fascinating story Gordon, and as you say Braithwaite was no doubt a very dangerous man, but what you've just said is that this all happened in the early seventies. He was behind bars from nineteen-seventy-two until a couple of years ago. The girl we've found beneath the floor of the old chapel was killed and buried there early to mid-nineteen-eighties, so that puts Terrence Braithwaite out of the running. HM prison service is his alibi. You can't get better than that'

The retired PC shook his head, 'Oh, but it doesn't. In fact, the nineteen-eighties puts him right in it.'

Taking on a puzzled expression Hunter said, 'I'm not with you Gordon. Braithwaite would have been in jail. You said he got life.'

'He did get sentenced to life, but he wasn't actually in prison for long. He was transferred to a secure hospital for assessment. In his case I think he went to Rampton, which is where he was released from. The thing I haven't told you is that in the early eighties his wife died and he was allowed out for her funeral. I can remember it because a telex came from headquarters about the arrangements. We thought the prison service had everything sorted so we didn't do anything different – you know put extra officers out on patrol. Just after the burial he told the guards he needed to go to the toilet and they allowed him to go to the vestry, which they thought was secure. But he found a key to the outside door and did a runner. There was mayhem. We were chasing around all over the place to try and find him but he'd disappeared. If my memory serves me right, he was on the run for five days before they finally re-captured him. He was found in the grounds at Whitby Abbey. The papers had a field day with that – the place where Dracula had landed in the book – and the link to his nickname. You can just imagine it can't you?' Smiling he added, 'He was interviewed, but he never told where he'd been all that time.'

* * *

DI Gerald Scaife again took briefing. He reported that they still hadn't managed to identify their victim – the HOLMES team were still trawling through the National Missing Persons Index to see if any of the names cross-matched with females reported missing during the 1980s. He said they were especially prioritising those from West Yorkshire, given Hunter and Grace's feedback from their interview with Gordon Jennings, adding that there were more records to check on the system than they had anticipated.

Then he handed over to Hunter, who, using the notes he had scribed as prompts, slowly went back over what Gordon Jennings had told him and Grace that afternoon. Pausing after ten minutes, licking dry lips and moistening them, he roamed his eyes around the room. He could see from the reaction in his colleague's faces that he had grabbed their attention. Then, pushing aside his annotations he added, 'I also talked to him about the fire at the chapel. He could remember it, although not the date, except to confirm that it was early eighties sometime, and that it was the start of summer – around May – June time. He told us that the chapel had stopped being used in the early seventies and had been boarded up, supposedly to stop thieves getting in, but it had been the target of constant vandalism and he'd cleared away lots of kids over the years who'd got in to play. He can also remember that a local tramp, who's now dead, used to doss in there from time to time. He said that there had been a couple of fires lit in there, but they were only small ones which had hardly caused any damage – kids making campfires, that kind of thing. However, there was one big fire that caused considerable damage. Apparently he was on duty that evening and was called to it following the attendance of the fire brigade. He said that whoever had started this fire had intended burning the place down. They'd piled rubbish and old prayer books on top of the altar and dragged together pews and started it. It caused a significant amount of damage inside, mainly to the floor and the pews, there was lots of smoke damage and, following that, the council did a proper job of securing it for safety reasons. He was given the names of a number of teenager's who'd been using the place as a den, and he did interview them, but all of them denied having anything to do with it and he had no evidence so the job was written off as undetected. He's kept all his pocket books and he's going to go through them and give us the date of the fire and the names of the teenagers he interviewed at the time.' He pushed himself back in his chair and skirted the room again. 'Another thing I also got from him was an immediate reaction when I asked him if anyone had ever reported a cow being killed and its head severed. He wanted to know why I was asking that, but I told him I couldn't tell him at the moment, and he told me that a local farmer had rung in the morning after the fire at the chapel. He remembered it because of the fire. He was making enquiries at the houses nearby and he was diverted away from them to take the report. The cow had been killed and beheaded and left in the field across from Chapel Lane. He said he'd never come across anything like it. He's going to go through his pocket books today to get us the date.'

DI Scaife checked that Hunter had finished and said, 'Okay, good work there. As soon as Gordon Jennings rings in with those dates and the names of the children he interviewed for the fire I'll prioritise it as a line of enquiry. Regarding Terrence Braithwaite, I want this picking up first thing tomorrow morning. Following everything we've just been told about him; I want to dig into every aspect of his life. District Admin have confirmed that the full case files relating to the Braithwaite investigation are still in the basement and those will be here first thing in the morning.' He looked at Hunter. 'I want you to go through the files and summarise them for us.' Taking back his gaze he scoured the room. 'I will also be allocating an enquiry to contact the probation service to get copies of what they hold about him on file, and I will also be tasking someone with liaising with the prison service to see what they have on record about him. I'm especially interested if he disclosed anything to hospital staff, or if he was involved in any treatment regime. What's really important is getting those dates that he was on the run and see if there is a link with the chapel fire. Once we get the dates we can also check and see if any females on the Missing Person's Index fit into the five-day time-frame.' He paused before finishing with, 'This just may be what we've been looking for everyone.'

* * *

Except for Hunter, no one hung around after evening briefing. He had stayed to formally document the notes he made of that afternoon's interview with Gordon Jennings and then he intended visiting the hospital to see how his former boss was before heading home. He had thought about him on and off throughout the day, and although not religious had found himself on more than a few occasions saying a silent prayer for his speedy recovery. Closing down his computer, he picked up his mug and finished the last dregs of his now cold tea, staring across the room at the incident board. Next to the first crime scene photograph depicting the skull of their victim was a blown up section of an Ordnance Survey map of the Chapel estate. It had two Post-it notes indicating where their victim had been discovered, and where their suspect – Terrence Arthur Braithwaite – lived prior to his arrest. It was all they had at the moment despite all their enquiries.

Hunter mentally rewound the day's interview, picking out the key elements as he scrutinised the map. The distance between the two locations was less than thirty yards. Surely, this wasn't just a coincidence?

* * *

In the Intensive Care Unit at Barnwell General Hospital a nurse told Hunter which bed Michael Robshaw was in. He made his way to the open door but stopped before he entered, taking a deep breath as he explored the ward. He immediately spotted Dawn slumped in a high-back chair next to his former boss's bed. Head askew, resting on one shoulder, she appeared to be asleep. His gaze drifted to the bed where Michael Robshaw lay unconscious.

He could hear the heart monitor next to him beeping away steadily. *That was a good sign, wasn't it?* Edging closer and taking in his appearance he couldn't believe this was the same man he had spent so much time with over the years. It wasn't the tube keeping him breathing, or the wires and cables monitoring his vital signs that shocked him, but the state of his face. The image reminded him of a swollen bruised beetroot. Hunter had dealt with many bad assaults over the years, and many murders, but never had he seen someone whose face had taken such a battering. He swallowed hard.

DS Leggate jolted awake. For a moment she looked startled

'Sorry gaffer,' he said, 'I just wanted to pop in and see how he is.'

Dawn pushed herself up the chair and tried to blink sleep from her eyes. 'Sorry Hunter, I'd gone there. What time is it?'

Hunter glanced at his watch, 'Ten past eight.'

'Gosh I've been asleep for almost an hour. That's the first time I've managed to get some shut-eye since I got here late last night.' Then, knuckle-rubbing her right eye and looking at Michael, she said, 'There's been no change in him since he was admitted.'

'Has he not come round?'

She shook her head. Stray strands of hair came away from her loose ponytail. 'They're keeping him sedated because of his head injury. The surgeon who operated on him said it was to release the pressure. They're going to keep him like that until they think he's ready or until he show's signs of improvement.' On a brittle note she ended, 'They've said that the next twenty-four hours are critical.'

Hunter stood by the end of the bed. He could see that Dawn looked shattered. Her face had none of its usual lustre – dark circles haunted her bloodshot hazel eyes and her face looked pale and drawn.

'What have they said? How badly is he injured?'

For a brief moment her eyes glassed over. She blinked and answered, 'They're mostly worried about the swelling to his brain caused by his skull fracture. Other than that he's got a fractured pelvis, right femur and a broken right arm.'

'Good God, it must have hit him with a hell of a whack. Was the car speeding? We've been told it's a hit and run?'

Dawn pursed her mouth, 'Traffic are telling me they now believe it was deliberate.'

'Deliberate?'

'They've got a witness who heard it and saw some of it. She lives in one of the cottages up from curry house. She'd just got out of the bath and heard the bang. She looked out of her window and saw the car reversing over him before driving off.'

'Reversing over him! Is she sure?'

'I spoke with the Traffic Sergeant and she tells me that the witness is confident about what she saw, and they've disclosed it to the surgeon, and he says the site and severity of the injuries would be consistent with that.'

'Christ! Deliberate?' Hunter locked eyes with Dawn for a moment, then he said, 'Any ideas who? Did the witness get a number?'

Dawn shook her head. 'She was so shocked that by the time she realised what was happening the car had driven away.'

'Any cameras around?'

She released a weak smile, 'Thinking like a detective. Can't help it can you? I've already asked the same questions.' Straightening her face, she said, 'There are none in the immediate vicinity, so they're looking at the roads around the location to see if they can pick anything up. To be honest Hunter they haven't got a lot to go on. The witness has no idea about the make of the car, other than it was a saloon, and because it was dark she can only say she thought the car was grey or silver.'

'But deliberate... Who would do this to him? It's a long time since he's been front line.'

'The only thing we can think of at the moment is the drugs related murder across in Parson Cross. I just reviewed it the other day. Michael played a key role in that, especially with the media. I don't know if you've seen any of the TV news lately Hunter, but it was Michael who announced that the police were openly declaring war on the drug gangs following the shooting. And since then there's been a massive police crackdown in Burngreave, where info tells us is where the perps live. Dozens have been arrested, and loads of drugs and assets have been seized, and although they've not yet charged anyone with the murder, it's certainly curbed their activities and created lots of anger and tension there.'

'So Traffic are looking to see if it's linked to that enquiry. Do they need any help?'

'Any help?'

'I used to be in drug squad. I've still got my contacts.'

'It's a nice gesture Hunter. And I know, like me, you want to get to the bottom of this, but I'm going to leave it to Traffic.'

'I really want to help with this. I'll make some enquiries. Do some digging around.'

'No you won't Hunter. You'll leave it to Traffic. You've got enough on with this job.' Her voice was sharp. She took a long pause, switching her look to Michael.

Hunter followed her gaze locking onto the swollen and bruised face of his former boss thinking about what Dawn Leggate had just said to him. He couldn't just do nothing. *Someone's going to pay for this!* He owed his former boss that.

CHAPTER EIGHT
DAY FOUR

Hunter stood before the bathroom mirror smoothing a hand over his freshly shaved face, at the same time casting his eyes over the grey hairs attacking the temples of his dark brown hair. He was sure their numbers had increased these past twelve months. *You're showing signs of age Hunter Kerr!*

Scooping up two handfuls of warm water from the sink, he closed his eyes and washed away the remains of shaving foam. As he straightened to check himself again he felt a pair of cold arms wrap themselves around his bare waist. The sensation made him flinch. He snapped open his eyes and caught Beth's image in the mirror, her chin resting on his right shoulder.

'I never heard you come back.'

'Sneaked in to see what you were up to.'

'Are the boys okay? I heard them earlier. They sounded lively this morning.'

'Football practice tonight after school.'

'You should have given me an extra nudge. I'd have got up with them and taken them to school.'

'I could see you were fast on.' Lifting her head from his shoulder she added, 'Anyway, I can see you need your beauty sleep.' She broke into a grin.

She always had a beautiful smile. It brought back the memory of the first time he'd set eyes on her. During his uniform period he had escorted a prisoner to the hospital following a pub brawl; the felon had needed treatment after having a bottle broken over his head by the wife of the man he was fighting with. While waiting for the doctor to stitch up the wound he had spied Beth. She had been a student nurse in A & E. They had briefly chatted while the doctor sewed up his prisoner and, on its completion, he had walked out of the hospital with a very sorrowful man nursing a sore head and her phone number. Two years later they had married. Now, with eleven-year-old Jonathan, and nine-year-old Daniel, they had just celebrated their lace anniversary and the excitement he felt whenever he saw her was exactly the same as that first time fifteen years ago.

Beth unlocked her hands and dragged her fingernails across his stomach. He felt his muscles tighten.

'Like my six-pack?' he said looking back at her.

'Six-pack,' she replied with a hint of sarcasm. 'You're going to seed Hunter Kerr.' Snatching away her hands she smacked his bottom.

He turned to grab her but she sprang away. 'You know what you are Beth...' he responded and chased her into the bedroom.

* * *

Hunter got up for the second time that morning – this time in more buoyant mood. He had been feeling down since returning from the hospital the previous evening. Seeing his former boss in that state had shaken him. He'd tried to watch television when he got home but he had found himself unable to concentrate and when he had gone to bed it had taken him an eternity to drop off. Making his way to the bathroom, the smell of bacon frying from the kitchen greeted him. It urged him on and he jumped into the shower, towelled quickly, threw on a pair of joggers and a T-shirt and hurried downstairs. When he reached the kitchen Beth was just dishing up cooked bacon onto thick crusted bread.

'The way to a man's heart,' said Hunter, leaning in and kissing her neck. She was wearing a short wrap. Black. It caressed her curves. The images of half an hour ago cascaded into his inner vision. He picked up one of the sandwiches and bit into it.

'Delicious,' he said chewing.

'Just like me.'

'This is better than you.'

Beth shouldered him. 'I'll take it back.'

He pulled away and, holding onto his bacon butty as if it was a prize, said, 'Fight you for it' and took another bite.

'What are you doing today?'

'I'm not on till two. I thought I'd go down to the gym and do a session with my dad before going into work. I haven't seen him or done any boxing training for over a week. What are you doing?'

'I've got a baby clinic at eleven. It'll be manic. In fact, all day will be. I looked on the computer before I left last night. My day's pretty well booked up with patients. Your mum's picking up the boy's after practice. Will you be home at ten?'

'Should be, I'm not planning on going to the pub.'

'How's the job going?'

'Slow start. Not got any positive leads at the moment. Still don't know who the girl is. We think she might be a prostitute.' He gave her a brief synopsis of his and Grace's conversation with Gordon Jennings.

'Sounds complicated.'

'Aren't they all? We haven't had an easy job for ages,' he said wiping the crumbs from the side of his mouth. 'As long as we get our man I ain't bothered.'

* * *

For the second evening running Hunter was alone in the MIT office. He was working through the items of evidence pertinent to the Braithwaite investigation. There were at least a dozen files to go through, plus crime scene photographs, and an exhibits list and he wanted to conduct most of the initial reading in relative silence.

Evening briefing had revealed no new leads, though the HOLMES team had narrowed down the missing persons list to two possible candidates who could be the victim since they had widened the search to include West Yorkshire's *Missing From Homes*. Grace had tracked down relatives of both missing women and left them a telephone message to contact her. When she had left earlier there hadn't been a response from either of the families. Retired PC Gordon Jennings had come up with the date of the major fire in the chapel and the names of the teenagers he had interviewed in relation to it, and actions had been allocated to trace and re-interview those people.

Hunter lifted his gaze from the dozens of sheets of paper that lay across his desk. He had already moved some of the piles of documents he had read and pushed them across onto Grace's desk. He was currently going through the victims' witness statements. From those he was moving onto the suspect interview notes. He was hoping that by the end of the evening he would have gleaned enough information from the case files to enable him to present a thorough account of Terrence Arthur Braithwaite's rape and killing spree at next morning's briefing. As he eased away his tie from his shirt collar and cast his eyes on the next statement he had chosen, he hoped to God this wasn't a pointless exercise, especially as he was the person pushing Braithwaite to the fore of the enquiry.

Hunter had just turned the first page when he became aware of heavy footsteps sounding outside in the corridor, heading his way. He lifted his head just as Barry Newstead drifted into the office.

Barry stopped in his tracks. 'Hey 'op mucker. You still here? Haven't you got a bed to go to?'

Hunter kept his finger over the paragraph he had started. 'I'm just seeing if I can get through the majority of this lot so I can brief the team tomorrow.'

He watched Barry walk to his desk. Hunter noticed he was wearing a suit he hadn't seen before, but whether it was new or not was debatable – it was so badly creased that it looked as if he had slept in it. Hunter knew that his size had something to do with it – Barry had always been big, and slightly overweight, yet for years he had carried it off, presenting himself as a man not to be messed with. However, of late, Hunter thought that Barry had lost his swagger. Especially these past six months. The bull neck he once had now showed signs of shrivelling and his jowls were starting to drop. He knew he'd not long had his fifty-seventh birthday but Hunter couldn't help but think he looked older, especially since he had stopped dyeing his hair and moustache. His rumple of thick curls and bushy moustache was now a mass of dark grey.

Hunter watched him flop down in his seat and unfurl a clump of papers he was holding. Barry flashed him a smile. He returned the gesture. *There's still fire in those eyes though.* He had first come across Barry Newstead when the detective had interviewed him following the murder of his sixteen-year-old girlfriend Polly: A murder which had recently been resolved. Then, when he had joined the police, he had been reacquainted with him in 1994, when he joined CID. Barry became his mentor and they had formed a remarkable partnership. Barry was one of the best thief takers he had met and a brilliant interviewer, he'd quickly learned so much from him, although there had been occasions when some of the tactics he employed to get confessions had disturbed Hunter. Nevertheless, he had always supported him, and it was Hunter who had invited him to take up the post of Civilian Investigator within the team eighteen months ago.

Barry waved the batch of papers he had just unfurled, 'Well I've got some more reading for you before you go home.'

Hunter's eyebrows knitted, 'What are those?'

'Copies of the newspaper reports about The Beast of Barnwell. Makes for good reading actually. When I first went into CID it had only been two years since Braithwaite had been caught. Most of the guys in there had been involved in the investigation and besides football and shagging it was all they ever talked about.'

'Do you recall much of that conversation?'

Barry threw him a puzzled look. 'Depends on what you mean. As I say there was always someone in the office who, at some stage, would bring something up about the case.'

'I'm thinking about the rapes he was charged with and the murder. Remember Gordon Jennings said he didn't think one of the rapes had been investigated properly. In fact, his words were that it had been knocked. What I'm getting at is, are you aware of any outstanding rape cases from your time in CID that could've been down to him? And any undetected murders as well. David Simmons, our historian friend, said that there was a rumour that Braithwaite was responsible for more.'

'I can certainly confirm that they thought he'd done more than what he'd been charged with. They were looking at a couple of indecent assaults locally on women that were pretty similar to his MO, and there was an unsolved murder of a prostitute found on waste land, just outside Sheffield city centre, from the early seventies, that they were looking at. Apparently, a van of a similar type and colour as his had been seen in the area where she was found and was never eliminated from that enquiry. I know for a fact he had at least two prison visits by us, but like every other interview he refused to talk. If you want my thoughts I certainly think we're onto something with Braithwaite. Using the armrests of his seat he pushed himself up, 'Do you want to take a shufti at these while I get us a drink.'

'Go on then. It'll give me something different to look at. I'm starting to get eye-strain with all these statements.'

Barry reached across and dropped the curled sheets of paper over the statement Hunter had been reading, stepped from behind his desk and ambled to where the tea making facilities were where he picked up two mugs. Holding them up he said, 'I'll just nip down the corridor and get these cleaned.' Then, he made for the door.

Hunter picked up the papers. They were A4 photocopied sheets of headline reports from the Barnwell Chronicle newspaper. They recounted the guilty verdict against Braithwaite. back in 1973. for the murder of Glynis Young, his escape and capture in 1984 and his subsequent release to freedom three years ago. He began to read.

Hunter had just finished the last report when Barry returned and placed two clean empty mugs on top of Hunter's paperwork.

'I'll get us a real drink shall I?' Barry said, and walked back to his desk where he brought out a bottle of blended whisky from his bottom drawer, held it aloft for a second as if seeking Hunter's approval, but without waiting for a nod pulled out his chair from behind his desk and wheeled it next to Hunter. Unscrewing the cap of the bottle he arranged the mugs and engaged Hunter's eyes. 'Would sir like ice?' he cracked a grin as he sat down.

Hunter laughed.

Barry poured them each a generous measure and picked up his mug and cradled it as if it was an expensive malt in a crystal cut glass tumbler.

Hunter picked up his own mug and took a swig, holding the whisky in his mouth a few seconds before swallowing. The warmth of the liquid tumbled down his throat leaving him with a satisfying afterburn. 'Just what the doctor ordered Barry.'

'Remember when we did this regularly?'

Hunter nodded. 'Not seen as the done-thing now mate.'

'The job's changed.'

Hunter thought about what he'd said. 'To be fair Barry, it had to.'

'The fun's gone out of it.'

Hunter studied his face. The laughter lines he always recalled him having had now been replaced by deep creases. Hunter wondered if it was simply age or the stress of being diagnosed with angina a few months ago. He said, 'Does that sound as if you're thinking of putting your ticket in again?'

'No chance.'

Hunter remembered Barry's initial retirement seven years ago. It hadn't been his choice. He had been forced out by the newly promoted District Chief Inspector, who, following a complaint by a prisoner that Barry had planted evidence, had entered a packed CID office, called him a dinosaur and likened him to Gene Hunt from *Life on Mars*. When Barry had retaliated by telling him he was proud of being likened to a 'real copper, and not someone who'd been arse-wiped all through his career, and wouldn't know a villain even if one'd slapped him in the face,' the Chief Inspector had made it known that he was going to nail him for his unorthodox and illegal methods and get him the sack. Following that outburst Barry had been advised by his DI to take retirement and he had reluctantly done so.

'Why did you come back Barry? Okay, I know I suggested it when I was working on the 'Demon' case, but you could have turned it down. You were well into retirement. Why come back to even worse bureaucracy and more restrictions than when you left?'

Barry's mouth tightened. 'I should be saying because of Jean dying, and I was lonely, and needed focus, but the bottom line is that even if she was alive today I would have still jumped at the chance following your invite. This isn't a job it's a way of life.' He lifted his mug, saluted Hunter and took a drink of his whisky. Nursing his mug and relaxing back in his seat he said, 'Pretty bad about Mike Robshaw eh?'

'I went to see him last night. He looked in a bad way. They've kept him sedated.'

'Do you know how he is today?'

'I tried to ring the gaffer but my call went to her voicemail. I'm going to call in on my way home again tonight.'

'If he's awake give him my regards.'

'Yeah, of course.'

'He was a good boss Hunter.'

'That's a real compliment coming from you Barry. Especially given your thoughts about bosses.'

Barry smiled. 'No, he was Hunter. His feet were always on the ground. He was old school. He'd been there and done it.' He took another drink. 'Do you remember the time we were interviewing that prisoner for a spate of distraction burglaries on elderly people. Mike came in while we were writing down his confession and asked us how we were going on and the prisoner accused us of fitting him up. Mike asked him what he meant and he told him that we'd bet him a tenner that we'd get him convicted. Do you remember? Mike first looked at him, then at us, and then put his hand in his jacket pocket, slowly took out his wallet and said, 'I think I'll have a tenner on that.'

Hunter broke into laughter. 'I'd forgotten about that Barry. Yeah I remember.' He stared into his mug, became thoughtful for a moment, then, lifting his gaze said, 'I hope he pulls through.'

Barry drained the last of his whisky. Putting down his empty mug he said, 'Fancy another nip?'

Hunter looked once more at his mug's contents. He still had quite a bit of whisky left. He shook his head. 'I'd like to say yes, but I've quite a bit to get to get through before I knock off. And now I've got these newspaper reports to summarise and fit into my briefing.' He switched his look back to the photocopied headlines Barry had dropped over his paperwork. His eyes settled on the report relating to the capture of the Beast following his escape after his wife's funeral during the 1980s. He glimpsed at the date of the article and suddenly the hairs at the back of his neck bristled. From his top tray he picked out the sheet of paper that contained the information about the two West Yorkshire women missing in the 1980s. Snapping up his head, wide eyed, he stared across the desk at Barry, 'Thanks to the date on one of these newspaper reports I think I might have just found out who our victim is.'

CHAPTER NINE
DAY FIVE.

Julie Adamson, as she now was, lived in a detached house on a large newly built estate in Pudsey. Before allowing Hunter and Grace into her home she kept them on the doorstep whilst she examined their police identification and looked them over. As they followed her through the hallway, Hunter took a glimpse of the 80s photograph he was holding; two teenage girls posing for the camera, one younger than the other. The youngest had long mousey hair and a pretty angelic face – it was her they were here about. The other girl, although some thirty-five years younger in the photo, clearly resembled the woman they were following along the hall.

She showed them through to a large open plan lounge dominated by a black corner suite. A large screen TV, above a replica Adams style fireplace, was on. It was showing a music channel video but the sound had been muted.

Julie displayed an anxious look as she switched off the TV with the remote, offered them the sofa and seated herself in a large matching armchair opposite. 'I'm guessing from the phone call you've found Ann Marie and it's not good news?'

Hunter gave the photograph another quick glimpse before offering it across for Julie to take. He couldn't help but notice that her light brown hair still had the same bob-style as that in the photograph. He replied, 'We don't know that yet Julie. This is the photograph we have on our system of Ann Marie. I can recognise you in it. Can you just confirm for me that the girl standing next to you is your younger sister?'

Julie took it from him. Her hand was shaking. She looked at it for only a couple of seconds before nodding and returning her gaze. 'That's the last photo we had done together. I was nineteen and she was seventeen. Mum took it before we went out together one night. It was just as things were starting to go bad with Ann Marie.' She handed it back. 'Have you found her? Is she dead?'

Hunter clipped the photograph of Julie and Ann Marie Banks into his folder, 'Honest answer Julie? we don't know. I can tell you we have found a body of a female who we believe died in the nineteen-eighties, but we're unable to identify who she is at the present time. There was nothing with her ID wise, and so the only way we can do that is by comparing DNA. We have a number of girls, including Ann Marie, on our system who are still listed as missing from the eighties and what we're currently doing is visiting everyone who reported someone missing back then. Where we find a family member, we are asking them to provide a mouth swab so we can cross-match the DNA.'

She returned a nod of understanding.

'I know we talked on the phone this morning but just for the record can I confirm that you reported your sister missing back in May, nineteen-eighty-four?'

Julie nodded again.

'And can you confirm she is still missing?'

'I haven't seen her since I reported her that day. I last spoke with Ann Marie on Saturday the twelfth of May, nineteen-eighty-four.' She bounced her look between Hunter and Grace. 'I still remember most of what we talked about. It was our last conversation. I've never forgotten it.' For a brief spell her look went vacant. Shaking herself from her dream-like state she said, 'When Ann Marie first went missing, because of the type of person she'd become, and because of the people I knew she hung around with I reported her missing because I thought she might have been in an accident, or something bad had happened to her, like the last time when she was taken to hospital. But when the police told mum and me that she'd disappeared and they'd no idea where she was I just knew she'd come to some harm. And although I clung to the hope that one day she'd just turn up, as time went on, and we'd not heard from her, I somehow knew deep down that Ann Marie was dead.' She looked at Hunter. 'You could say I've been expecting this.'

Out the corner of his eye Hunter could see Grace had begun taking notes. 'As I said earlier Julie, we don't know if it is Ann Marie, we still have other people to speak to who reported girls missing.'

'It won't be a shock if it is her you know.'

'Julie, a couple of seconds ago I picked up on something you said about expecting to hear that Ann Marie had been taken to hospital. You said 'like the last time'. What did you mean by that?'

She pointed to Hunter's clip folder. 'Ann Marie left home not long after that photograph was taken – a big bust up. Three months later the police came to our house and told me and mum that she was in hospital. She'd been beaten up. The police told us she'd been found unconscious in an alley.' She glanced between Hunter and Grace again. 'That was when we also found out the life she was living. You know she was on the streets don't you?'

Hunter dipped his head in affirmation. 'We've got it recorded that Ann Marie received a police caution for prostitution.'

'That was down to that boyfriend of hers. Jamie bloody Baxter. Waster of this parish.' She spat out. 'She met him a just few months before that photo was taken. You can see how attractive she was. She had lots of lads fancying her but for reasons best known to her she took up with Jamie. Mum warned her about him but she took no notice and the next thing we knew she was taking drugs. We found out Jamie was a dealer. He used to push stuff at soul nights you know. Wigan Casino and all that. He ended up getting arrested eventually but not before he'd damaged Ann Marie.'

'Sorry to hear that Julie.' Hunter saw that her neck had turned blotchy. He thought it to be a sign that she was getting agitated. 'I know this is uncomfortable for you but we need to know a few things about Ann Marie.' He paused to give her some breathing space before saying, 'Tell me about the time she was in hospital. Do you know exactly what happened to her?'

'Only that the police said they'd found her unconscious and that she'd been beaten up. They asked if we had any idea who might have done it because apparently she'd refused to tell them what had happened. We gave them Jamie's name and I know they questioned him but it never came to anything. Me and mum went to see her in the hospital. She was in a right state. We'd tried to get her to tell us who'd attacked her but she just kept telling us she didn't know. Mum got a bit angry with her over it.'

'Do you remember the injuries she had?'

She thought for the briefest of spells before answering, 'A couple of broken ribs and a broken wrist. She had a black eye as well.'

Hunter quickly exchanged glances with Grace. He could see in his partner's eyes that like he, she was registering that their victim had the same injuries. Goose bumps rippled his skin. He said, 'Can you tell us, if it's not too difficult, a bit about Ann Marie's background? I'm afraid we've only got the most basic of details about her on our computer.'

Julie Adamson's mouth tightened and she slowly shook her head. 'It's a good job mum's how she is you know. This would probably see her off.' She stared at them a moment and added, 'Mum's in a care home. She's got dementia. Doesn't even know me now. Talks about Ann Marie going missing all the time, as if it was just yesterday, bless her.'

'And your dad?' asked Grace.

'Dad's dead. He died a long time ago before all this happened. I was only eight. It was an accident at work. He was electrocuted by a faulty machine. Mum brought us up on her own. Struggled at times. That's why I sometimes get so bloody angry when Ann Marie's name comes up. I think about all she put mum through when she knew how hard it was for her.'

'I'm sorry to put you through this,' said Hunter, 'But could you tell us a bit about Ann Marie, so we can get a picture of her.'

Julie Adamson huffed. 'Do you know why I get angry?' She didn't wait for a response. 'It's because I know what she was once like – before that Jamie walked into her life and got her into drugs. Don't get me wrong neither of us were angels, but I would never have thought Ann Marie would end up being the person she was. We were so close, right up to her being seventeen. There's only two years between us. Ann Marie was a bit of a tomboy compared to me. I was the one who played inside with dolls while she'd sooner be out climbing trees. When we were in our early teens we were inseparable, but then I started work at Woolworth's and that's when she started seeing Jamie Baxter. I knew a bit about him from school. I remember him being this lad from a rough family who was always getting into scrapes – fighting. And he was also a bit of a bully. But the drugs thing we didn't know about until he'd got his hooks in her and then it was too late. Don't get me wrong mum did her best once she found out and tried to get Ann Marie to finish with him. To appease us she told us she had, but she hadn't, she was seeing him behind our backs.'

'So things got strained between you?'

'Once she got in with Jamie we didn't recognise her. I kept having a go at her to dump him and she kept promising she would but she kept saying that it was hard because she loved him. I got on to her about the drugs and she just said they were only uppers and that they were harmless. It was so frustrating. Even I couldn't get through to her.' She glanced up to the ceiling for a few seconds. Then, returning her gaze said, 'She got worse. She stole money from me you know. I caught her. We had this blazing row and mum got involved and told her she had enough to put up with, without what she was doing, and that's when Ann Marie stormed out. She moved into a flat with Jamie. She was eighteen.' She broke off, rubbing her face with her hands. After a few seconds of silence she continued. 'It wasn't the same after that between me and her. I bumped into her a couple of times in the High Street and she used to come into Woolworth's and ask to borrow money, but I knew what it was going to and so I said I couldn't. She used to kick off in the store and she was ejected by the manager on quite a few occasions. I lost my job because of her.'

'I'm sorry to put it like this Julie, but do you think that's how Ann Marie got into prostitution then?' asked Hunter.

She nodded. 'It was a few years after she left home. Or at least I think it was. She split up from Jamie when she was nineteen. He went to prison after he was caught breaking into a chemist, which was no surprise, and Ann Marie couldn't afford the rent so the landlord kicked her out. She came back home, and asked mum if she could have her room back and that she'd change. Mum took her back and she repaid her by stealing from her purse.' She shook her head in disgust. 'We both had a go at her and mum told her to get out. I've never seen mum so angry. The next I heard of Ann Marie was about six months later. A couple of mates in the pub said that they'd bumped into Ann Marie, and they told me that they barely recognised her. That she looked a bit of a wreck. She'd apparently tried to cadge some money off them and told them that she was sharing a flat with a girl in Chapeltown. And then I got the phone call from her that night when she was locked up. "Could I come and collect her" she said, she'd "got no money for a taxi." That was when I found out she'd got herself arrested for prostitution. I was mortified. I was so bloody embarrassed when I walked into that police station, I can tell you. When I asked for Ann Marie, the officer on the desk looked at me as if I was something on the bottom of his shoe. I just wanted to curl up into a ball and disappear. And when I saw her for myself I couldn't believe she was the same person. She was nothing like the Ann Marie I knew. She'd lost weight. She looked like someone from Belsen.' She paused, then said, 'To be honest she did look like a prostitute. I never told mum. I daren't.'

'Did you take her back to her flat that night?'

'I did, but I didn't go in. It looked a bit of a dump to be honest. It was above some shops. I just dropped her off and drove off. I was so annoyed with her. Afterwards I felt so guilty – as though I was somehow to blame for what she'd become. I thought I should have tried to help her.'

'You shouldn't have felt guilty,' interjected Grace. 'She was nineteen. Grown up. It was nothing to do with you what she'd become. You've said yourself what she used to be like when she was younger. If you need to blame anyone blame Jamie Baxter.'

Julie Adamson nodded. 'Yes I guess so. I know what you're saying, but I couldn't help thinking at the time.'

Hunter jumped back in. 'Just going back Julie, it says on our system that you reported Ann Marie missing in May, nineteen-eighty-four. Her arrest for prostitution was six months before that. Did you keep in touch with one another?'

She nodded. 'Strangely enough we did. A couple of days after her arrest I came out of work and she was waiting for me. I'd got a job as a care assistant with the council and she came to the home where I was working. She said she wanted to apologise to me and said she'd done it because she had no other means of making money. We started to keep in touch after that. Not regular as such, but certainly a couple of times a month, she'd either meet me when I'd finished work or we'd meet up at a pub and I'd buy her a couple of lagers.'

'Did you ever talk about what she was up to?'

'If you mean did I ask her directly if she was still working the streets, the answer's no, but we did talk sort of indirectly. I mentioned once that I felt afraid for her — that I thought it was dangerous what she was doing. She just laughed and told me not to worry. She said her flat mate looked after her and that they mostly worked together, that sort of thing. I did ask her once about the drugs — if she was still on them? She said she was trying to get herself off. She was in a programme. She begged me not to give her a hard time so I didn't ask her anymore.'

'So what about her going missing?'

'Well, as I said earlier, the last time I talked to her was Saturday the twelfth of May, eighty-four. She used the phone in the hallway at the back of the shop where her flat was. I normally rang her but I remembered this because she rang me. It was about half six time. She sounded excited. She said she'd met someone, and that he was nice and he was going to get her a job. I said that was good news. She said she was going out with him that night. He was picking her up in his van. To be honest, I wasn't sure that what she was telling me was the truth and she must have sensed it because she burst out laughing and said, "Honest Julie, it's not like that. He's nice. He's not a punter or anything like that. We're going for a drink and talk about a job." That was basically it. She said she'd give me a ring the next day and tell me how it went. Then she said bye, and hung up.'

'Did she tell you his name?'

Julie shook her head, 'No, she never mentioned it. She was only on about a minute. She was excited. She just wanted to tell me the good news.'

'You said that Ann Marie said he was picking her up in his van? You're sure he said van?'

'Definitely, because I can remember thinking the van must be something to do with his job.'

Hunter thought about the piece of carpet they had found with their victim. Duncan Wroe, the crime scene manager, had said that he was certain the carpet had come from the back of a van. Things seemed to be slotting nicely into place. This was too much of a coincidence. 'But she never rang?'

'No. I rang the flat on Sunday evening. There was no answer for ages and then her flat mate answered and I asked to speak with

Ann Marie. She said she wasn't there. I asked her what she meant. She said she'd last seen her the previous evening – that a guy had come and picked her up and that they'd gone out for the night and she hadn't come home yet. I asked if she knew where she was but she said she'd no idea. Ann Marie hadn't told her where they were going. I told her I was worried, and Lesley – that was her flat mate – said for me not to be, that the man seemed nice. She said that as soon as Anne Marie came in she'd tell her to give me a ring. She didn't, so I rang the flat again but there was no answer so I tried the next day and that's when I spoke with the man who owned the shop who was also their landlord. I told him I was Ann Marie's sister and that I was trying to get hold of her. He said he'd not seen her Saturday afternoon and he wished he knew where she was because she owed him rent. I asked him if I could speak with Lesley instead and that's when he told me he'd not seen either of them since Saturday evening when he'd locked up. The shop was always shut on Sunday's. I asked him if he could check their flat and he said he'd already been banging on their door that morning, because they owed two months' rent, but they weren't answering. He said if he didn't get their money by the end of that day he was kicking them out and then he hung up. I rang again that Monday evening but no answer and that's when I went around to the flat the next day. I spoke with the owner and he told me that the pair had done a runner, owing him two months' rent and that he'd bagged up their stuff. He said he was keeping it and they couldn't have it until they paid up. I told him this wasn't like Ann Marie and that I was worried. He just kept saying they owed him money and they'd done a runner. He said I had to tell him when she got in touch or there'd be trouble.'

'So what did you do?'

'I asked if I could see the flat. He said there was nothing to see. He'd bagged everything up. I insisted and said I was ringing the police and so he let me have a look upstairs.'

'And?'

'It was as he said – nothing to see. Apparently he'd tidied up the place and bagged up their bedding and clothes. I called the police and they asked me if I could go to the station to make my report. I did so and spoke with a PC Townsend. When I told them him about what I knew and what the shop keeper had done with Ann

Marie's stuff he sided with him and just suggested that Ann Marie had gone because she owed money and that she'd turn up. He also asked me if I knew they were both prostitutes. I was so angry. I asked him what that had to do with me reporting my sister missing. I think I embarrassed him and he promised he'd do some enquiries and get back to me.'

'And did he?'

'To be fair he did. A couple of days later. He still thought there was nothing serious about Ann Marie's disappearance or Lesley's. He thought they were lying low because they owed money and that they'd turn up. He said Lesley was well known to them and that they were doing patrols in the area where she worked.'

'By that he meant where she worked as a prostitute?'

Julie nodded.

'Do you know Lesley's full name?'

She shook her head. 'I'd only met her once. She was with Ann Marie once when she came to meet me at the care home. Ann Marie only introduced her as Lesley her flat mate.'

'And did you get another visit from the police?'

'We rung them every day for about ten days to see if they'd heard anything or found her, and then two detectives came to the house and asked me and mum lots of questions about Ann Marie. You know like you're doing now – about her background, her friends, boyfriends. We told them about Jamie Baxter and how he'd got her into drugs and I told them what she'd told me about this man she said she was meeting.'

'So at that stage they started taking Ann Marie's disappearance seriously?'

'Yes, but I told them it was too late by then and got a bit annoyed. Mum calmed me down. They promised they would do everything they could to find her and they did come back to us on several occasions and kept us up to date. They told us they'd questioned Jamie and he'd got an alibi – he was with his new girlfriend the Saturday she'd disappeared. They'd quizzed the shop keeper and recovered Ann Marie's and Lesley's clothing and they'd looked at the flat but they said everything appeared to be okay. There was no sign that there'd been a struggle or anything in there. They asked us if we had any idea where she might be, but we hadn't a clue. Ann Marie was twenty-one when she disappeared.' Julie looked from Hunter to Grace. 'This body you've found, do you think it's Ann Marie?'

'Hunter shrugged his shoulders. 'I honestly can't say at the moment. As I said earlier the only way we'll know, I'm afraid, is by a DNA comparison. We need to take a mouth swab from you if that's okay?'

She nodded. 'I've got a daughter of my own you know. I've called her Ann Marie. She's twenty-two herself and got her own place. She knows about my sister going missing and I ring her every day to see if she's all right. In fact, if I don't ring before a certain time she rings me. It's made me so overprotective.'

Statement taken and DNA sample obtained, Hunter and Grace said their goodbyes on the doorstep of Julie's home.

Hunter was about to turn to make his way back to the car when Julie engaged his eyes.

She said, 'I'd like to bury her – put her with dad. Mum would want that. It just seems right.'

Hunter watched her eyes start to glass over. He wanted to say that it might not be Ann Marie, but somehow he knew different. Everything that had been said pointed to their victim being her younger sister. He said nothing. Instead he offered up a sympathetic smile and turned on his heels.

* * *

'I'm sure this is our victim,' said Hunter, taking the reins at evening briefing. He was standing beside the incident board pointing to an A4 size copy of a photograph of a mousey haired, thin faced girl, with heavy blue/grey eye make-up. She had a strong jaw. 'We've got to wait for the DNA result but I'm convinced that the person we've found in the old chapel is twenty-one-year-old Ann Marie Banks, from Chapeltown, Leeds, who was last known to be alive on Saturday, the twelfth of May, nineteen-eighty-four.' He tapped her photo. 'This is the last photograph we have of her and she was seventeen in this. Her older sister Julie says that even though she was four years older than that photo when she disappeared, it bears a strong resemblance because she looked a lot younger than her age, although she did say that when she went missing she had lost some weight and her face looked gaunt because of her drug use.' Hunter went on to outline the circumstances of Ann Marie Banks' disappearance gained from that morning's interview. 'From our talk with Julie it has thrown up some very interesting information which totally convinces me that the body is that of Ann Marie Banks. First, our victim certainly fits the profile in terms of height and size and hair colour, and secondly, we have the old injuries to her ribs and wrist when she was beaten up.' He took a step forward from the board. 'What is also interesting is the van aspect. Julie Adamson told us that when she last spoke with her sister, she told her that she was going out that Saturday evening with a man and that he was picking her up in his van. As we know our victim was found lying on a piece of carpet that is believed to have come from the back of a van.' He tapped the photograph of the white jumper and pink trousers. 'We have shown Julie Adamson the clothing our victim was wearing but she doesn't recognise any of it, however, she does recognise the loop earrings. She said her mother had bought Ann Marie a similar pair for her sixteenth birthday.' He took a breath and looked to Dawn Leggate, to see if she wished to respond. He could see she looked tired. Her hazel eyes no longer held their sparkle. He wasn't surprised – she was putting in visits to the hospital to see Michael in between her incident room work. In fact, she had only got back from visiting him ten minutes prior to evening briefing. He had bumped into her as she was closing the door of her office and had asked how he was. She'd told him that though there were signs of improvement Michael still wasn't out of danger. He had been taken back to theatre that afternoon to have his fracture pin-and-plated and he was still heavily sedated. It must be a really worrying time for her he thought as he held her gaze.

When she didn't respond he prompted, 'I don't know what your thoughts are boss, but for me everything fits.' She gave him a slow nod. 'It certainly looks as though you might have discovered who our victim is and, if it is her, somewhere to start our enquiries. Good work. I've asked for the DNA sample to be prioritised so we could have a result as early as tomorrow morning. She momentarily closed her eyes and rubbed at her temples. Blinking her eyelids open she said, 'You've also gained some information about Ann Marie's flat mate?'

Hunter responded, 'Yes boss. Grace has made some checks since we got back and we believe that woman is Lesley Jane Warren. Interestingly, Lesley is also listed on the Missing Person Index. She was officially reported missing by her mother twelve days after Ann Marie's disappearance. That report was made following the visit by the detectives investigating Ann Marie's disappearance. Thanks to Julie Adamson, we know that Lesley Jane Warren was alive on Sunday the thirteenth of May, nineteen-eighty-four, because she spoke with her on the phone. But after that she simply disappeared without trace. Extensive checks were made by the police at all her local haunts and with all known associates but without gain. Lesley was known by police in Chapeltown; she had been cautioned twice for prostitution and she also had a conviction for shoplifting. She was twenty-three years old back then.'

SIO Dawn Leggate threw Hunter a look to check he had finished. When he returned a nod she said, 'At the moment, although it looks as though our victim is Ann Marie Banks, without a DNA match we merely have speculation. What is significant is that on the date she went missing Braithwaite was AWOL from prison and it coincides with the fire at the chapel. And on that note that is where I want to leave things for now. If we get a hit tomorrow, then it certainly throws up new lines of enquiry. Especially with regard to her flat mate.

* * *

Doctor Anna Wilson listened to the rain outside machine-gunning the roof of the forensic tent. For the past ten minutes she had noted it getting louder and faster with each passing minute, and now, for the first time since the weather had changed she could feel the cold: The forensic suit she was wearing offered no protection whatsoever to the drop in temperature. She checked her watch. 8.30p.m. Time to call it a day, and time to tell her team to pack up their equipment – the mix of experienced staff and students were working with the ground penetrating radar outside the inner cordon. *Gosh! They must be soaked through.* Even though she had heard the rain getting heavier she had been so focussed on finishing excavating the last section of the grave-site by the end of that day that she hadn't given a thought for her team nearby. Stabbing her trowel into the damp soil and gripping its handle, she eased herself up, slowly straightening out her spine. It had been a long day. She was about to call out to her team and tell them to pack up when the voice of her supervisor shouted up, 'Anna, I think we've found something!'

CHAPTER TEN
DAY SIX

'Can I have your attention everyone,' called Dawn Leggate, lifting her voice above the chatter as she strode to the front of the room. 'I think you've already heard, but I'm making it official – we've found another body buried in the construction site!' She parked herself on the edge of a desk. 'I was called away from the hospital last night. Doctor Anna Wilson and her team have found more human remains with the ground penetrating radar, and what's interesting is that they are less than a dozen yards from where we found our first victim. Duncan Wroe turned out last night, together with a forensic team and they've secured the site ready to start work on the excavation this morning. As yet, we don't know what we will find. I have been told that the remains are only a couple of feet below the surface – roughly the same depth as our first victim.' She paused momentarily, glancing at the incident board. Then continuing, she said, 'This is a game changer. Until Doctor Wilson excavates the site we won't know what we've got, but given last night's revelation about Ann Marie's flatmate, Lesley Jane Warren, I am going to begin preparations for another body find. And I am opening out the search parameter. I have a meeting with the POLSA Inspector this morning and we are going to grid-mark the area to conduct new searches. With regard to our enquiries, until Doctor Wilson uncovers the remains and tells us what we've got, we still focus on our first victim.' She began tapping the tips of her fingers, 'We chase up that DNA result. We need it urgently. We really could do with knowing if our victim is Ann Marie Banks, especially as the murder MO of this victim fits with the others. And we plough through the existing lines of enquiries you've all been allocated.' She slid off the edge of the desk and hand smoothed the front of her skirt. 'You have enough to get on with guys.'

* * *

Detective Constables Tony Bullars and Mike Chapman traced Susan Braddock to a semi-detached house in the nearby town of Goldthorpe. She answered the door after the first couple of loud knocks from Tony. In her early fifties, with short dark hair, she eyed them with intense suspicion. Tony flashed his warrant card and introduced them. 'We're making enquiries into the body we've found on the construction site at Chapel Meadows.'

She responded by screwing up her face, moulding puzzled features.

Tony returned his identification to his inside jacket pocket. 'We think you might be able to help us.'

She slackened her brow. 'I don't understand.'

'We believe you used to play around the old chapel with some friends when you were younger – back in the eighties?'

Now her face changed to one of bewilderment. 'Well, yes, but how…'

Tony interrupted, 'Susan, your name was given to us by a retired police officer called Jennings, who used to be the community bobby for the Chapel estate. The body we've found was buried beneath the wooden floor of the old chapel and he's told us that he once interviewed you and your mates about a fire that was started in the chapel in May, nineteen-eighty-four?'

She blushed slightly, 'Good God! Bobby Scott you mean?'

Tony nodded.

'Crikey, I remember that now. I was only thirteen. He scared the bloody life out of me and my mates. My mum wouldn't let me go out for a fortnight after that. He accused us of trying to burn the old chapel down.'

'Yes we know. He's told us a little bit about it. Can we come in and have a chat?'

'But it had nothing to do with us. We got blamed because we used to play there.'

Tony took a step forward. At six-foot-tall, with an athletic build, and a clean-shaven strong jaw with cleft chin, he was a commanding presence. 'We could still do with having a chat with you.'

His door-step action caused Susan to back up into the hallway. She said, 'I don't know how I can help you. And what's the fire to do with this body you've found?'

'I can explain all that,' Tony replied, flashing his blue/grey eyes and taking another step forward.

Susan Braddock turned and started walking back into the house, shrugging her shoulders. Tony and Mike followed, closing the door behind them. She took them into the kitchen.

She called over her shoulder. 'I was just making a drink. Do you want one?'

Tony glanced at his partner who returned a nod. Tony said, 'Coffee would be great. Milk please, two sugars for me and none in the other. My colleague's on a diet.'

She smiled as she filled up the kettle, 'I'm always on a bloody diet. It's not working.' Following a pause she asked, 'Have you spoken with any of the others?'

'You're the only one we've managed to trace so far.' Mike Chapman replied. Mike was a complete contrast to his partner. Four years' senior to Tony, at 34, with unruly greying hair he looked a lot older, and whereas Tony was tall and slim, he was chunky, despite having lost three stone over the last six months. He had recently grown a goatee beard and moustache which, although trimmed, still looked untidy on his face.

'How did you find me after all this time?'

'Facebook.' Tony answered.

She gave him an incredulous look, before bursting into laughter. 'Well I wasn't expecting that. Facebook.'

'It's how we get a lot of our breakthroughs these days. It's almost our first port of call when we're trying to trace someone. It's also how we catch a lot of our villains would you believe? One recently did a selfie whilst he was doing a burglary near here and put it on for his mates to see. I mean how stupid is that?'

Susan gave another short laugh and switched on the kettle. 'Bobby Scott used to scare the shit out of us as kids. He was bloody huge. As soon as we saw him we'd run a mile.'

'He's still a big fellow and he's in his seventies now,' said Mike.

'We never started that fire you know. He tried to say it was us but it wasn't.' She bounced her gaze between the detectives. 'Honest. I'm telling the truth.' The kettle boiled itself off and she made three coffees. Handing Tony and Mike one each she said, 'I've seen it on the news about the body you've found but I don't see how I can help.'

Tony responded, 'To be fair Susan we don't know if you can. What we're looking at is the probability that fire at the chapel was started around the same time as when the body was buried there.'

Her face suddenly paled.

Tony picked up on it. He said, 'Is there something the matter?'

She spluttered and set down her coffee, 'Jeez! We knew something was wrong that night, but we never told Bobby Scott when he interviewed us – we were too scared, because we knew we shouldn't have been in the chapel.'

'What do you mean Susan?'

She covered her mouth and looked shocked. 'Talk about visiting the past...' Shaking her head, she added, 'I think we might have seen something.'

'What do you mean you might have seen something?'

'It wasn't as much seen, as what we heard.'

'Can you tell us what that was?'

She shot a glance to Tony. 'Did you say May, nineteen-eighty-four?'

Tony nodded. 'That's when the fire was, according to PC Jennings, he wrote it down in his pocket note book. It was actually the thirteenth – a Sunday evening. Does it ring any bells?'

'It being the Sunday evening it does, though I can't remember the month, and nineteen-eighty-four was right because, as I say, I was thirteen. I remember it being Sunday because we always used to go there the night before school. We used it as a sort of a den. The place was really creepy and we'd go there as a sort of dare. It was somewhere we could have a crafty smoke and we'd play hide-and-seek, that kind of thing. Steve – Steve Simpson who used to live in the next street used to tell us ghost stories and all about the supernatural. Scared the shit out of us.' She broke into a smile and pulled her eyes away, drifting them to the window, as if reminiscing.

'So you were there that night of the fire?'

She brought back her gaze. 'Yes, but as I say we had nothing to do with that. It was the other two people who broke in.'

'Two?' Tony shot a quick look at Mike and then fixed her eyes. 'You say two people?'

'It's a long time ago now, but I'm sure I can remember thinking there were two. To be honest I didn't see anyone exactly – it was their voices I heard. I'm sure it was two men. We were upstairs in the gallery at the time. Steve was telling us another one of his stories when we heard them breaking in downstairs. We thought at first it was Bobby Scott coming to get us and we were crapping ourselves, but then when we heard their voices we realised it wasn't. We kept our heads down thinking they'd have a quick look around, realise there was nothing worth nicking and then bugger off, but they didn't. I could hear this groaning and dragging noise and so I peeked over the balcony...' She broke off and her face lit up. '...That's it, it's coming back to me now. I looked over the balcony but it was too dark to see anything clearly, but I could see two people. They were just below us and I could see they were bent over this long bundle. Steve told me to get down in case they saw us. Everyone was bricking it. None of us dare move.'

'Did you look over the balcony again?'

'No I kept my head down.'

'Can you remember what else you heard? Anything they said?'

'Not what they said. They seemed to be groaning more than anything and I could hear them dragging something. I guessed it was the bundle they had. Then I heard them smashing up the floorboards.' She took a long look at Tony. 'It's all coming back to me now. We never told Bobby Scott this because we thought we might get into trouble.'

'This is really important Susan. Think about what you heard?'

'She thought for a moment. 'I can remember floorboards being pulled up and then some scraping. I can remember whispering to the others about taking a look at what they're doing but Steve told me not to. He said they might be murderers and they're burying a body. She took another look at Tony. 'He said it as a sort of a joke to wind us up because we were so scared, but I mean, what you're telling me is that was probably what was happening, aren't you?'

Tony checked with Mike before answering, 'It's certainly looking that way Susan.'

'Bleeding Hell. Wait till I tell my mates. They won't believe it.'

Mike asked, 'You know when you said you saw them bent over something. Can you remember anything of what that might have been? The shape or anything? Could you tell if it was a body?'

She gave them a look that told Tony and Mike she was thinking about the question. After several seconds she shook her head, 'I really did only have a quick look and, as I say, it was dark by then. It was hard to see anything at all.'

'But you're confident when you say there were two of them?' Mike again.

Her mouth tightened. 'I'm sure I saw two. I mean it's so long ago and it's the first time I've thought about this since I was thirteen. We all made a pact not to talk about it after Bobby Scott interviewed us because we were scared about what we'd seen and we'd told him a lie by saying we weren't in the chapel that Sunday.'

'And the voices you heard – were they men's voices?'

She nodded vigorously. 'Definitely.'

'Young or old?'

She studied for a moment. 'Old.' Then she paused. 'Do you know I'm not sure when I say old. Like I say I was only thirteen. They were men that's all I can say. They were whispering, but like loud, but I couldn't hear what they were saying. We were right up in the gallery. All I wanted was to get out of there. Do you know what I mean?'

Tony nodded. 'You said you heard floorboards being ripped up. Beneath it is soil. Did you hear any digging with shovels or scraping or anything like that?'

She appeared to be thinking about the question again. After a while she answered, 'I'm not really sure. I could hear this smashing up and that's when we decided to get out of there. We sneaked out to the back corridor. There was a window that went out onto an outbuilding and we climbed out of that and just legged it. When we got to the meadow we hid ourselves in the grass and stayed there for a while. Steve kept joking about them being murderers. Then we saw the smoke coming from the chapel and Steve said to leg it before the cops come, so we did. That's when we got our heads together and said none of us were to say anything. When Bobby Scott interviewed us we all kept to our story.' She gave Tony an innocent look. 'You can understand can't you?'

Tony nodded. 'Sure I can. I think I would have done the same at thirteen.' He studied Susan's features for several seconds. He couldn't help but think that she had just handed them some very important pieces of their jigsaw.

* * *

Dawn Leggate made her way to the incident board, picked up a red marker, wrote a name below the word 'victim' and turned to face her team. She tapped the board. 'I've had it confirmed ten minutes ago. The remains found six days ago are definitely that of twenty-one-year-old Ann Marie Banks.' She studied their faces. She could see looks of acknowledgement. Doubts had finally been answered. The DNA confirmation meant that they could progress their enquiries. 'Now we can start delving properly into her past. It's not going to be easy given the time-factor but we already know a little about Ann Marie thanks to her sister.' She took a short breath. 'We know that at the age of eighteen she started to go off the rails after she met a guy called Jamie Baxter, who got her into drugs and most likely into prostitution. He's someone I now want tracing and questioning. Secondly, we know she worked the streets and we know she was caught on Manningham Lane in Bradford and given a caution. See if we still have intelligence regarding her activities and see if there is anything on the system about punters around that time. And thirdly, we also know that she was badly beaten up and hospitalised. The detectives who investigated her disappearance might be a good starting point, although I'm guessing they'll be retired now.' She set down the marker pen. 'The flat she was living in... We know it's a charity shop now, but I need to know who the owner was when Ann Marie was living there. We know he bagged up Ann Marie's and Lesley Jane Warren's stuff because he told Julie Adamson that he'd done it. I want him interviewed and eliminated as well. I want to know what that room was like shortly after her disappearance. See if the detectives searched it and noted anything untoward. And check if it was forensically examined at the time. If not, I want that done now.' She brought together her hands with a clap. 'Most importantly, we need to trace the man who Ann Marie was meeting that evening. Get his name and my guess is we have her killer.' Taking a pause, she said, 'The most likely person to know this is her flat mate. However, I have a bad feeling about her as well. The fact that she disappeared within twenty-four hours of Ann Marie going missing, has not been seen since, and especially now that we've found another body nearby. Doctor Wilson and her team are still excavating the grave but, if I was putting money on it, I'd say this is going to be Lesley Jane Warren.' She took another pause before continuing, 'Susan Braddock's information has thrown up a new angle. Gordon Jennings' pocket book clearly dates the night of the fire at the old chapel. It is the day after Ann Marie was last known to be alive. We now know for definite that it is Ann Marie's body buried there and Susan Braddock says she heard and saw someone dragging something inside the chapel. And although she is unable to describe anyone she is confident two people were involved. Both of them men. I am certain that what she and her friends witnessed was Ann Marie's body being brought there to be buried and that the fire was started to cover and protect what the killers had done.' Turning, she tapped the map of the Chapel estate. 'As to location, while I shouldn't jump to conclusions, this is right on the doorstep of Terrence Arthur Braithwaite who has already been raised as a suspect. This morning I had the helicopter do a 3D image of the area, and when we overlay it over the old ordnance survey map, these latest remains are buried within the garden boundary of Braithwaite's old house on Chapel Street.' She scoured the faces of the detectives. 'There is more regarding Braithwaite which, although forensically we can't prove it's him at the moment, it certainly makes him a person of interest.' She broke off a second, observed a few of the faces, saw that a couple were making notes, and then continued, 'We know that on the eleventh of May, nineteen-eighty-four, he escaped while at his wife's funeral and wasn't re-captured until five days later. The day after his escape is when Ann Marie Banks said she was meeting a man who was picking her up in his van, and the next night is more than likely when she was brought here to Barnwell and buried in the old chapel, witnessed by Susan Braddock. That is too big a coincidence don't you think?' She saw a few nodding heads. 'At first I was sceptical about Braithwaite, even given the fact that he was on the run around the time of Ann Marie's disappearance, but given the discovery of this latest body almost in his garden it's something we can't afford to ignore.' Dawn looked to her team again. 'The question is, if one of the people Susan Braddock heard and saw was Braithwaite, then who was the other? Everything we've heard from Gordon Jennings indicates that he was carrying out his attacks alone. This latest information would suggest otherwise.'

CHAPTER ELEVEN
DAY SEVEN

Sitting at her desk, Dawn Leggate set aside the photographs she'd received that morning following yesterday's excavation of the second crime scene. The dozen different images were of the skeleton they had removed from the muddy shallow grave: The remains were human and female. Her hands and feet had been bound with rope and a piece of rag pushed into her mouth as a gag. Like Ann Marie Banks she had been strangled, but unlike Ann Marie, no severed cow's head had been placed across her chest. Trying to shake away thoughts of what this latest victim must have gone through before she died, she picked up the photograph of Lesley Jane Warren the HOLMES team had printed from the Missing Person Index. She studied the pretty smiling freckled face with the Purdey hairstyle and asked herself, *is it you?* Laying it down over the other photos she wondered how such an innocent looking girl had ended up on the streets – selling herself. With Ann Marie Banks it had been down to her boyfriend introducing her to drugs. *What's your story?*

Momentarily, she closed her eyes and rubbed at her temples. Fighting off exhaustion, she was re-visiting everything she had seen, and every piece of information she had been given that day, doing her damnedest to compartmentalise it before evening briefing. A knock at her door broke into her concentration and she opened her eyes as DI Gerald Scaife entered.

A smile lit up his face. 'We've got a result with the corroded Yale key they found with the body yesterday.'

'By the smile on your face something tells me I'm going to like this.'

He nodded. 'Mike Chapman and Tony Bullars got a copy made of it this morning and took it across to the shop in Chapeltown where Ann Marie and Lesley Jane Warren had their flat. The upstairs is only used for storage now but it still has the original door and lock. It's never been changed. And guess what?'

'You're going to tell me it fits; I hope?'

He nodded again. 'Absolutely! I think we can be pretty certain now that the body is that of Lesley, unless another female had a key to the flat. We're still trying to track down members of her family. Her mum and dad are no longer around but her Missing from Home report listed two brothers, and we think we've found one of them living in Halifax. I've sent a request to West Yorks for them to visit the address we've got and see if it is him. With a bit of luck we should have DNA confirmation in a couple of days.'

'Great news Gerry. What about a forensics examination of the old flat?'

'That's been arranged for tomorrow. Mike and Tony have spoken with the current owners, who are the Salvation Army, and they say that the rooms upstairs have not undergone any changes since they bought it back in two-thousand-and-one. They've certainly not decorated it and Mike tells me the carpets look right for the eighties.'

'And what about the owner, when Ann Marie and Lesley were living there? Have we managed to trace him?'

'The Salvation Army bought it from a Harry Wainwright. Mike's spoken with the Captain from Chapeltown Church who was involved in buying the place. She's going to get on to the solicitor they used because she remembers Mr Wainwright telling her that he was buying a bungalow somewhere near Scarborough to retire to. With a bit of luck, we should have an address for him tomorrow.'

'Good news again. Anything else I need to know before briefing?'

'We're still trying to track down Jamie Baxter – Ann Marie's boyfriend. We think that he might be in prison. Our intelligence system had him flagged as a suspect by SOCA. We think he was busted in a big drugs operation three years ago. I've sent off a prison request for confirmation. And we've also got the name of one of the detectives who dealt with Anne Marie and Lesley Jane's disappearance. It's like you thought boss, he has retired. We've e-mailed the Pensions Department and requested his address.' Scaife took time out while Dawn made some notes in her journal. When she lifted her eyes, he took it as a signal she had finished and continued, 'And the background enquiries you wanted doing with regard to Terrence Braithwaite; the prison service has confirmed that he spent the majority of his time at Rampton Special Hospital and they have an extensive file on him. It's all on paper so they're going to try and get a copy of it across to us within the next day or two. We've also spoken with the probation service who were involved in his re-settlement. There were a number of joint meetings with the police before he was released, and it was decided that because of his age, and condition – apparently he suffered a stroke while at Rampton – that he should be placed in a bungalow well away from this area. He's currently living in Bridlington. They're e-mailing me full details.'

She gave him a nod of acknowledgment. 'It seems as though some pretty solid work's been done today.' She picked up her journal. 'Give me five minutes Gerry and then I'll be through for briefing. I'm ready for calling it a day and starting afresh tomorrow.'

Watching DI Scaife leave, shutting the door behind him, Dawn leaned back in her chair and let out a heavy sigh. She felt totally drained and she could feel a headache starting. Squeezing her eyes shut she willed it away. It had been another long day and it wasn't over yet. She still had to call in at the hospital to visit Michael before she went home. She was getting increasingly anxious about him. It had been four days since the accident and, as yet, he'd shown no sign of recovery. The consultant had reinforced only that morning that his injuries were very serious and the healing would be a slow process. Before returning to his rounds he had done his best to appease her by gently touching her arm and telling her that, 'miracles are not going to happen overnight,' but she wished they would. Most frustrating was the state of the investigation – they were still nowhere near discovering who was responsible for running him over. She just wanted this nightmare to end.

Dawn entered MIT and made her way to the incident board, pushing errant strands of hair from the sides of her face back over her ears. She gave the white board a quick glance before meeting the expectant faces of her team. It now listed two victims. Ann Marie Banks's information and timeline had been fully updated, providing her date of birth and her flat address, together with the time and date of the last known contact with her – the phone call from her elder sister. The photograph of her aged 17 from the

Missing Person Index had been placed next to the photo of her skeletal remains, as if to give the bones some formal identity. All that had been heavily underlined. Next to that, the name of Lesley Jane Warren had been scribed with an added question mark. Dawn recognised Gerry Scaife's neat handwriting.

Below Lesley's name, five photographs had been bunched together. They were duplicates of ones she had seen earlier on her desk. The first one depicted soil-stained, clothed skeletal remains partially covered by clumps of mud. The victim wore pink and white nylon shell-suit bottoms and a pink Sweater shop jumper. She knew from that morning's visit to the construction site that this was the grave shot prior to the bones being removed. The second photo showed the victim laid out on a plastic sheet with her wrists and ankles bound. The third was of a skeletal corpse after it had been stripped and laid out on a metal gurney. That was the shot before the examination by Dr Anna Wilson. There was another image of the two lengths of rope used to bind her, and the fourth photograph showed a pitted and corroded brass coloured Yale key and a gold coloured cross and chain.

'We believe that the second body that was found yesterday is that of Ann Marie's flat mate Lesley Jane Warren. At the moment that is only a "possible" because we have yet to formally identify her. We think we've traced a brother of hers and shall be requesting a DNA sample tomorrow. What makes us believe that this is Lesley, is the fact that in the pocket of a pair of shell-suit bottoms she was wearing we found a Yale key which fits the lock to the flat she shared with Ann Marie in Chapeltown. Thankfully the door hasn't been changed since the pair disappeared.' Dawn flicked open her journal and picked up on her recent notes. She took a prompt from a date she had written. 'Like Ann Marie, the last contact we have with Lesley was back in nineteen-eighty-four. In her case it was Sunday the thirteenth, roughly twenty-four hours after Ann Marie was last seen. Ann Marie's elder sister, Julie, rang the flat in Chapeltown early on the Sunday evening and Lesley answered. As we know she asked to speak with Ann Marie and it was Lesley who told her that Ann Marie hadn't come home from the previous night – that she'd last seen Ann Marie when a man had come to the flat to take her out for the evening. That is all the information we have prior to these two disappearing. To date we have no eye witnesses as to their last known movements. Julie phoned on several occasions after this but got no answer until the Tuesday, when the shopkeeper, who we now know is Harry Wainwright, answered, and told her that neither of them were at the flat, and expressed his belief that they had done a runner, because they owed him rent money. We have an enquiry out to speak with Harry Wainwright, but only as a witness at this stage. If that is still the case once we interview him, then what we have, is that both these girls disappeared on the weekend of the twelfth and thirteenth of May, nineteen-eight-four, and that is the last we know of their whereabouts until we found their bodies this week. Besides the phone conversation between Julie Adamson and Lesley Jane Warren in which Lesley made a comment about "a nice man with a van" picking up Ann Marie, the night she disappeared, the only other thing we have of significance is the information provided by Susan Braddock, who you will recall, as a thirteen-year-old, back in nineteen-eighty-four, saw and heard what she describes as two men dragging something into the chapel. We know that this was on Sunday the thirteenth of May because of the fire in the chapel that night, which was recorded by retired PC Gordon Jennings in his pocket book.' Following a short pause, she said, 'Doctor Wilson carried out a post-mortem this afternoon, and although she is unable to determine any areas of assault on the body because of its state, she has been able to disclose that she died as a result of strangulation, exactly the same way Ann Marie met her death. Though unlike Ann Marie, her hands and feet were bound with rope and a rag had been inserted into her mouth, most probably as a gag. The clothing, rope and rag have all been submitted to forensics for DNA analysis despite the condition they're in.' She snapped her journal shut and studied her team's faces. 'Things have taken a dramatic turn everyone. We have someone out there who has killed and buried two young women back in nineteen-eight-four. The question is, is it the same killer or killers? I would like to say I have an open mind on this but two females murdered and buried within twenty-four hours of each other, and only ten yards apart, that surely is too much of a coincidence. And if we take into account Susan Braddock's testimony the likelihood is that it's two killers. At the moment the finger of suspicion is clearly pointing at one man who has already been convicted of a series of rapes and one murder, but frustratingly, at this stage, all we have is lots of circumstantial evidence. We don't have anything forensically to link him, and so we have to rely on old fashioned policing and look into every little aspect of Terrence Arthur Braithwaite's life. Also, on the off-chance that I could be accused of being biased, and to make sure I haven't missed anything or anyone, before I make the decision to bring him in, I'm also allocating other lines of enquiry to determine if we have any other persons of interest who lived in that locality during the nineteen-eighties that we should be looking at.' She took a deep breath and added, 'What I also need to tell you is that the press have got wind of the second body. They have already tried to get hold of me and I've drafted a response to the Press Office confirming the second find. I haven't yet confirmed the identities of our victims but once I do...You know what the press are like. Especially if they discover that both our women had been prostitutes. We're going to have Ripper-like headlines.' Taking another deep breath, she said, 'I have also had the Chronicle reporter raise a question about Braithwaite, they are already looking at a Beast angle. You don't need me to tell you what the headlines will be once we reveal that Ann Marie was buried with a cow's head, so for now I'm keeping this under wraps for as long as I can. I will be liaising with the Press Office tomorrow to determine how we handle this...' She paused, sighed and added 'As if we didn't have enough on our plates. What I ask of you lot is that if you get waylaid by any of the press, or during your enquiries you are asked questions about the investigation you give away as little as possible. Savvy?' On that note she ended briefing.

Dawn stayed by the incident board watching the squad pick up their things and filter out of the office. She caught Hunter looking back over his shoulder, offering her a reassuring smile. She felt her chest tightening. The pressure was getting to her.

* * *

Shortly after 9p.m. Hunter turned off the main Attercliffe Road into a deserted side road that accessed a number of small businesses, many of them back-street garages. The street was poorly lit, with many of the street lamps no longer working. It was a secluded area he knew well from his policing past and was the ideal location for the meeting he had arranged. Two hundred yards along the road, he found the derelict building he was seeking. The rusted gate still hung precariously on its top hinge, just as he remembered, and was open. He swung his Audi in through the gap, entering a weed infested compound hidden by old concrete fencing and parked up next to a rusted Bedford lorry jacked up on bricks. In front of him was a large red-brick, Victorian building, which in its heyday had been a prosperous engineering firm but was now in bad state of repair.

Keeping the engine running, Hunter set the handbrake and turned off the headlights. The last thing he needed was to draw attention.

Next to him sat Barry Newstead.

'Are you sure you're okay with this?' He said, looking out through the windscreen at crumbling and cracked algae-damp brickwork.

Barry released his seatbelt, 'I said I was didn't I? I've got a lot of time for Mister Robshaw. I'd do anything to help catch who did this to him. Who's this guy you said we're meeting?'

'He's a snout from my drug squad days. He's called Shaggy.'

'Shaggy?'

Hunter smirked, 'Shaggy. He looks like the cartoon character from Scooby Doo, but with dreadlocks. You'll see what I mean when he comes.'

'And you think he might be able to give you a lead?'

'What he doesn't know about what's happening on the streets around here isn't worth knowing. I'm going to see if he's heard anything about Mike being run down.'

'Does the gaffer know you're here?'

'She doesn't know anything about this.'

'Oh.' The word was long and drawn out.

Hunter shot him a sideways glance. 'I'm doing this for Mike! I owe him.'

Barry shrugged his shoulders, 'Yeah, I know. I just wanted to know what the state of play was, that's all.'

'I just want you here as my back up – corroboration you know.'

'I'm fine Hunter. No need to explain.'

'I'm not going to do anything. I'm just gonna see what he knows and then pass it on. I know Shaggy well. He won't have said anything even if he's been interviewed, but he'll tell me.' Hunter rolled down the window. Instantly a cold chill hit him and made him shiver. It was a typical late September evening – the temperature had dropped away sharply since dusk. He settled back in his seat.

For the best part of ten minutes they sat there, neither of them speaking, just listening.

The sound of scrunching footsteps coming closer made them both sit up. Alert, Hunter sharp-eyed the broken entranceway just as a man, head tucked into the collar of an army combat coat, came into view. Tall and slim with untidy dreadlocks and a wispy chin beard Hunter could see that Shaggy's outward appearance had not changed, even though it been six years since he'd last clapped eyes on him.

He stopped at the gate and looked their way.

Hunter guessed he was checking out the car. He knew he wouldn't recognise it, and with its tinted windows the sight would more than likely be unnerving him, so he opened his door, activating the interior light and stepped out.

Lifting his head out from the collar of his coat and, giving the street a quick check, he entered the yard and made for the car.

Hunter greeted Shaggy with a fist-pump and opened the back door for him.

He slid into the back seat, closing the door. Within seconds the inside was filled with a pungent smell that was either cannabis or patchouli oil. Hunter guessed the former and kept his door open a fraction but turned off the interior light.

Shaggy said, 'Long time, no see man. Who's your partner?'

Looking over the top of his seat Hunter replied, 'This is Barry. He works with me.'

Barry reached behind and they shook hands.

'Not DS then?'

Hunter answered, 'Not Drug Squad, no Shaggy. CID. We're in a murder squad. I moved a few years ago.'

'So this is about Sonny is it?'

'Sharp as ever Shaggy, I see.' He watched him crack a grin and added, 'It's sort of about Sonny.'

'Sort of?'

'Well it's not just about that job. But going back to that, whatever you know about it would be helpful.'

'I know only the word on the street. It's probably what you already know. They say it was Jazz Roberts and Danny Harris from Burngreave who carried out the hit. The word is that Sonny was trying to take over Jazz's turf. Taxed a few of his crew – took their gear and cash. He was disrespecting them man, so they taught him a lesson. I hear Danny was the shooter. Did him on his own doorstep to send out the message. You know all this. You've busted them both already.'

'We've nicked them Shaggy, but haven't got the evidence to send them down and nobody's prepared to go official. We could do with finding the shooter. Is that something you could do? Find out where the gun is?'

Shaggy's eyes drifted over Hunter, buffeting the wall of the derelict building. For a good ten seconds he was silent then he dragged back his gaze and said, 'You're asking me a big thing here Hunter. It's like you say, no one wants to go official. If this gets out... These guys don't mess around – you know what I'm saying?'

Hunter nodded. He was only too aware of the danger his former informant could be putting himself in. He engaged with Shaggy's hazel eyes. 'You know me Shaggy. I've not let you down before and I'm not going to now. No one will find out anything about what you and me have discussed. We don't even need to meet if that's too difficult. Just a phone call is enough.' He paused and added, 'There'll be a few grand in it for you.'

'It's not the money I want Hunter. If I do this, it's in return for the favour you did me. I've not forgotten you saved me from going inside when my Rosa was pregnant.'

'Do you think you'll be able to find where the gun is then?'

'I'll see what I can do Hunter. As I say, I'm a bit out of the scene now, but I still know a few people. I'm guessing it's a shooter they've probably bought in – you know for this one job. I've not heard about the Burngreave lot having guns before. They usually use knives.'

'Do you think you can speak to a few people?'

'Look I'll ask around. No promises.'

'Good man.' He paused again, studying his informant's pale craggy face. He knew he was roughly his age but the man looked a lot older than thirty-seven. Drawing back his gaze he said, 'Now this is the other thing I want to ask you.'

'What's that man?'

'A colleague of mine got knocked down a few days ago. He's in a bad way.'

'The cop on the news. That CID Chief?'

Hunter gave a quick nod, 'We think it was deliberate. We don't know if it's linked to Sonny's investigation or not. You haven't heard anything on the streets have you?'

Shaggy shook his head, 'No man. Nothing about that. You want me ask around about that as well for you?'

'I'd much appreciate it Shaggy.'

'No problem man.' He opened his door and swung out a leg. Reaching over he shook Hunter's hand, and stepping out lowered his head and said, 'Good to see you again man, though I think you looked cooler with the long hair and ear ring. You've got CID written all over you now.' He pronounced CID as Sid.

Hunter couldn't help but release a smirk as he watched Shaggy ambling towards the broken entrance gate. For a brief moment, memories of his drug squad days – previous clandestine meetings with Shaggy – flashed inside his head. He had always come up trumps – he hoped it was going to be another successful outcome.

CHAPTER TWELVE
DAY EIGHT

At morning briefing, Detective Superintendent Dawn Leggate informed her team that Lesley Jane Warren's brother had been spoken to the previous evening and he had agreed to give a DNA sample. She also said that they had identified the address in Scarborough where Harry Wainwright had retired to. The bungalow was actually just outside, in the little village of East Ayton. She told the team that they had also tracked down one of the detectives who had worked on the disappearance of Ann Marie Banks and Lesley, and lastly, confirmed that Ann Marie's boyfriend, Jamie Baxter, was in Armley prison, serving eight years for conspiring to supply class A drugs. Before bringing the briefing to a close she allocated priority lines of enquiry to visit and interview the latter three individuals and ended with an excited clap, galvanising everyone into action.

***

Hunter and Grace had been allocated the task of talking to Terrence Arthur Braithwaite's key worker when he was in Rampton Special Hospital, and they had an appointment with a man called Kevin Crompton, who was now a drugs counsellor with the NHS in Barnsley. Grace had rung him before going off duty yesterday and had already had a brief chat about some of the work he had done with Braithwaite. He had revealed to her that he had conducted many one-to-one therapy sessions with him and had a file of very interesting material which he had been cleared to discuss.

Hunter had just come off the motorway and was stuck in slow-moving, nose-to-tail rush-hour traffic heading into Barnsley town centre. One hand on the steering wheel, he unfolded a scrap of paper he'd removed from his jacket pocket to check the address they had been given. He saw that they needed to turn off at the next junction, by the traffic lights, and he was willing the line of vehicles in front of him through the green light he could see up ahead.

Suddenly Grace piped up, 'Did you go and see Mister Robshaw again last night?'

Hunter gave her a sideways glance. The question took him by surprise. Swallowing hard he replied, 'No I was knackered. I sacked it early.' He normally shared everything with Grace, but given that he had gone against Dawn Leggate's orders last night he had already decided that his and Barry's meeting with Shaggy was between them and no one else.

'I was just asking, because the gaffer didn't say how he was this morning.'

'I saw her before briefing. She says they're turning off his ventilator this morning to see if he can breathe on his own.'

'Fingers crossed eh?'

Hunter didn't reply, simply nodded his thoughts as he dropped the address slip into the centre consul and indicated left. 'It's just down here,' he said pulling away from the line of traffic.

Five minutes later Hunter was turning into a car park and seeking out a parking spot. There was one in the visitor section by reception, and he parked their pool car and turned off the engine. Picking his folder off the back seat he looked at Grace and said 'Okay?'

She nodded, 'I'm optimistic about this.'

'Me too. Can't wait to hear what he has to tell us.'

They weren't waiting long in reception. Kevin Crompton appeared within a few minutes, immediately introducing himself with a soft voice and a welcoming smile.

He was tall and slim, in an athletic way, and wore a blue checked Oxford shirt and jeans. With his short trimmed, almost white hair, and a clipped goatee and moustache, Hunter judged him to be in his late fifties or early sixties.

Shaking their hands, he pointed Hunter and Grace down the corridor he had come from, towards his office which was the second one along. He had left the door ajar and he showed them in.

The first thing Hunter noted as they entered was how warm the room was – almost stifling. The next was its untidiness. Paperwork, especially files, seemed to be strewn everywhere.

Kevin Crompton's desk was large but even that was chock-a-block with documents.

In that instant the untidiness reminded Hunter of his own desk. He still hadn't managed to organise and tidy his files ready for next month's move to the new murder suite.

'You want me to tell you about my sessions with Terrence Arthur Braithwaite.'

The counsellor's voice brought back Hunter's thoughts.

Kevin offered them two chairs and seated himself behind his cluttered desk.

Flicking open a heavyweight file he said, 'You said it's in relation to a murder investigation? I'm guessing it's to do with the two bodies you've found buried on the old Chapel estate that's been all over the news these past few days?'

Hunter and Grace nodded.

'Can I ask exactly what interest you have in him? Have the bodies been there a long time? He did almost thirty-two years at Rampton you know?'

Hunter checked with Grace and then said, 'Yes we know that. And yes, the bodies we've found have been there a long time. The thing is, his name's cropped up a couple of times during our recent enquiries and it's made us very interested in him. We know a fair bit about the crimes he was convicted of, but we don't know anything about his background and, as you've spent a lot of time and done a lot of work with him, we're interested in whether he's ever disclosed anything that might be relevant to our present investigation.' Hunter explained about the discovery of the bodies and, keeping back the victim's occupations and how they met their deaths, he revealed the name of Ann Marie Banks and told him that they believed the other victim was her flatmate Lesley Jane Warren. He then mentioned that their disappearance in nineteen-eighty-four coincided with the time Braithwaite was on the run after his escape.

'My, I can see now why you're interested in him. When that happened I was doing therapy work with him. I was the one who had to break the news to him about the death of his wife. He took it very badly. He asked me if he could go to her funeral and made the official request. There was some intense debate about whether he should go or not, but at the time Terrence Braithwaite was engaging with us and so the Governor agreed. There was hell to pay when he escaped. You can just imagine. The press had a field day.' He shook his head. 'Internally, there was an enquiry and, along with several others, I took some flack for supporting his release, but we were not held responsible, thank goodness, and so I was allowed to continue my work with him when he was recaptured. And I was with him when detectives interviewed him about where he'd been and what he'd been up to, but as you're probably aware he refused to say anything.'

'You can see now why we've got an interest in him?'

Kevin dipped his head, 'So when you say you want to know about his background what do you mean? Any specifics?'

Hunter shrugged his shoulders, 'Anything and everything, as I say all we know about Terrence Braithwaite is what we've got in our old files and a little from the Probation Service. We know nothing about his past. It might not be worth anything at the end of the day, but it least it will give us an insight into the type of person we'll be dealing with when we interview him.'

The counsellor stroked his chin, 'What I'm about to tell you about Terrence Arthur Braithwaite will probably put him at the top of your list.' He had a momentary glimpse at the file in front of him and then looked up at Hunter and Grace. 'I know I said Terry engaged with us – that was true in the nineteen eighties, but it took us a long time to get there with him. You're probably aware of his performance in court when he was found guilty?'

Hunter said, 'You mean when he tore open his shirt and showed off his tattoo?'

'Yes. Quite a performance. It made everyone in prison wary of him – prisoners and officers alike. He was monitored for quite some time. He was put on the sex-wing because of the rapes and he immediately started being disruptive – a mirror performance of what he'd done in court – so they put him in solitary. Within days of being released from there he attacked a prisoner who he said had tried to rape him. He almost killed him. He was put back into solitary and assessed.' Pausing a second he continued, 'There's no doubt Terry had a personality disorder, but back in the seventies there was no radical treatment for people with psychological problems. Once they were assessed as having a disturbed personality they were medicated and farmed out to a secure hospital, but not a great deal was done with them. It was mainly group work – touchy feely stuff – treating themselves in effect. That's what happened with Terry. He was sent to Rampton, but for the first few years he had no diagnosis and very little treatment. All that changed in the eighties, which is where I came in. I first worked with him in nineteen-eighty-two, though, as I said, initially Terry was very hard work. I tried methods of looking at his behaviour but he wouldn't open up. Sure, he'd talk, but I felt it was staged, rehearsed. I didn't know if he was playing games or simply refusing to engage with the programme. Without a shadow of a doubt he trusted no one. No one at all, and so I had to change my approach to build up that trust, even so, there were times when he was very cold and unresponsive – showed no emotion whatsoever. It took me a good year before he started to engage fully and that's when I started unpicking his past. And now this is the interesting stuff!' Kevin eased himself back in his chair and smiled, 'Terry had a very complex early life. I learned that his father left home when he was four, and he was brought up by his mother, who he described as a very strong person, she provided everything for him but gave him very little love and later became an alcoholic. Early on in our discussions, whenever we touched on his relationship with his mother, he exhibited feelings of rejection and sometimes hate. Sometimes it manifested in flashes of anger – verbal ranting as opposed to physical violence. He told me that when he was young his mother was like any other normal mum –got up with him, and packed him off to school, kept the house clean, did the ironing, but things changed as he got older. When he was eleven she stopped getting up with him and he had to get himself off to school. She stopped washing his clothes regularly, and the kids at school started calling him *smelly* and he was bullied. He suddenly had a number of *uncles*…' Kevin air-fingered uncle. '…one of whom sexually abused him when he was ten. What was really disturbing about this is that he told me that this *uncle* was found dead one night in the back yard of the flat where they were living at the time. He had apparently fallen down the steps while drunk. Terry told me it was an accident. Repeated that to me several times and smiled all the time. It was very disconcerting and made me realise that there was more to the story than he was telling me'

'You mean he was responsible?' Hunter interjected.

Kevin rolled his head. 'This is not my official comment, but yes I thought so. I probed him several times about this during many sessions but he never expanded on the circumstances. All he would repeatedly say is that there was an inquest and that the coroner ruled it was an accident.'

'But you believe he pushed the man.'

'As I say, I have my belief, but no confession.' He locked onto Hunter's eyes. 'See what I mean when I said interesting?'

Hunter nodded back.

'After that he said it was just him and his mum, but she drank heavily and he had to sort out everything for the both of them. His life became very chaotic. He got a job as a butcher's delivery boy and they just about scraped through on his wages. He said that despite his best efforts to stop her drinking she wouldn't give up. He told me that sometimes she would go on a bender and get hysterical and crazy and then be out of it for days. Regularly, when he came home, she'd be lying in a pile of vomit and he'd have to clean her up and put her to bed. He said that she died when he was seventeen. It was another "accident", as he put it. He told me he'd gone out on his deliveries one Friday, and when he'd got home at tea time he found his mother dead at the bottom of the stairs. She'd broken her neck. The police put it down to a drunken fall. The neighbours confirmed her problem with alcohol.'

'You think he killed his mother as well then?' asked Hunter.

Responding with a quick shrug he replied, 'Again I talked to him several times about this, but he never changed his story, other than to say it was an accident, though I have to say he never showed any remorse or sympathy when he talked about her or the incident.'

'So what happened to him after that?'

'He said he fended for himself. He progressed from delivery boy to butchers' apprentice and made a living. He kept on the flat and kept himself to himself. And I mean that literally. When I asked him about friends, all he would say is that he was too busy earning a living for friends.'

'What about socialising – going out for a drink.'

He told me it never really bothered him. He said he used to go out but he'd been banned from his local for fighting so kept away.

He said it wasn't his fault – he was picked on, like at school, and just stood up for himself.'

'What about relationships?' asked Grace.

'Didn't have any as far as I'm aware. He never admitted to dating or having girlfriends. He used to say he was never really interested in girls.'

'But he got married. How did he meet her?'

Kevin nodded. 'Sheila you're on about. Circumstances brought them together, not any arrangement. She was seven years older than Terry. Lived at sixteen Chapel Street. He used to deliver to her apparently. Terry said that he just used to chat with her when he delivered. He used to tell her about his upbringing and about the death of his mother, and he told me that she offered him empathy and kind words and she used to make him a cup of tea whenever he made his delivery. Then her husband got killed in a mining accident and things got hard. He said he returned the kindness by helping her out with her rent and bits of meat. He eventually moved in with her. He told me it was the first time anyone showed any kind of love for him.' Kevin shook his head, 'Quite sad really. I've met a lot like him in my work.'

Hunter said, 'Not an excuse to be a killer and rapist though?'

The counsellor cracked a grin, 'No, I'll give you that. I'm not defending him, believe me. In fact, Terry's upbringing mirrors that of a lot of the people I deal with – a bit like the ones you come across?'

Hunter acknowledged with a nod. 'Can I just ask you something else about Terry?'

'Fire away.'

'We've spoken with the community bobby for the Chapel estate. The officer's retired now, but he told us about Terry being caught for some burglaries in the late sixties. Did you ever talk to him about those?'

'Yes, as part of Terry's programme we discussed those during many of our sessions. You always needed several sessions with Terry before you got something from him. He used to ask me why I needed to know all this, so I told him that I wanted to know how he got involved in those offences, especially given the fact that he had a regular income and also that he'd found solace and love after all the sadness of his early life. I was surprised by his answer.'

Hunter's eyebrows knitted. 'Oh, what was that then?'

He paused momentarily and looked away thoughtfully. Then, bringing back his gaze said, 'Before I tell you what he said about the burglaries let me tell you about a session I had with him before that. I'm telling you this because it was something that happened in Terry's life before he committed the burglaries and I think you'll find this more interesting and relevant.' Pressing the tips of his fingers tightly together he steepled his hands. 'I used to focus a number of his sessions on his personal life. Once he introduced the subject of his wife I was interested in the relationship he had with her and so probed him about that and his home life. Again, he skirted around a lot, but there was one time when he told me he'd got depressed once because he'd lost his job at the butcher's. I asked him about that, thinking he'd brought it about himself, but he told me that the shop started to struggle in the mid-sixties because a supermarket had opened on the High Street and the butcher couldn't afford to keep him on so let him go. He wasn't out of work long though. He got a job at the pit but he said he hated it. Hated going there every day he told me, but it was the only job he could do which gave him the wage they needed. The strange thing about this conversation was that in one breath, what he said came over as being very bitter towards the butcher for giving him his cards, and in the next, he said it was a good thing because the shop got burned down and he would have been out of work anyway.'

'What!'

Kevin nodded sharply, 'A familiar theme appearing here eh? I asked him if he knew how that had happened and he just shrugged his shoulders, but he started grinning again when he told me that the fire brigade put it down as an accident. Apparently the butcher used to boil the bits of pork he couldn't sell – pigs heads and feet, that kind of thing, in a huge floor-standing vat to make pork pies. Terry told me that used to be one of his jobs. Well, the way he told the story, was that the fire was put down to the gas burner setting fire to some bits of sawdust that were sprinkled around the floor. The butcher and his wife had to be rescued from their flat above the shop and the place was gutted.'

Hunter delivered a wry smile, 'I suppose it's too much to ask if you got a confession out of him?'

'Terrence Braithwaite never confessed, even to the murder and the rapes he was found guilty of. Although I correct myself on that, he did confess about the burglaries he'd done, which is where I get back to your original question.'

'What did he say about those?'

'We talked a lot about the burglaries. In fact, it was the one series of offences he didn't mind talking about, but what was strange about this was, when I asked him why he'd carried them out, expecting him to say something along the lines of "for gain," he didn't say that. What he actually said was that he did them for the buzz. He told me that he got a real thrill from carrying out a crime.'

'That's the first time I've heard a burglar say that. They usually come up with some lame excuse that they were drunk or high on drugs.'

'It's not exactly a surprise to me. Therapy is the one time prisoners can get things off their chest without repercussions and so they usually are a little more honest. I have had other offenders say similar things, but I wasn't expecting that answer from Terry, especially because of how he'd skirted around all the other things.'

'One of the things I'm particularly interested in is what the bobby told us, that during one of his burglaries, an allegation was made by a fifteen-year-old girl who was in bed at the time with flu, that he sexually assaulted her. She said that he fondled her breasts, but he denied this and he was never charged with it.'

'I am aware of that allegation and I did put it to him. He went into some depth to explain that job. Basically, he said that he never expected her to be in the house. He told me that he'd seen the back upstairs window open, got up onto the outhouse and climbed in and found her in bed. She woke up, and he said he'd panicked and tried to stop her screaming, by putting a hand over her mouth. He said he hadn't fondled her. She'd made that up.'

Hunter caught something in his voice as he trailed off. He said, 'I'm sensing that you didn't believe him?'

'It didn't fit with the response about him doing the burglaries for thrills. I just couldn't imagine Terry Braithwaite going into a panic. Now if he'd have said, when she woke up I simply turned and left I would have believed him. It would have been something I would have expected him to do.'

Hunter nodded. 'So you think he did sexually assault her?'

'Again, he never confessed, but that type of behaviour is what I would expect from a sexual predator, which is ultimately what he became when he went on to rape. As you're aware, sex offenders all start off committing minor offences – stalking, minor sexual offences, things of that nature. This incident could well have been his trigger. And, as you know from your case files, each of the rapes he carried out, progressively worsened with regards the violence towards his victims, finally ending with the rape and murder of a seventeen-year-old girl.'

'You said earlier that Terry never confessed to the rapes or the murder he was convicted of; did he ever say anything about them?'

'I did say he never confessed, but I recall on one occasion he made the comment "The police got lucky. They'd have never have caught me if it hadn't been for that fisherman." Every time I went back to this comment he said he didn't want to talk about it.'

'So he never went into detail about those attacks?'

Tight-lipped Kevin shook his head.

'I know you also said earlier that Terry had been interviewed in prison about other offences he might have committed, and that he refused to talk to detectives.'

Kevin nodded, 'I sat in on those interviews. Detectives interviewed him three times but he didn't say a word, just smiled at every question. They were very unnerving interviews. Your colleagues were very frustrated to say the least.'

'I can imagine it. Especially in the seventies. They would never have expected any villain not to say anything.' With a smile he added, 'I think you know what I mean?' Hunter chose not to respond. He knew only too well what Kevin was alluding to. Barry Newstead had told him numerous stories of detectives resorting to strong-arm tactics to gain confessions. Pausing he said, 'Did he ever say anything to you, or hint, that he had carried out other attacks on women.'

'I can see that question is very relevant to your current investigation, but my answer is never. We had many sessions talking about this, especially after his escape and capture. I asked him many times about where he'd been – where he'd hidden? Who had he seen? Every time he'd just say he didn't want to talk about it. Terry was probably my most difficult patient.'

Disappointed, Hunter stored the counsellor's response. He had hoped that during his incarceration at Rampton, Terrence Braithwaite would have disclosed something which would link him to their enquiry. Preparing to finish the interview he said, 'Just one more question Kevin. Throughout any of your sessions with him did you ever get the impression that he wasn't working alone when he carried out his attacks?'

'Alone?'

'That he maybe had an accomplice?'

The counsellor cocked his head. 'Do you know it's funny you should say that. My immediate answer is no. He never said anything directly about either working with anyone or anyone being present during his attacks on those women, although there was one session early on in my time with him where I asked him how he felt after he had killed Glynis Young. I was trying to get him talk about his emotion, especially given that he'd already told me that he got a rush from the thrill of committing his crimes, and he said something, which again, took me completely by surprise.'

Hunter straightened, 'Oh yes.'

'He said "Death is a beautiful thing."' He bounced his gaze between Hunter and Grace. Seeing them returning nonplussed looks he said. 'It's a quote attributed to serial killer Charles Manson. And, he also quoted me something else which came from the Manson trial. It was attributed to one of his followers. When I asked him about the attacks – the rapes, and especially the significance as to their seasonal timing – you know Halloween, his reply was "Every day was Halloween."' He watched their reaction change. 'I asked him why he'd said that – wondering if it was something he'd just heard and was quoting it, but he knew exactly who'd said both quotes and he also said he was a great admirer of Manson.'

'Did you push him on that?'

'Of course. Charles Manson was one of my case studies at university. I was interested to know why he was drawn to such a famous, charismatic, evil character. I wanted to know just how much he knew about the man and his deeds and particularly why he was an admirer of him. In a nutshell, the response he gave me was that he wanted to be revered like Manson; for people to sit up and take notice and be afraid of him. Most of all he wanted to pit his wits against the police. Remember, he had already been caught and served time for burglary. It was his way of getting them back. The thing about Terry was that he believed he was better – intellectually brighter. He displayed many of the personality behaviours of someone with a psychopathic disorder. Remember what he said about getting caught for the murder of Glynis Young – the police got lucky. The fact that he associated himself with such a person as Charles Manson was, while disturbing, also fascinating.' Kevin paused, studying their faces. 'Now, it might also be very relevant to your investigation. Do you know about Charles Manson?'

Hunter hadn't expected for the interview to run out in this way. The drug counsellor had him hooked. He answered, 'To be honest, not a lot, other than snippets I've seen on TV, historical crime cases, and also stuff I've picked up from time to time in books or magazines about him. I know that he and his hippy cronies murdered a load of people back in the late 60s. A famous actress was among his victims if I recall.'

Kevin nodded, 'Sharon Tate. She was Roman Polanski's girlfriend – the film director. She was carrying his baby. Six of her friends were murdered as well in the same house. And, the so-called cult also killed two elderly people the night after. It was one of those shocking cases that made everyone sit up. But the thing people always get wrong about that case is that they cast Charles Manson as the psychotic killer. He wasn't. Manson never killed anyone. He got his followers to carry out the killings. He was actually convicted of murder under California's conspiracy laws.'

'I never knew that.'

Kevin nodded again. 'That's why I find your question very relevant now. You see Charles Manson was a very enigmatic man who manipulated and influenced a group of young people into believing he was a Christ-like figure who could give them a better life. He introduced them to LSD and established his own religion. Some of their practices were based on those immortalised by an early twentieth century ceremonial magician called Aleister Crowley who was an occultist.'

Hunter felt the hairs on his neck and back stand up. 'Can I stop you a second there? I don't know if you know this, but they found a load of occult symbols painted all over the walls in his cellar when they arrested him after the murder of Glynis Young. The retired bobby I've mentioned told us this. He said there were pentagrams and upside down crosses – things of that type. And he'd painted female heads on the walls of the cellar and daubed them with animal blood.'

'Well that is interesting. I can't remember seeing this in his file. I must have missed it. It would have given me a better insight into him, especially given that Aleister Crowley was dubbed The Wickedest Man in the World. He was one of the inspirations behind Charles Manson's teachings to his followers. If Terry was on the same wavelength…' His voice trailed off.

For a good few seconds no one said anything.

Inside his head Hunter was running everything through at supersonic speed. When he got to the end he said, 'So if I'm getting this right, if he was such a fan of Charles Manson then there could be the possibility that he followed in his footsteps by, either coercing someone else into carry out the attacks, or manipulating someone else into helping him?'

Kevin took on a look of deadly seriousness. 'Terry Braithwaite has a powerful personality, and it's not beyond the realms of possibility to think that he could have manipulated and transferred his offending behaviour to someone else. Just who that person is, you'll have to find out yourself because he never told me.'

* * *

The hospital corridor to the wards was busy. Hunter weaved his way past streams of people visiting their loved ones, avoided the queues for the lifts, and made his way up the stairs to the ICU ward. He met Dawn Leggate inside the entrance leaning against the wall, sipping from a cardboard cup.

She met his gaze and issued a weak smile.

'Hello boss, is everything okay?' He chinned in the direction of the ward where Michael Robshaw lay.

She sprung her shoulders off the wall. 'Yes, Mike's fine. I'm just getting myself a coffee. His daughter, Rachel, has come up from Bristol. I'm giving her some time with him.'

'Has he come round then?'

'Not fully. They've taken him off the ventilator and he's opened his eyes a couple of times, but he's not registering anything. The nurse says that's normal. He could be like this for a good couple of days. The main thing is he's breathing on his own now and the swelling to his brain has started to go down.'

Hunter caught what he thought was the sound of her suppressing a sob. He saw that her eyes had filmed over and, feeling a tinge of embarrassment mixed with sorrow, he diverted his look to a poster on the wall about infection control. At that moment a flashback jumped inside his head of his and Barry's clandestine meeting with Shaggy. He had a sudden urge to tell her what he was doing to help catch her partner's attacker, but at the same time he recalled that she'd already ordered him not to do anything that would prejudice the enquiry and he pulled himself up. Masking any emotion he said, 'I only called in to see how he was. I'm glad to hear that he's turned the corner. I'm not going to stop if his daughter's here as well – three's a crowd as they say.' He started to turn.

'Okay, no problem. If he comes round I'll tell him you've been. I know he'd appreciate what you're doing.' After a brief pause she said, 'I forgot to say at briefing, good job today Hunter. I was so much in a rush to wrap things up so I could get here that I forgot to mention it.'

He looked over his shoulder and saw that her eyes now glistened; she'd blinked away the film of tears. He replied, 'Oh thanks boss.'

'No. Credit where credit's due. You and Grace did a good interview today. You got some good information. I certainly think now that we need to be looking at Braithwaite in more depth. In fact, I want you and Grace to go and interview him.'

Hunter threw a questioning glimpse. 'Oh?'

'There's not enough to arrest him yet but following your meeting today I think we should be talking to him about where he was and what he was doing during his time on the run in nineteen-eighty-four. I certainly think we've got enough to invite him in for a chat so I want you to fix that up tomorrow.'

'Yeah sure. It'd be interesting to see what he says, or if in fact he says anything at all. He hasn't been very cooperative in the past.'

'Oh, I know you Hunter. I'm sure you can be very persuasive.' She flashed a mischievous grin.

Dismissing his previous thoughts he responded, 'I'll look forward to that. There's nothing I like more than getting under someone's skin. Especially someone like Braithwaite. I'll get in early tomorrow to fix that up.'

With that he said his goodbye and made his way back to the exit, his head awash with thoughts. Jumping to the fore was how he was going to approach the interview with Terrence Braithwaite and he knew for certain he was going to have difficulty getting to sleep tonight thinking about it.

CHAPTER THIRTEEN
DAY NINE

The incident room was silent. DC Tony Bullars was just taking his seat after telling the squad about his previous day's visit to the charity shop where Ann Marie Banks and Lesley Jane Warren once had their flat. He told them that a forensic team had moved in and were slowly clearing the room prior to carrying out an examination; they were especially looking for signs of blood following DC Mike Sampson's revelation.

Earlier, Mike had introduced the threads of yesterday's conversation with Harry Wainwright, the previous owner of the shop. Mike had opened up by telling the squad that in spite of his eighty-four years, Harry was in remarkably good health and spirit, and could remember and relate a considerable amount about the two women during their time as tenants there. Not surprisingly, Harry had mentioned several times how difficult the girls had been, in particular with regard to regular default in the paying of their rent. With a little embarrassment, he promised Mike that he hadn't known about them being prostitutes when he had agreed to their tenancy, and that it had only been pointed out to him by a number of his customers once the women had moved in. He had initially wanted to get rid of them, but he said that Ann Marie was a very persuasive girl who he had some sympathy for, and also that he was a bit of a soft touch and so he had let them stay. Although Harry had got to know the pair, regarding them as bright and bubbly, he had never been privy to their personal lives, telling Mike that the only time he became aware of either girl's families was after they had gone missing. Mike had spoken at some length about the events before and after their disappearance and Harry had been consistent in his response. He had only become aware that they had gone following a phone call and visit from Ann Marie's elder sister. He told Mike that he genuinely thought that the pair had just done a moonlight because they owed him two months' rent and so he had changed the lock on the back door so that the only way they get in to their flat was to come into the shop. Within days he had emptied their wardrobes and cupboards of clothes. He told Mike that he could remember thinking at the time that he had been surprised that they hadn't taken any of their personal clothing, and they had also left a few nick-knacks – photos, bits of make-up and toiletries on the sides. But on the other hand he'd said that none of it was expensive, so he'd guessed that they were probably going to try and sneak in on a later date or come and beg him for their tenancy back once they'd got enough money together and paid him what they owed. Mike had asked him what state the flat had been in following his discovery that the girls had left and Harry reluctantly confessed that what he had told the two detectives who had visited him following the girl's disappearance wasn't the truth. He said that when he was first questioned by them he had told them that the flat was okay. That nothing had been out of place. He'd said that not to hide anything, but because he didn't want any hassle over two prostitutes who had done a runner. He had then gone on to tell Mike that he'd only gone up to the flat following Ann Marie's sister's phone call to see if anything had happened to either of them. When he let himself in he found a chair upturned by the table, a smashed cup on the floor, and a small photograph frame smashed by the fireplace, but when he'd had a look around the flat, and found neither of the girls there, he'd assumed that the girls had either had a party or a bit of a fall out between themselves and nothing more. It was only after several more visits from the detectives that he realised something more serious may have happened to them but he dare not tell the police that he had lied for fear that they'd consider him a suspect. He'd finished off by telling Mike that there had been no more tenants following Anne Marie and Lesley Jane's disappearance, because he didn't want any similar problems, and that the flat hadn't undergone any decoration or change while he had owned it.

Thanking the two detectives for their input, Dawn Leggate rose from the chair she had commandeered before briefing and made her way to the incident board. More had been added to each of the victim's timelines, and a photograph of Terrence Arthur Braithwaite from his 1971 arrest file, had been stuck up, with spidery lines linking addresses, photographs and newspaper articles: The board was beginning to tell a story. She pointed a finger at a post-it note placed over the large map of the Chapel estate, identifying the house where Braithwaite once lived and said, 'I want to know everything about sixteen Chapel Street. See if there are any photographs around of how it looked when he was living there. We'll make a press appeal. And given that our latest body was found close to the rear garden of Braithwaite's house, and what Gordon Jennings has told us about what he saw painted and drawn over the walls of his cellar, I want that place excavating. The cellar wasn't examined at the time so I want it doing now.' She tapped a manicured nail over the shaded houses on Chapel Street. 'I want a thorough job on that place – dig up the cellar if necessary. And lastly for today, get back on to Probation and Rampton hospital; see if there is anything in his files about associates or friendships he struck up while in prison. Also see if they have a list of his regular visitors.' She pulled back her hand, 'I'm told that we should have the DNA result from Lesley Warren's brother by this afternoon. We'll know soon if our second victim is Lesley or not.'

* * *

It had been a long time since Hunter had been to Bridlington. As a child, his parents brought him here for day trips and he seemed to recall a more vibrant town. Today, mid-week, it was quiet, and nowhere near as warm as on his previous visits – though it was the start of autumn, he reminded himself.

He and Grace sat on a bench overlooking the old harbour, eating fish and chips, shying away from a bracing wind coming off the North Sea.

'It's a long time since I've done this,' said Hunter, breaking off a piece of battered fish, while eyeing a couple of large seagulls who were monitoring them predatorily only a few yards away.

'Brings back memories does it?' asked Grace. Then, before he had time to respond she said, 'How do you want to play this with Braithwaite?'

Hunter gave her a sideways look. Grace was staring out to sea, her tight black locks tumbling across her face in the wind. He noticed that her summer freckles were starting to fade. 'He's turning up with his solicitor so we can't go in too hard. I thought about you leading it. He's only ever been interviewed by men in the past and wasn't very forthcoming as you know. It'd be interesting to see if you have a different effect on him.'

She glimpsed sideways, 'I hope that's not a sexist comment, Sergeant.'

He grinned and gave her a gentle shove. 'You know what I mean.' Although he considered himself a good interviewer, he thought that Grace was better in some situations; whereas he generally steamed in with direct questions, her pitch was softer; she was more patient in her approach; her build up was slower – she had this knack of soothing the interviewee with empathy until she got what she wanted. Then she went for the jugular. Given that Terrence Braithwaite wasn't being arrested, and could therefore leave the station at any time, this interview called for that tactic. 'If you can get him to open up, one of the main things I'd like you to focus on is where he got his head down while he was on the run for five days in nineteen-eighty-four. It'd also be good if you could get him to talk about his escape. The report in his prison file states that, after the graveyard service, he asked to go to the toilet and his guards let him use the one in the church vestry after checking that the door to the outside was locked. After they discovered he'd escaped they found that the outside door had been opened with its key, but how he'd managed to get hold of it they had no idea. The detectives investigating the escape interviewed the vicar, and he'd told them that he'd noticed that the key had gone missing from the hook where it was normally kept several days beforehand, and that he'd mentioned it to the churchwardens and the cleaner. They were also interviewed and confirmed this and they hadn't been able to help as to its disappearance. The conclusion was that they believed Braithwaite had just got lucky – that it had fallen from its hook and gone underneath a piece of furniture or something and he'd just found it by chance. But knowing what we know now what is more likely is that it was taken by his accomplice and then hidden for when he carried out his plan. It would be good if you could sway the interview to how he got hold of the key as well.'

'You're not wanting a lot, are you?'

'I have every faith in you getting a full and frank confession so that by tonight we can wrap this enquiry up.' He put a couple of chips into his mouth and gave her another friendly nudge.

* * *

Bridlington police station lay in the older section of the town. It was a large Victorian stone building with high windows. From reception, they were shown to an interview room and left alone. It was a room almost identical to the ones back at Barnwell; its four walls covered by fabric soundproof cladding and its furnishings a table and four chairs. A recording machine rested on the table.

Choosing the plastic chair nearest the door so that anyone wanting to leave had to get past him, Hunter slipped off his jacket, slung it over the back, and tucked his legs beneath the table. He was just checking that the recording equipment was working when there was a sharp knock on the door. It was the receptionist. She had brought Terrence Braithwaite and his solicitor. Hunter passed Grace a quick glance which, without saying anything, was his 'are you ready' look and she responded immediately with a brief nod.

Grace greeted them, thanked them for agreeing to this interview, and pointed out the empty seats across the table.

Without getting up Hunter offered up a faux smile while running his eyes over his adversaries. Terrence Arthur Braithwaite had changed considerably from the photograph that the prison authorities had given them with his file. In fact, had Hunter seen him in the street before today he would have passed him by without giving a him second glance; the thick dark hair, evident in his prison shot, was now battleship grey and longer, covering his ears and collar, and gone was his beard and moustache. Although there were some similarities to the photo clipped to his file; his wide nose hadn't altered and those unusually dark brown eyes still sat deep in their sockets. What Hunter couldn't miss was the slight droop to the left side of his mouth and the limp in his left leg, reminding him that Braithwaite had suffered a stroke five years ago while in Rampton: It was one of the reasons why he had been released on licence, and because it was felt he was no longer a danger to the public. As Hunter watched this seventy-three-year-old easing himself down, his broad upper body tensing, displaying strength rather than frailty, he wasn't convinced.

Sitting next to him, removing a legal pad from a briefcase, was his solicitor. The man introduced himself as Saville Chambers who worked for the firm of Sheffield solicitors that had represented Braithwaite during his trial in the seventies. Saville was smartly dressed in a well-tailored pinstripe suit and looked to be in his early fifties. He had close cropped light brown hair, and a clean-shaven, pinched face with protuberant ears. Testing his pen on the top yellow sheet, he looked up and said, 'My client has informed me that you wish to speak with him regarding an investigation you are involved in but that you have not been specific about the nature of that. Can you expand on this?'

Grace settled herself at the table, leaned forward and rested her arms, intertwining her fingers. She answered, 'We are currently involved in an investigation following the discovery of two bodies close to where Mr Braithwaite used to live in Barnwell, and because of that he is one of a number of people whose name has cropped up during our enquiries and we would merely like to eliminate him.'

'Eliminate him, so he's not a suspect?'

Straight-faced she replied, 'Mr Braithwaite is not a suspect at this stage. All we want to do is talk to him about a particular period in his life which would help us with our investigation.'

'And that period in his life is when may I ask?'

'The nineteen-eighties. Nineteen-eighty-four to be precise.'

'You are aware that my client was jailed in nineteen-seventy-three and didn't get released until three years ago?'

'All will be revealed with my questions Mr Chambers.'

'Fine. And can I just clarify that should Mr Braithwaite wish to leave at any stage during your questioning he can do so without any hindrance?'

She looked at Terrence Braithwaite, 'Mr Braithwaite is not under arrest and he can leave this police station at any time, but we would appreciate it if he could answer some questions we have for him.'

Terrence Braithwaite traded his gaze with Grace and responded, 'I am at your mercy Detective Marshall, but before we start may I ask how your daughter is after her ordeal. Robyn, isn't it? It must have been a terrible time for you.'

Grace pulled back her hands and stiffened. She felt her skin bristle and her chest tighten. Suddenly her thoughts were launched back to that night just over twelve months ago when the serial killer they were chasing abducted her eldest daughter. Catching the pleasure written all over Terrence Braithwaite's face besieged her. She could feel anger rising.

Braithwaite said, 'Oh I'm sorry Detective Marshall I didn't mean to upset you, I was merely asking after Robyn's welfare.' His voice was slow and steady.

Hunter leaned forward, 'Detective Constable Marshall's daughter's welfare is none of your concern Mr Braithwaite, now can we get back to the questions?'

Terrence Braithwaite diverted his eyes and fixed Hunter, 'Oh I'm sorry Sergeant Kerr I was only enquiring after your colleague's daughter. I didn't mean to offend.'

'Well, as I say this interview is about you.'

'Of course, of course. My apologies once again.' He wiped some spittle which had dribbled from the corner of his mouth. 'And you Sergeant Kerr, you're looking well despite your own personal ordeal.'

'Ordeal?'

Winking he replied, 'Your father wasn't it? Got involved in some nasty business didn't he?'

Hunter's voice rose, 'Mr Braithwaite my father has got nothing to do with you, now can we get on with this interview?'

Terrence Braithwaite's mouth bore a lop-sided smirk.

His solicitor placed his pen down on the table with a loud retort. 'We appear to have got off to a bad start here. I think we should take a short break.' His pale blue eyes switched between Hunter and Grace. 'Shall we say five minutes and begin again?'

Hunter switched off the recording machine and pushed back his chair. 'I think we'd better Mr Chambers. He glared across the table, his eyes wide and fierce.

Grace pulled herself up. Fighting back a sudden bout of anxiety and avoiding eye contact with Braithwaite she said, 'I'm just going to get a drink of water.'

'And I could do with going to the toilet,' said Saville Chambers, pushing aside his legal pad. The only marks he'd made on it were from his pen testing.

In the ladies room, Grace supported herself with locked arms on the edge of the sink and stared into the mirror. She could feel that her breathing was ragged and fought to bring it back under control by taking in great gulps of air. *How the fuck had she let the interview be taken away from her?* It took her the best part of two minutes to get back to normal breathing. *The bastard!* She cursed him as well as herself. She'd let Terrence Braithwaite get under her skin back there, but it won't happen again, she told herself, pushing herself upright and checking her composure. Straightening her blouse she mouthed, 'You're mine, Terrence Arthur Braithwaite' and made for the door.

Outside in the corridor she met the solicitor coming out of the gents rolling his hands over one another.

Suddenly, from the interview room a loud clatter resounded followed by a dull bang and a yelp.

Grace froze momentarily. She and the solicitor locked eyes and then both spurred into action, rushing to the interview room door.

Grace got there first and flung it open. She was confronted by Hunter standing yards from the table holding up his hands in surrender. His face bore a surprised, almost shocked look. The other side of the door she caught sight of Terrence Braithwaite. He was bent over the table, his face in his hands, blood trickling through his fingers, splodges falling onto the oak veneer surface. His chair was lying sideways on the floor. She was conscious of the solicitor breathing over her shoulder.

Hunter cried, 'He did that!'

Braithwaite glanced up, a pained look in his deep set eyes.

His solicitor brushed past Grace and placed a pair of caring hands on his client's shoulders. 'What's happened Terry?'

'I'll tell you what happened,' growled Hunter stepping forward, 'He smashed his own face on the table and he's trying to make it look as though I've done it.'

Terrence Braithwaite mumbled, 'Sergeant Kerr attacked me over nothing.'

Grace stared at Hunter trying to read the look on his face. She knew from past experience that her partner had a sharp temper, and she had witnessed him manhandle suspects a little too fiercely at times when they've decided to resist, but she had never known him assault a person during an interview before. This was totally out of character, and she wondered if Braithwaite had continued to taunt Hunter while she'd been in the toilet. Diverting her gaze back to Braithwaite she saw that he was attempting to stem the flow of blood coming from his nose and mouth. What had started out as a very promising day had deteriorated to rat-shit.

* * *

Hunter and Grace were back in Detective Superintendent Dawn Leggate's office, standing before her.

She was bracing herself back in her chair, her face flushed. 'Don't you think I've got enough problems on my plate at the moment?'

Hunter almost stood to attention, a mixture of hurt and fury swirling around inside. Not only had he been unable to convince Grace that he had not attacked Braithwaite on the journey back to Barnwell, but now he was suffering the same torment from his boss. It felt like the Spanish Inquisition. Suppressing his annoyance he responded, 'I can put my hand on my heart ma'am and say that I did not assault Terrence Braithwaite.'

'For Christ's sake Hunter don't call me ma'am – you make me sound like the bloody Queen Mother.' She shook her head. 'I've had a superintendent from East Yorkshire on speakerphone bending my ear for the best part of half an hour this afternoon accusing me of sending across officers under my jurisdiction to assault a vulnerable pensioner in one of his police stations. Even if you didn't assault him it's bloody embarrassing having my, and my officer's professionalism challenged. Don't you see that?' She turned to Grace. 'Did you witness what went off?'

Grace swallowed hard. Biting down on her lower lip she answered, 'No, I'm sorry I was in the toilet boss.'

'So we just have Braithwaite's word against yours Hunter?'

Hunter nodded, 'I promise you, boss I didn't do anything. Braithwaite bashed his own face on the table.'

She huffed loudly. 'I really could do without all this.'

'I'm sorry boss. Genuinely I am. I never asked for this to happen.'

'And neither did I. You cocked up a simple job.' She spat back.

Hunter wanted to respond. He resented being accused of something he hadn't done, but he knew now wasn't the time to say anything. His SIO was under pressure, not only because of the murder investigation but also with what was going on her personal life. He just wished she would cut him some slack.

Taking a deep breath, she said, 'Braithwaite's solicitor has lodged a formal complaint. You know what that means – Professional Standards will want to interview you both. I suggest the pair of you get your heads down and prepare your statements before you go home. Now let me get on with my job.' With that she dismissed them with a flick of her hand.

* * *

Dumping her bag down on the kitchen work surface Dawn Leggate caught her reflection in her make-up mirror. She barely recognised herself; her face seemed thinner and so pale. She looked tired. She was tired. In fact, she was exhausted. Things were taking their toll; she had just spent thirteen hours in the incident room and another hour by Michael's bedside – who still hadn't come round, adding to her angst.

Once it's over, and Michael's out of the woods, then I can switch off and take a break. She knew what she needed; opening the fridge door she took out a chilled bottle of wine, poured herself a glass and took a large swallow. Instantly the crisp, fruity taste refreshed her taste buds while the coldness hitting the back of her throat invigorated her. She took another swallow, holding this one in her mouth she tipped back her head, closed her eyes and savoured the flavours. A sudden sense of guilt overcame her. She knew she'd been hard on Hunter: Been hard on Hunter and Grace. She should have given them the opportunity to explain the circumstances of what had gone on instead of dismissing them like naughty schoolchildren. She needed to make amends for her behaviour. As their senior officer, she knew she should have behaved more professionally. They were the best on her team and she should have made it known she was supporting them. She knew that Hunter could be a loose cannon at times, but assault someone in a police station? Provoked or not, she knew that wasn't his style. She'd speak to him first thing to tomorrow morning and make amends. Finishing her glass of wine, she poured herself another. Suddenly she realised how hungry she was. With the fridge door still open she scoured the shelves; three eggs, a tomato, a piece of withered cucumber and an out of date packet of mixed salad. She sighed. What with everything that had gone on she'd not had time to shop. Without warning tears filled her eyes. She felt herself filling up. Seconds later she started to sob.

CHAPTER FOURTEEN

In his kitchen, Terrence Arthur Braithwaite made himself a cup of tea, a huge grin smearing his face as he stirred the teabag around in his mug. He was thinking about Detective Kerr. His nose was still sore and swollen but his actions had been worthwhile. He had already made an official complaint and knew the consequences of that would be that the detective would be warned to back off. He squashed the teabag against the rim of his mug and dumped it in the bin, musing on the next step. Although Detective Kerr and his female partner were off his back, there was still the worry of the skeletons they had unearthed, although he was pretty sure that when they buried them they'd left no evidence which would lead back to him, nevertheless he needed to make plans. What did they say about failing to plan?

As he opened his fridge to get the milk, music started up next door. Status Quo – *Down, Down*. It was blaring, the beat vibrating the walls.

That fucking moron!

He had already had several run-ins with Eric over the loud music. When it had first happened, a week to the day after he had moved in, he had ignored it, especially knowing that his neighbour had been seriously injured in a motorcycle accident and was wheelchair bound. But then the frequency of it started to wear him down, especially when it had gone on until well after midnight. After three weeks of enduring thunderous rock music he'd decided to nip around and have a quiet word: ask him if he could turn it down a fraction and not play it so late into the night. He had gone around the morning after one of Eric's late night sessions that had kept him awake until 1a.m. The kitchen door was open and a stripped down motorcycle was the first thing that presented itself to him, oil leaking from its engine, staining the floor. He'd banged on the door but got no response and so he'd gone in. The kitchen was a tip. Filthy pots everywhere. The table was full of engine bits and motorcycle memorabilia. Eric had been in the front room. It was only 10.30 in the morning but he was drinking strong foreign lager from a can. He'd introduced himself and then started to mention the music. He asked Eric if he could play it not so loud. Instead of being neighbourly Eric had laughed at him. Told him to fuck off, and said 'I'll play it as loud as I want old man.' That had instantly got his back up. If he'd have still been in prison he'd have sorted him out. There and then. But he hadn't been in prison. He was a free man and wanted to remain that way and so decided better of it and left, fuming with anger. He had only just got back inside his house when Eric had started up again, cranking up the volume even louder. Deliberately winding him up. The fat bastard! It had gone on like this – at least three times a week – for the past two years.

Stirring milk into his tea, he slammed the fridge door shut and slung the spoon into the sink. One day he was going to shove those vinyl's right down his fucking throat!

CHAPTER FIFTEEN

DAY TEN

Following a restless night Hunter rose early, slipped on his joggers, hoody and trainers and ran to work. With every pounding footfall he mulled over yesterday's events, cursing Terrence Braithwaite for what he done and beating himself up for not seeing it coming. His feelings were just as bitter towards Grace and Dawn Leggate; it was as if they didn't believe him. Maybe he could believe it of his boss because she didn't know him that well, but not Grace. That hurt him.

Taking longer than normal in the shower in the gents changing room, he changed into the suit he kept in his locker and made his way upstairs to the MIT office. He was the first in. Checking the incident board to see that nothing new had been added, he made his way to his desk, skirting around the boxes surrounding his workspace. Sitting down, he took one look at them and reminded himself again that he needed to sort out his files before the impending move. Dragging back his gaze he settled his eyes upon the accumulation of paperwork in his pending tray, and let out a heavy sigh as he picked out a bundle and laid it across his jotter.

He had just read the opening paragraph of his first report when he heard the office door open. Glancing over his shoulder he saw Detective Superintendent Leggate struggling to push her way through; she was fighting to slip one arm out of her coat while juggling with her handbag and briefcase. Deliberately avoiding eye contact he returned to his paperwork.

Seconds later she was standing over him, depositing her bags and her coat on Grace's desk. 'I owe you an apology,' she said, 'But first I need a coffee. Can I get you a tea – that's what you prefer isn't it?' With that, she made her way to where the tea and coffee making facilities were on top of a small filing cabinet and began messing with the cups and kettle.

Hunter looked up and saw her looking back over her shoulder.

Dawn said, 'I shouldn't have treated you the way I did – you and Grace. Of course I believe you Hunter. I know that you don't always work to the rules, and you certainly don't like anyone to get top side of you, but you're no bully.'

Hunter observed her face. In that moment her words resonated around inside his head and he could feel relief swamping his body. For some strange reason he found himself choking back tears – he never felt like this. Swallowing hard he said, 'Thanks boss that means a lot to me. I honestly swear that I never laid a finger on him.'

She held his gaze a good few seconds. 'I believe you Hunter. I'm going to speak with Professional Standards this morning and see who's handling the complaint. I'm going to have my say before they come and interview you. I know that's what Michael would have done if he was still your boss.' She returned her eyes back to the boiling kettle. 'Now how do you like your tea?'

* * *

Dawn stuck a black and white photograph of a Victorian single storey terrace with wooden sash windows and a panelled front door up on the whiteboard, and jabbed a finger at it. 'Sixteen Chapel Street,' she said, looking around the room. She saw that she had her team's fullest attention. 'The home of Terrence Arthur Braithwaite, kindly supplied to us by The Chronicle. This is what it looked like in nineteen-seventy-two following his arrest for the murder of seventeen-year-old Glynis Young.' She gave the photo a quick glance and then continued. 'Yesterday a team began excavating the foundations of this house and we are hopeful that by the end of the day all the rubble will be cleared and we will have full access to the cellar so we can begin a forensic examination. Whether we find anything or not is in the lap of the gods but, following the discovery of our two bodies, one of them buried by the boundary of this address, it's something we can no longer afford to miss.' She paused, roaming her eyes amongst her squad. 'Now everyone, update. The DNA result has come back for our second victim – I can confirm she is Lesley Jane Warren. That means we can focus just on the flat in Chapeltown where both she and Ann Marie lived. A forensics team are on their second day there and they have found some blood in the lounge carpet and on the stairwell leading to the back hallway. That has already gone off for analysis to see if it belongs to either of our victims. Following that discovery, I've spoken with the Press Office and we're going to do a reconstruction, focussing on the weekend they both disappeared from that address. I am also going to organise a plea to the street workers who were associates of Ann Marie and Lesley. Its thirty-five years ago now – many of them will have moved on and will more than likely not want to talk about their past. However, let's not that daunt us. It just means we'll have to work that much harder. It will be going out on Crimewatch and the regional news. Our prompt for viewers will be the beginning of the Miners' Strike.' She saw some of her team screw up their faces. 'I know, not something I would have chosen, especially given South Yorkshire's role in all that, but it's something which will help highlight the date when they were taken and killed. And on that note it's fair to say that the killer of Ann Marie and Lesley is one and the same, and the person that tops our list is Terrence Arthur Braithwaite.' She tapped her fingers over his head-and-shoulders mug shot. 'And what we also need to look at, especially given what Susan Braddock has said, is that he was working with someone else. Who that person is, we have no idea and so this is what I want you to concentrate on.' She removed her hand from Braithwaite's photograph. 'From today we start peeling back the layers of Braithwaite's past. We go back to Rampton Secure Hospital and get a list of everyone whoever visited him while he was held there. We speak with Probation – see what they have in their records regarding associates. And we make discreet enquiries around where he currently lives and see if anyone has noticed any one person in particular regularly visiting Braithwaite. We also request his phone records. If he did murder Ann Marie and Lesley with someone else, then more than likely they will still be in contact with one another. What we won't do now is re-interview Braithwaite. Following what happened yesterday, we know that is not going to get us anywhere.' She focussed her gaze upon Hunter and Grace, 'And that bears no reflection on you two. Braithwaite is a lot more cunning than we anticipated.' She brought back her eyes and skirted them around the team. 'Or at least he thinks he is. He's going to be on his guard now, but if we stay focussed he will slip up and that's when we pounce.'

* * *

Hunter drove to the construction site at Chapel Meadows. Beside him sat Grace. They had been given the task of liaising with the forensics team who were examining the cellar of Terrence Braithwaite's old home. Along the journey they'd hardly spoken a dozen words until they pulled up by the entrance and Hunter turned off the engine, then Grace rested her hand on his wrist...

'I'm sorry Hunter. I should have backed you up better than I did.'

He turned to face her, ready to tear a strip off her but, catching the pleading look in her dark brown eyes, a sudden feeling of guilt overcame him. With a softened tone he answered, 'Yes you should have.'

'It was just such a shock. I saw him holding his face and the blood and I thought about how he'd goaded us.'

'And you put two-and-two together and came up with five!'

She gave his wrist a squeeze. 'I am sorry. Forgive me?'

'I have to admit I am miffed. I know my temper can get the better of me sometimes but I would never do anything which would cause you problems. Cause myself problems yes, but not a colleague.'

'And I know that Hunter. I should have spoken up for you.' She gave his wrist another gentle squeeze. 'Friends?'

He relinquished a smile with a quick nod, 'Buy me a McFlurry with extra smarties after this and we're quits.'

Uplifted she responded, 'Deal. And I'm glad that's out of the way. I couldn't have done with looking at your sullen mug for another minute longer.' She shouldered him, flashed a wide grin and sprang open her door. 'Come on let's see what we've got.'

Hunter nipped the keys out of the ignition and opened his door. He felt the instant drop in temperature. A light cold wind seared his face. He dragged his overcoat off the back seat and started to pull it on as he got out of the car. As he pushed the door to he caught sight of a group of people rushing towards them. Reporters! He spotted Chronicle journalist Zita Davies, her long blonde hair flapping in the wind, heading up the posse. Although he had a good relationship with her he didn't wish to talk with her right now. He already knew from that morning's news that the press had speculated correctly as to why they were digging up Braithwaite's old cellar, and were already liking the enquiry with that of Fred and Rose West. The last thing he needed right now after yesterday's debacle was to be put on the spot by a bunch of hacks hankering after this afternoons' headline.

Darting a quick look at Grace he called, 'Come on get your skates on,' and fob-locking the car he put in a burst to the entrance, flashing his warrant card and skipping past the uniformed officer in plenty of time before the press horde got near enough to nab them.

He could hear the pack hollering after them but Hunter never looked back as he tacked his way to the new crime scene, Grace at his shoulder.

The short journey was a lot more difficult than either of them had anticipated. The ground was a lot firmer than their last visit, but it was still like trudging through freshly ploughed soil and within thirty seconds Hunter could feel his calves stiffening.

They stopped by the inner cordon, a necklace of blue and white crime scene tape embraced a large blue tent. The sound of a mechanical digger scooping up rubble came from inside. Standing by the entrance was someone in a full forensic suit, writing on a clipboard. With the hood up of the baggy, shapeless all-in-one, and facemask, Hunter couldn't make it out if the person was male or female. Hunter called out but never got a reaction. He formed his hands into a megaphone and bellowed. This time it worked. The person lowered their clipboard and slid down their mask. Hunter saw that it was CSM Duncan Wroe. He shouted, 'Just seeing how it's going. We've been given the liaison job.'

Duncan stepped towards them, 'Well you're going to be hanging around a long time Hunter. We're only half way into the cellar. The rubble's impacted.'

'Nothing doing then?'

'We've exposed the walls and we've found some of the painted symbols that were mentioned, but I can't see us clearing it out by the end of today. It's going to be tomorrow before we can start excavating.'

'Well we've got nothing else to do today. We might as well hang around just in case.'

'There's tea and coffee in the temporary incident room if you want to hang around in there.' The Crime Scene Manager chinned towards the Portakabin Hunter had taken possession of ten days earlier when they had found the first body.

Hunter turned to Grace, 'I'm sure I saw a portable telly in there. Come on, it's ages since I watched daytime TV.'

* * *

Hunter was just pulling his car out from a parking spot at Barnwell Police station to head off home for the day when his mobile rang. He braked and picked it off the passenger seat. It was Shaggy. He hit the answer button.

He hadn't even answered before Shaggy was demanding, 'Hunter is that you?'

Sensing the stress in his voice Hunter replied, 'What's up Shaggy?'

'I need to see you urgently.'

'What's it about?'

'I don't want to speak over the phone.'

'Can it wait? I was just about to go home.'

'Not really. I need to see you tonight.'

Hunter took a deep breath. 'Okay I'll be with you in an hour. Same place?'

'Yeah, same place. One hour.'

Hunter ended the call, scrolled down his contacts and auto-dialed.

* * *

On Attercliffe Road Hunter eased off the accelerator and gently squeezed on the brake as he coasted his Audi towards the couple of cars waiting at the stop light by the junction. This was where he turned off the main road. Outside it was raining lightly and the road shimmered with reflective light from cars and street lamps. Hunter started tapping the steering wheel, waiting impatiently for the lights to change. Next to him he gave Barry a quick look. 'Are you sure you're okay doing this again?'

'No problem Hunter, we'll only be a few minutes with him won't we?'

'I hope so. I wouldn't have bothered turning out but he sounded really rattled on the phone. If he's got something I'll ring the incident room at Ecclesfield and let them deal with it.'

There was a moments silence and then Barry said, 'I bet you're frustrated with what's gone on with Braithwaite?'

'Frustrated is a fucking understatement.' He paused and added, 'You believe what happened don't you?'

'Course I do. You're more subtle than smashing someone's face into the desk.'

'I'm annoyed because I just didn't see it coming.'

'I wouldn't have seen that coming. I tell you what though it show's you had him rattled. Talk about desperate measures call for desperate things. That has all the hallmarks of a guilty man.'

'I'm also a bit frustrated for the team because it means we have to back off until we can get the evidence to bring him in properly'

'We can always abduct him and waterboard him. If it's good enough for the CIA'

Hunter let out a laugh and then returned his attention back to the traffic lights. As he did so, a silver Subaru whipped across the junction into the side road Hunter was taking. He tried to get a glimpse inside the car but its speed and the blacked-out windows prevented him and he missed getting the registration number because of the two waiting cars in front.

He had a bad feeling about this. At this set of lights most cars went towards Sheffield – there was nothing down the road the Subaru was heading except small independent garages and a couple of car dismantlers. The street wasn't even a short-cut – it came back onto Attercliffe Road.

Shooting Barry a sideways glance, he caught the concerned look in his colleague's face, as if he'd read his mind, and gunned the engine, yanking down the steering wheel to overtake the car in front, realising, as he jolted forward, that he'd not left enough room to pull out. He cursed in frustration and beeped the horn to get a reaction. Its brake lights flashed on. Hunter banged the horn again, muttering beneath his breath, 'Move out of the fucking way.'

Then the lights changed. The two cars in front pulled sluggishly away, almost as if snubbing him. Hunter lurched forward, his Audi's wheels spinning and squealing as he bolted through the lights and took a hard left.

Hunter could feel his heart racing as he stamped hard on the accelerator. The back end snaked momentarily causing the four-wheel-drive to kick in.

A hundred yards ahead he caught the red flash of brake from the Subaru. A second later it was gone – disappearing from view around a bend.

Up front, in half-light, Hunter saw someone lying crumpled at the edge of the road, and even though he couldn't make out any features, Hunter instinctively knew this was Shaggy. Something bad had happened to him! He braked hard and the Audi scythed before dipping to a halt.

Snapping off his seat belt, he was out of the car before Barry, catching his hip on the front of the bonnet as he dashed to his informant's aide.

The blazing headlights of Hunter's car confirmed it was Shaggy. He lay on his back, his knotted hair fanned out like the snakes on Medusa's head. His eyes were wide, full of panic.

In that instance Hunter spotted him clamping his chest with both hands, thick red blood flowed between his fingers. He was taking desperate breaths and moaning. 'They've shot me Hunter,' he gasped.

'Who did this Shaggy? Was it Jazz or Danny?'

He opened his mouth again, but all he released was a cough. A cough that spluttered blood. It spurted over his bottom lip onto his chin.

'Hold on Shaggy,' Hunter cried, 'We're getting you some help.' Back over his shoulder he could hear Barry on the phone yelling for an ambulance and the police. He forced his own hands down over Shaggy's in an attempt to stem the surge of blood from the wound, but the stream wasn't stopping. After a couple of seconds Hunter could feel the breathing in Shaggy's chest getting shallower; he was catching his breath and he knew that, despite the pressure he was bearing down, the life blood was leaving his body.

'Hang on mate.' He said again. This time he made his call softer – he was aiming to calm him.

Shaggy issued another cough. More blood liberally left his mouth and he made a gurgling sound. His eyes rolled backwards and then his eyelids slowly shut. He let out a choke and became still. Hunter stared at his face. It was the second time in his career that someone had died in his arms.

* * *

Hunter pulled up his hands and stared – there was blood all over them: not only on his hands, but down the front of his shirt and on his trousers. He reached down and tugged off his trousers and dropped them into the evidence bag held in the outstretched hands of the Crime Scene Investigator. As he did so he tried to catch his colleague's eyes, but the civilian officer, with whom he'd worked beside at numerous crime scenes, shied them away. Hunter knew it was nothing personal – this was the man's job. After all he was being treated as either a suspect or a significant witness in a killing. He knew that Barry in the next room was suffering the same uncomfortable fate. He felt exposed and vulnerable even though he knew everyone in the room, including the DI from the rubber heel squad standing by the door, gaoler-like, preventing his escape. The DI was looking straight at him – his eyes unwavering. Hunter pulled away his eyes, a guilty breath catching in his throat. He'd been investigated before, but never for anything this bad. For a moment he reflected and thought about Barry in the next room. He'd dragged him into this. This was his fault. He also thought about the next few hours; the grilling the pair of them would be subjected to. Outside he caught a raised voice back along the corridor. Female. Detective Superintendent Dawn Leggate. It sounded as if she was heading towards them and at a fast rate of knots judging by the decibels getting ever louder. This he didn't need.

* * *

In the shower room at the station Hunter rested his forehead against the tiles, letting the warm water cascade over his neck and shoulders and run down his back. The water washed away the dried blood. He watched the red-stained water stream into the shower tray and trickle down the plug. It strangely reminded him of the times when he had cleaned his art palette after finishing a painting. But this wasn't paint. This was blood. Shaggy's blood. And he'd got him killed!

* * *

An hour and a half later Hunter trudged out of the interview room feeling totally jaded following his grilling by Professional Standards. A DI had led the interview; it was always like that – one rank above – and he'd cut him no slack. The DI exposed every transgression he had made against procedures. He'd messed up good time and he knew it.

He made his way up to the office where he found Barry sat at his desk. Barry greeted him with a smile but Hunter could tell it was half-hearted.

Barry said, 'How did it go?'

'Fucking nightmare! And you?'

'I did my best but they had me on the ropes Hunter. I think it would be fair to say they've got us by the short and curlies. They've suspended me.'

'Me too.' Hunter took a deep breath. 'I'm sorry about this Barry.'

'Don't apologies Hunter. You didn't make me go – I volunteered remember.'

Hunter sighed, 'Still it's down to me.'

'And it's not finished there.'

Hunter threw him a questioning look.

'Ma'am wants to see us before we go.'

'Oh fuck!'

'Oh fuck exactly.'

Hunter felt scruffy in his T-shirt and joggers as he stood outside Dawn Leggate's office, but that was the only spare attire he had in his locker following the seizure of his blood splattered clothing. Barry was wearing crumpled jeans and a shirt.

Dawn's door was ajar and Hunter rapped softly.

'Enter.' Dawn called from inside. Her voice sounded brusque.

Hunter pushed open the door and stepped in, an image flashing inside his head: it reminded him of his first visit to the headmaster's office at secondary school following his school-playground fight with Simon Drayton. His stomach had knotted then.

Dawn was sitting behind her large desk, straight-backed in her chair, her face bearing a look that could kill.

Hunter was about to speak when she said, 'What the fuck were you two playing at?'

Hunter thought her Scottish accent made her question sound even harsher. He opened his mouth to answer an apology, but he never got the chance, as she continued, 'I'd already told you Hunter not to get involved. Instead you go wading into an area where someone has already been shot and killed, wearing no protective body gear, and exposing a vulnerable witness who's got killed for Christ's sake. The papers are going to have a field day with this. The pair of you...' she aimed a finger at both of them, 'broke every rule in the book. You both know there are rules for dealing with informants, especially in situations like this, and you ignored them. You go steaming in and as a result an innocent man has been killed.'

'But we didn't go steaming in boss.' Hunter replied.

'Did I ask you to speak?' Her finger was now jabbing.

'No boss.'

'Well don't then, not when I'm fucking talking. I wouldn't mind but you can't even get your story right between the pair of you – both of you telling Professional Standards it was each your idea. I don't know you haven't got one fucking brain cell between you. And now you're fucking suspended for God's sake.' She lowered her hand. 'As if I haven't got enough on my plate. Now get out of my office, both of you, before I say something I'm going to really regret.

Backing out of Dawn's office, closing the door behind him, Hunter gazed at Barry. He looked deflated. He said quietly, 'That was some bollocking.'

'She certainly didn't pull any punches,' he whispered gruffly. Setting off down the corridor, he called back, 'I don't know about you, but I need a fucking drink.'

CHAPTER SIXTEEN

At Bridlington bus station Terrence Braithwaite waited for the bus to York. He had on a baseball cap and kept his chin tucked into his overcoat. He knew that detectives would eventually pick him out on CCTV but he wasn't going to make it easy for them. Once he got off the bus, though, that was where their surveillance of him would end. He had already determined that the preparations he had in hand for the next part of his journey would ensure that he completely disappeared off the police radar. Checking his watch, he saw that he had another ten minutes to wait before the bus departure. He was first in line and a small queue had formed behind him. He didn't look sideways because he didn't want anyone to make contact with him — neither eye nor voice. He wanted no one to remember him. The sudden ringing of his mobile made him jump. He knew who this would be because only one person had his number. He took a few steps away from the person behind, dragging his large holdall with him and answered with a soft 'Hello.'

'Did you see what was on the fucking news?' The agitated voice rasped.

In his mind's eye Terrence could see him hyperventilating, probably in the toilet or the back yard at his workplace. He was always like this when the pressure was on.

Covering his mobile with his hand, speaking low he said, 'I told you not to ring unless it's urgent.'

'It is fucking urgent for God's sake they're digging up the cellar. Haven't you seen?'

'Course I have. Don't worry it's me they're after. They don't even know about you.'

'It won't take them long, forensics and all that. They'll soon put two and two together.'

'No they won't, they're cops. We're smarter than them. We got rid of the evidence remember. It's still at the cottage isn't it?'

'We need to get rid of it Terry.'

'Don't worry I'm on my way there right now. The key's still in the same place isn't it.'

There was a pause down the line before the man answered 'Yes.' There was surprise in his voice.

'And the supply of food is still well stocked?'

'Yes I was up there six weeks ago and swapped some – got rid of the out of date stuff.'

'Good. There's no need to worry then. I'll be keeping my head down there. Now you need to calm down and remember what we talked about. You don't do anything different to what you normally do. And don't ring me again. You know where I am. Drive across in a fortnight, fetch some fresh stock and we'll catch up.' Terrence paused, listening. The man's breathing had steadied from his initial outburst; a good sign that he still had a calming influence on him. He checked him with, 'Okay?'

There was another pause before the man answered, 'Okay.'

'Good. Now don't ring this number again. My phone will be off from lunchtime so you won't be able to get hold of me. And keep it together. They have no idea about you. Just act as normal.'

With that Terrence ended the call. For a moment he held the phone in front of him, staring at the screen until it went into sleep mode. Then he smiled to himself. Things hadn't changed after all this time – he could still control him.

Slipping his mobile back into his coat pocket, out of the corner of his eye, he ran his gaze back along the line, checking if it looked like anyone had overheard the conversation. Three women immediately behind were deep in conversation. Others appeared to be keeping themselves to themselves. No one was giving him a second glance. At the end of the queue he caught sight of a young woman who looked to be in her mid-twenties, with long dark hair. Although her head was bent – it looked like she was reading one of those e-books he had heard about – he couldn't help but think how strikingly beautiful she was. He let his eyes linger over her and found himself getting hard. It was just the boost he needed.

CHAPTER SEVENTEEN
DAY ELEVEN

Once more Hunter found himself unable to sleep. Not only was he still smarting from Dawn's rollicking, but each time he had attempted to close his eyes the images of Shaggy's last moments swirled around like a zoetrope inside his head. Finally, at seven a.m. he gave up, crept quietly down stairs and made himself a mug of tea. He drank it staring out through the French doors, watching a not too lively dawn emerging from behind the distant hilltops. Hearing the boys rousing upstairs he boiled the kettle again, setting another cup for Beth. Making two teas he climbed back upstairs, calling for Jonathan and Daniel to make their way to the bathroom, and as an afterthought added, 'And make sure you brush your teeth properly.' Pausing on the landing, listening at his son's door, he heard them get out of bed, and stepped into his own bedroom and set Beth's drink down on her bedside cabinet. Her eyes were still shut though he could see she was stirring. He kissed her head. 'I'll sort the boys. You just get up and wave them off.'

She blinked open her eyes, 'Aaw, thank you.'

'I spoil you. And I'm not going anywhere am I?'

Beth forced herself up, brushing straggles of hair from her face. 'Hunter Kerr I hope that's not a voice of resignation I can hear. Stop feeling sorry for yourself, you've only been suspended. You'll only be off a couple of days while they investigate.'

'I could lose my job over this!'

'You do exaggerate. Course you won't lose your job. It's not your fault that guy you were meeting got killed.'

'It is in a way. There're rules in place now. It's not like the old days. I shouldn't have dealt with him the way I did. And I went against the gaffer's orders.'

Beth propped herself up, 'I'm not having you moping round the house all day feeling sorry for yourself. You did what you thought was right under the circumstances and I'm sure they'll see it like that.' Pausing she added, 'I tell you what we're going to do – we're going to get the boys off to school and then you and I are going out for the day. I'll ask your mum and dad to fetch them from school in case we're late.'

Hunter was about to say that he had too much ringing around to do, but Beth held up her hand to stop him. She said, 'No arguments. It's a long time since you and I have done something together.'

Loading their waterproofs and walking shoes into the boot, Hunter and Beth drove Jonathan and Daniel to school, dropped them off, and then began their drive to Robin Hood's Bay; Beth had chosen the destination – it was one of their favourite coastal haunts and it had been a good few years since they had been there.

Just like all the other times, the journey was sluggish, driving in nose-to-tail traffic right up to Pickering, but once they started the climb onto the moors, and passed The Hole of Horcum, the roads opened up allowing Hunter to put his foot down all the way to Sleights, which was where he turned off onto the winding country lanes – the final leg to the sixteenth century coastal resort that was once a smugglers haven.

Parking in the village's main car park at the top of a hill, they were met with a sharp wind as they got out of the car and they donned their coats and walking boots quickly before holding onto one another to begin the steep descent down to the harbour.

They chose the footpath because the cobbled roadway looked slippery, but the trek wasn't easy – lots of steps made up the route, and so they took their time, window browsing in the quaint shops on the way down. Twenty minutes later they made it to the slipway that led to the beach and here they stopped to take in the sea view. The tide was out and Hunter was thankful because the sea was kicking up quite a swell; it meant they could stroll along the beach without being caught by the spray being thrown up.

Beth grabbed hold of his arm and bit by bit they negotiated the seaweed clad slope to the bottom where Hunter cast his eyes across the bay. Scudding clouds filled the sky but it didn't look like it was going to rain and so they set off towards the distant jutting headland where Ravenscar sat atop.

Hunter loved the sea, and despite the roaring and crashing noise the waves made as they pounded the large rocks that dominated the seashore, somehow the sound was melodious and relaxing. With each step he could feel his stress levels diminishing.

'Glad you came now?' Beth asked softly.

Hunter wrapped an arm around her and pulled her close. 'Definitely. I needed this.'

They walked for half an hour before turning back to the harbour where they headed for the fish and chip shop in the narrow alleyway behind the harbour wall. It was the second time in a week that Hunter had eaten fish and chips but he couldn't resist the temptation; although it was a good few years since they had been here he had commented on how nicely cooked and fresh the fish had been. Finding a place to sit at the bottom of the harbour wall with Beth, Hunter ate his meal with his fingers, taking in the refreshing salt and seaweed air and listening to the seagulls squawking around them. As he took in the sights and sounds, thoughts of the previous evening drifted into his head. As well as feeling guilty about what had happened to Shaggy, at the same time he couldn't help but feel resentful that Professional Standards had authorised his suspension when all he had been doing was his job. It was one of those moments that he wished he had something to fall back on so that he could tell them to shove the job up their arses.

'What are you thinking about?' Beth's voice brought back his attention.

'Nothing.' He answered still staring out to sea.

'You're thinking about last night again aren't you?'

He was thoughtful for a few seconds before replying, 'Yes. I can't help but think that I got him killed.'

'Hunter we had this conversation earlier. You just listen to me. You didn't get him killed. How many times have you dealt with informants and something's happened to them?'

'Loads, but nothing's ever happened, until last night.'

'Exactly. You said yourself he called you because it was urgent. What happened to him was going to happen whether he met up with you or not. He knew something and someone wanted him silenced. There was nothing you could have done. In fact, you and Barry could have got shot as well. You want to think yourself lucky.' Beth scrunched her empty polystyrene tray shut and brushed up next to him. 'I'm just glad it wasn't you Hunter.'

Hunter pulled her close and kissed the top of her head. 'Me too. Love you.'

They meandered back to the car park via the back streets, a more gradual climb that passed a café, where they called in and grabbed a cup of tea each before calling an end to their day at 3p.m. Hunter wanted to make a dent in their return journey before rush hour started.

Entering the car park Hunter felt his mobile vibrate. Taking it out of his pocket he saw that he had three missed calls from Grace, two from Barry and two from Dawn Leggate. It reminded him that all the times he had visited this place he had never been able to get a signal down by the harbour. He dare not ring Barry on this phone because he had already been warned not to contact anyone involved in the investigation, so he brought up Grace's number and was about to return her call when his mobile rang. He didn't recognise the number, but somehow he had the feeling that he should answer it and so swiped the screen. 'Hello, Hunter Kerr.'

'Detective Sergeant Hunter Kerr?' the female voice repeated.

Hunter thought she sounded anxious. 'Yes,' he replied.

'Sergeant Kerr, it's Rosa, Steve's wife.'

Hunter was about to ask who Steve was and then he twigged. Shaggy! He caught himself. He hadn't anticipated this call. He could feel his chest tighten and, feeling awkward, he said, 'I'm sorry about Shaggy, Rosa, I never meant for him to get hurt.' He found himself stumbling over the words.

'I don't blame you Hunter. I know you wouldn't have got Steve hurt. He trusted you. That's why he wanted to help you. You helped him in the past. I know that.' She stifled back a sob and said, 'It was Danny who shot him.'

'Danny... Danny Harris. How do you know that?'

'Mark told me before he ran off.'

'Mark?'

'My son. Steve's step-son.'

'How does he know? And did you say he's run off? Why?'

'It's a bit of a mess. He's involved.'

'Involved?'

'I don't mean involved, as in Steve's death, but he's got himself involved in Jazz and Danny's drug dealing. Last week Steve found out that Mark had been running drugs around the estate for them. He searched Mark's room and found Danny's gun. We were mortified. As you know, me and Steve have done bits of weed in our time but never any hard stuff or anything to do with the gang's round here. We had no idea Mark was into it. It's come as a complete shock. And when Steve found the gun, well, he just went mental with Mark. He told us that Danny had asked him to hide it for him after he shot Sonny. He's been terrified ever since the shooting. He's not a bad lad he just got drawn into things through his mates. Steve gave him an ultimatum – told him he had to go to the police and that if he didn't he would. Mark snatched the gun back and ran out of the house and we've not seen him since. That's when Steve rang you.'

'Where's Mark now, Rosa?'

'I don't know. I'm worried. I haven't seen him for three days, but he rang me last night after Steve was shot and told me he didn't have anything to do with it, it was Danny. I don't want the same thing happening to him as what's happened to Steve. You need to find him before they kill him as well. It's bad enough losing Steve, I don't want to lose my son as well.'

'Have you any idea where he is?'

'No. I can only think he might be with Danny and he's told him about Steve finding the gun. Why else would Steve have got shot? That's why I'm worried. Please Hunter, he's just a kid.'

'Look Rosa, I need to speak with my boss about this.'

'Can't you deal with it Hunter?'

'I can't Rosa.' He didn't want to reveal he'd been suspended over what had happened to her husband – she wouldn't understand. He replied, 'This is beyond me. We'll need to turn out a team to capture Danny, especially if he's armed.'

'But what about Mark? What's going to happen to him? It'd crucify me if he went to prison.'

'He won't go to prison if all he's done is run Danny's drugs around the estate, especially as everyone knows what Danny Harris is like. His reputation. They'll see it for what it is – that

Danny forced him. But they will want to speak with him about hiding the gun – he's a material witness.'

'I want him back home Hunter. I don't want anything to happen to him.'

'Tell you what Rosa, send me Mark's phone number. We should be able to do a trace and find out where he is.'

There was a slight pause and then Rosa said, 'I'll do that. Please bring him home safely. I know he wouldn't have known what was going to happen to Steve. He was his step-dad but he treated him like a real dad. I know Mark, he'll be worried stiff about this. I don't want him to do anything silly.'

'I'm sure he won't Rosa. Once you send me that number I'll make a phone call to my boss, and if in the meantime he contacts you or comes back you ring me straight away. It's important you do that.'

'Sure, I will. Thank you Hunter.' With that she hung up.

Thirty seconds later he had a text message. Hunter opened it and saw that it was a mobile number: Mark's. He switched back to his phone contacts and dialled Dawn Leggate.

She answered, 'I thought you were avoiding me.'

Her voice sounded as terse as last night. He replied, 'Sorry boss, I took a run out to Robin Hood's Bay with Beth. I've had no signal. I've just seen you've rung me.

'Even I believe that.'

'It's the truth. Honest.'

'I said I believe you.' There was a brief pause and then she said, 'I've been ringing you about your suspension. Putting aside that you went against my orders – which I haven't mentioned to Professional Standards by the way – that's between you and me, and I'll sort out some suitable punishment later, but what I'm ringing to tell you is that I've asked them to fast-track your case. You don't deserve it but I need you back on my team as soon as possible. I'm guessing that once everything's investigated you'll probably receive words of advice for going against procedure. It's not helped, though, by both you and Barry sticking to the same story about who's idea it was to meet with your informant..'

'It was my idea boss. I took him just for back-up.'

'I know that Hunter, but Professional Standards don't. They think there's something suspicious about you both saying neither of you knew. You could have at least got your story right.'

'I never thought that Shaggy was going to get shot, did I?' He could feel his voice rising. He took a deep breath to get a grip of himself; this wasn't Dawn Leggate's fault. He added, 'Sorry boss.'

'You will be when this is finished. Your actions have really cocked up my investigation. I'm two down and they won't give me any more resources.'

Hunter found himself apologising again.

'Anyway, I rang you because I wanted to give you the heads up as to what's happening about your informant's killing. Thanks to that sighting you had of the Subaru just before the shooting, they caught it on CCTV coming back onto the main road and managed to track it back to Burngreave. They also got its number – and guess what?'

'What?'

'It's registered to Danny Harris. An operation is being put together as we speak. They're trying to locate the car and him and hoping to do a dawn raid tomorrow.'

'I may be able to help there, boss.' He told her about the call he had just received from Rosa and how she had given him her son's mobile number. 'She thinks he's with Danny so if you do a trace it'll give you his location.' He read off the number to his Detective Superintendent.

'That's great Hunter. I'm going to hang up now and pass this on to the team straight away. I'll ring you tomorrow as soon as I hear anything. Oh, and watch the news tonight, we've just found Braithwaite's immediate neighbour in Bridlington murdered. A man called Eric Wheelhouse. His body was discovered this morning during enquiries. I'm told the scene is a right mess. I'm about to go up there and liaise with the SIO and see for myself. The guy has multiple stab wounds and he's been gutted like a fish. The man was disabled – severed his spine in a motorcycle accident – and they found him in his wheelchair with his entrails draped over his lap and get this – he's had his ears cut off and head phones had been put on covering the mess. The man's stereo was on full. A couple of Braithwaite's other neighbours tell us he's had a beef with Eric over him playing his music too loud. Certainly settled his score with him – the sick bastard.'

'You've got Braithwaite locked up then?'

'No he's done a runner. Oh, and one other thing, we've found the remains of a body in the cellar of Braithwaite's old house. We're going to try and hold that back from the press for a while following the murder in Bridlington. Things are certainly hotting up here.'

'Just a shame I can't be involved.'

'Well you've only yourself to blame for that haven't you. Now, not being rude Hunter but I need to pass on this number you've given me. I'll keep you in the loop and as soon as I hear anything I'll call you.'

On that note Dawn Leggate ended the call.

Hunter momentary looked out across the top of the bay. The clouds were starting to darken. He became conscious of Beth messing about by the boot, taking off her waterproof jacket and walking shoes. It was time to make tracks home.

That evening Hunter spent time with Jonathan and Daniel on their Play Station. It was a long time since he had been able to do this and after tucking them into their beds he settled down in front of the television. Once again it had been a fair while since he had actually been able to sit down and take in some television, and he watched an episode of The Bill despite Dawn's phone call bleeding into his thoughts, distracting his viewing. Just before ten o'clock he poured himself a glass of whisky, Beth a glass of wine, and then sat back down to watch the news. The murder in Bridlington was the lead story – the anchorman's excited tone broadcasting it as major breaking news. They showed aerial footage taken from a helicopter of Braithwaite's home adjoining the murder scene. There was plenty of forensic activity around the two bungalows, their entire frontage protected by a large oblong tent. The victim had been named as forty-eight-year-old Eric Wheelhouse. They'd also got hold of the latest body found in the cellar of Braithwaite's old address. They played previous footage showing the two places where they had found Ann Marie Banks and Lesley Jane Warren; their shallow graves still cordoned off. Then the shot panned out to take in the new excavation site, which was a pile of demolished rubble upon which sat a blue forensic tent. White suited forensic officers were captured going into the tent. Some background history of Terrence Braithwaite's murder trial in nineteen-seventy-three was aired, making great play on his nickname The Beast of Barnwell, and the broadcaster was speculating that there could be more bodies. The broadcast came to its close by relaying back to Braithwaite's present home. A reporter had door-stepped one of the neighbours for a quote – a woman who had no idea who she was living next door to and said she was shocked because he seemed such a quiet man and so ordinary. As if a serial killer is going to disclose his true nature Hunter couldn't help but snort to himself. He was surprised how quickly they had connected the killings and wondered how long it would take the newshounds to find out Braithwaite had already been interviewed at a police station and released. Someone was going to have to answer that awkward question and he was certainly glad it wasn't him.

CHAPTER EIGHTEEN
DAY TWELVE

Hunter came away from Bramall Lane football ground in reasonably good spirits having seen his beloved Sheffield United scrape a draw from the derby game against Doncaster Rovers. It hadn't been a good game but he told himself that at least they hadn't lost again. He shepherded Jonathan and Daniel through the throng of supporters all heading for the railway station. He was trying his best to hurry Daniel along, checking his watch that they would make it to the station in time to catch the next train home, when his mobile rang. He tugged it free from his coat, saw it was Grace, and answered.

'To what do I owe this pleasure?'

'Hi Hunter, are you okay?'

'Good actually. Just coming back from football with the boys. I haven't seen Sheff U for ages.'

'Did they win?'

'Drew with Donny. It wasn't a memorable match. I won't be in a rush to waste my money again this season. Pausing he asked, 'Have you rung me for anything special?'

'I just wanted to let you know how things were going on. I felt a bit guilty over the Braithwaite thing and now this with your informant I thought I'd just cheer you up.'

'That's appreciated. I'm enjoying the time off but I miss the banter.'

'Miss me as well I bet.'

'Don't miss you,' he chuckled.

'Well if that's your reply I'll hang up now.'

'Don't you dare.'

She let out a shallow laugh, and said, 'I don't know if you've seen the news but they've found another body at Braithwaite's old address on the Chapel estate and we believe he's also murdered his neighbour. We're gearing up for an all-out search for him.'

'Thanks Grace. The gaffer did ring me yesterday and told me. And I caught it on the news. Any idea who the body is in the cellar?'

'It's another female and youngish – mid-twenties. She was strangled like the others. We haven't found out who she is yet. She's been buried a lot longer than Ann Marie and Lesley; looks like she was put down there in the seventies. The thinking is that he killed her before he was caught for the Glynis Young murder. It also looks as though there could be another body in his cellar as well. The floor is old bricks and there are two areas where they've been disturbed. They started work on the excavation this morning.'

'The gaffer told me about Braithwaite doing a runner and I saw that forensics are going through his bungalow in Brid. Any idea where he's gone?'

'No, he's well and truly gone to ground. A neighbour saw him leaving his house with a big holdall yesterday morning and we've got a sighting of him at Bridlington bus station. We know he got a bus to York and that's where it ends at the moment. We've requested CCTV from the bus company and we're trawling through CCTV in York to see if we can find him.'

'Anything from his house?'

'Nothing. It's spotless. He's thoroughly cleaned the whole place. If you didn't know he'd lived there you wouldn't have a clue as to who the owner was. He's taken every scrap of paper with him, every bill, anything that might have had his name on it. The lot. It doesn't look as though he had a computer and we can't find evidence that he owned a mobile. He even took the house phones with him so we can't check logs, though thankfully we can get his phone records. He really is a canny guy.'

'Anything from his neighbour's house?'

'Not yet. The place is a dump. I tell you what though, Braithwaite obviously had issues with Eric Wheelhouse. He really went to town on him with a knife. They've found a hundred-and-sixty-two stab wounds on his body. There's no part of him that's not been stabbed. The pathologist says he was disembowelled with surgical precision. Apparently a similar technique used by Jack the Ripper.'

'Well, Terry Braithwaite was a butcher wasn't he.' Pausing he asked, 'Have they found any of his associates?'

'None listed on his record. We're still waiting for copies of the visitor log from Rampton to see who came to see him while he was inside, as well as his file from Probation, but from speaking with his Probation Officer she had him down as a bit of a loner. There's something else we've found out on that footing that is really interesting'

'What's that then?'

'Well you know we've made media appeals about the use of the flat where Ann Marie and Lesley lived.'

'I know the gaffer was going to prioritise it. I haven't seen the news about that though.'

'It was on the local news two nights ago. Well, as a result, we got back one very interesting response from a witness who thinks she saw Lesley being abducted, although at the time she didn't realise that was what she was witnessing.'

'Oh, go on then.'

'A woman in her fifties contacted us yesterday. Apparently she used to live in the house that backs onto Harry Wainwright's shop. She was a young teenager back in the eighties, and she told us that on the night Lesley went missing she was hanging out of her bedroom window having a crafty cig, because her parents didn't know that she smoked, and she saw a small dark blue minivan parked at the back of Harry's shop with its doors open. She was curious because she'd not seen it there before, and she also knew that Ann Marie and Lesley were prostitutes because she was friendly with Ann Marie, and her Mother told her to keep away from them. Anyway, that Sunday evening she told us that she saw a man with dark wavy hair and a beard, which fits the description of Braithwaite, together with a thin woman, with blonde hair, bundling something large wrapped in a sheet into the back of the van and then they drove off. She put the time at round about seven o'clock because they had just had their tea.'

'A woman!'

'Exactly.'

'And the witness is sure about the date – Sunday, thirteenth of May, nineteen-eighty-four?'

'Absolutely. Apparently Harry went to their house a couple of days later to ask her dad if he had seen anything, and told him about the girls doing a runner, owing him rent money. Her dad said no of course, and she decided not to tell Harry because she liked Ann Marie. She thought it might have been friends of Ann Marie's helping her do a moonlight and moving her stuff.'

'But if it was Braithwaite putting Lesley's body in the back of the van, that goes against what the witness Sue Braddock told us about hearing two men in the old chapel.'

'Unless he had more than one accomplice. A man who helped him bury Ann Marie and a woman to help him bury Lesley.'

Hunter furrowed his brow, 'Well, whoever this woman was, it can't have been his wife. She was dead. He buried her that Friday.'

'It's not finished there.'

'No?'

'No. Following on from that information we've interviewed the man who helped catch Braithwaite back in nineteen-seventy-one when he killed Glynis Young; the fisherman who saw him trying to rape her at Barnwell lakes and intervened. Banged on the roof of his van as he drove away and that's how he was caught. Remember?'

Hunter remembered.

Before he could answer Grace continued, 'Well he's a good seventy-five now, but he's still sharp as a knife, and we specifically asked him if he had seen anyone else with Braithwaite, or anyone hanging around at the time of the incident and he had. He told us that he thought he saw a young blonde haired girl sat in the front of Braithwaite's van. Apparently he did tell the investigating officers this at the time but they tried to say that maybe he was confusing it with Glynis Young, because she also had blonde hair. By the time they had finished interviewing him he wasn't quite sure and so it was never put in his statement for court and he was never asked. We went through everything again and he still remembers that event as if it happened yesterday. He's certain he saw Braithwaite attacking Glynis in the back of the van and that a young blonde haired girl was sat in the passenger seat watching the whole thing.'

'Wow. So you're now thinking that this young blonde haired girl in nineteen-seventy-one is the blonde haired woman in nineteen-eighty-four?'

'That's what it looks like.'

'Bloody hell Grace!' As soon as he expressed his thoughts he regretted it, shooting a look at the faces of his two sons.

Daniel was looking back scornfully. He said, 'I'm telling mum you swore.'

Hunter mouthed the word 'sorry' and then returned to his call. 'Listen Grace I've got to go for the train or I'll miss it. Thanks for filling me in. Hopefully I'm going to be back at work within a week but I'll keep in touch and let you know how things are going. If you hear anything else ring me.' With that he finished the call, checking the time on his phone. He had four minutes to catch his train.

* * *

Hunter saw the boys to their beds, said goodnight to them and following a quick shower decided to go and visit Michael Robshaw at the hospital. Kissing Beth, he told her where he was going, that he wouldn't be long and drove the short journey to Barnwell General. Visiting time had just started when he got there and he was surprised to find Dawn Leggate already on the ward, sitting beside her partner holding his hand. Evening briefing must have been early he thought, hesitating momentarily, wondering if she was still angry with him. Catching the hint of a smile on her lips he breathed a sigh of relief and continued approaching the bedside. Hunter saw that his former boss's eyes were still closed but he noticed a marked difference in his appearance for the first time since the accident; most of the dark bruising had gone, as had the swelling. He looked more like his old self. Pulling up a chair opposite and dipping his head as he sat down he asked, 'How is he? Any improvement?'

'Apparently the nurses say he's had a good day. He's had his eyes open a couple of times and he's asked for a drink for the first time.'

'That's good.'

She nodded. 'I'm glad you've come.'

'It's the least I can do. If it was the other way around I know he'd come and visit me.'

'I'm sure he would.' Dawn glanced at Michael's face, released his hand and gently stroked his cheek. Then, returning her gaze to Hunter she said, 'I'm glad you've come because I can update you about Shaggy's shooting. It's good news.'

'They've got them?'

She nodded. 'Yes, they've got both Danny Harris and Jason Roberts – Jazz. They traced Mark's phone to a flat in Burngreave and found them all together during a raid this morning. And they've recovered a gun. It was hidden in the toilet cistern along with a couple of kilo of amphet. Early indications are that it looks like the one used in both Sonny's and Shaggy's shooting.'

'Good result then?'

'It's thanks to your information. Especially getting Mark's mobile number. We got them before they could get rid of everything.'

'What about Mark?'

'Can't shut him up apparently. He's telling them everything; who's involved in the drug dealing and where they keep their stashes. He's told them about Sonny's shooting – Danny asking him to hide the gun and he was apparently in the back of the car when they shot his step-dad Shaggy. They threatened the same would happen to him if he said anything, but his mum's persuaded him to talk on the promise of moving them off the estate. They're sorting out a new place where they can go as we speak. They're in a council flat so it's going to be easier. They're getting them some emergency accommodation for a couple of days and then they'll probably be moved well out of the area where nobody can find them. Start a new life.'

'It's not going to be easy for them. It's a decision I wouldn't like to have to make.'

'Me neither Hunter. The main thing is Danny Harris and Jason Roberts are not going to be in a position to go looking for them. They're well and truly screwed. They're not going to be seeing the light of day for a very long time with two murder charges on their toes.'

'Are they saying anything?'

Dawn shook her head, 'Nope. Both "no commenting."'

'Well that's up to them. With this evidence they've blown it.'

'My sentiments exactly.'

'What about what's happened to Michael. Anything about that?'

Her mouth tightened. 'Mark's been asked about it but he says he's not heard Danny or Jason talk about any accident, only about the shootings. The team have recovered Danny's car and the DCI overseeing the investigation tells me it doesn't look as though it's been involved in any accident, so it's back to square one.'

'Christ, that's frustrating. Is there nothing come back from traffic about it?'

'Nothing. They've only got that one witness; the woman who heard the bang as she was drying herself after her bath, and looked out of her bathroom window and saw the car driving off and Michael lying on the road. They've gone through loads of CCTV footage, but there's nothing that matches the car's description on any of the roads going away from the scene around about the time of the accident. They're thinking now that maybe the car was parked up somewhere nearby, in one of the side streets, and that the driver legged it and then maybe went back the next day to pick it up when they were sober, so they're extending the search time parameters.'

'That really is frustrating. I hoped we were going to get a breakthrough.'

'You and me both.' Dawn sighed, 'Hey ho, mustn't get downhearted, there's still some work to do. I'm not giving up hope.'

'What about Braithwaite? Have you managed to track him down yet?'

She shook her head. 'We've got everybody out searching for him. You saw the news about the Wheelhouse murder?'

Hunter nodded. 'Grace gave me a call. She told me about how many times he'd been stabbed and everything. Horrendous isn't it?'

'And all because he was playing his music too loud. There's no doubt in my mind that Braithwaite's one sick evil bastard. The sooner we get him locked up the better.'

Hunter pursed his mouth and held Dawn's gaze. A moment's silence passed between them and then Hunter asked, 'I know it's not appropriate boss, but has anything been said about Barry's and my reinstatement, especially now they've got Danny Harris and Jason Roberts banged up.'

'I'm speaking with Professional Standards tomorrow to see if they can hurry things along. All I can see that will happen to you now is that you'll get a slap on the wrist, they'll probably recommend that you need some re-training on informant handling and then you'll be back in the fold. I'm afraid you're going to have to spend a few more days at home doing boring domestic duties, but it's nothing more than you deserve, going against my orders.' She issued a half smile.

'Lesson learned boss.'

'I bloody well hope so Hunter. Now do you fancy a quick beer? The back of my mouth feels like sandpaper.'

* * *

In a nearby pub, Dawn Leggate swiftly downed two halves of lager and then said her goodbyes leaving Hunter to finish off the remains of his beer. As she made her way across the car park to her car she thought about what she still needed to do before her day ended; there was her daily journal to complete and a list of priorities to prepare for morning briefing. As she took her car keys out of her bag she was already determining that she was going to do that with a sandwich and glass of wine in front of the TV watching the news. She had just popped the locks of her Mercedes and was about to open the driver's door when her mobile rang. Quickly, she pulled it out of her bag and glanced at the number. She didn't recognise it, but wondered if it was someone from the Sheffield team who wanted to update her about the arrests of Harris and Roberts and so she answered, 'Detective Superintendent Leggate.'

She was met with an initial silence and was about to repeat her name when the man said, 'Dawn.' She stiffened, feeling the hairs on the back of her neck bristle and with a sudden feeling of dread she replied, 'Jack?'

'Hello Dawn.'

Her stomach emptied. For some strange reason she felt scared and vulnerable and quickly glanced all around. Except for her the car park was empty. 'Jack why are you ringing me?'

'I just wanted to talk.'

Taking a deep breath, she answered, 'Well I don't. You and I are through. You shouldn't be ringing me. You've already been warned for harassment.'

'I just wanted to tell you I'm sorry.' He paused and then said, 'And I wanted to tell you I've lost my job.'

'Well you've told me. Now I'm going hang up and I don't want you ringing me again.'

'I want some money from the house.'

That scared feeling disappeared as soon as he finished his sentence, replaced by one of anger, 'You are fucking joking! That's my house.'

'It's *our* house! We were married.'

'No Jack, it was *my* house. My grandmother left me that house in her will. You're not having one penny from it. Now leave me alone Jack, or I promise, I will make a complaint against you.'

There was a few seconds quiet and then he said, 'This is not finished Dawn.'

Viperously she spat back, 'Last warning Jack.'

Another instant of stillness followed and then he said, 'How's Michael by the way. You're to blame for his accident you know Dawn.' Then the call ended.

Suddenly a sick sensation engulfed her and she tightened her hand around her mobile as if she was squeezing the life out of it. Reaching for the car door she couldn't help but look back over her shoulder with an element of fear.

CHAPTER NINETEEN
DAY THIRTEEN

Dawn sat her desk staring at her scrawl in her journal. She must have looked at it at least a dozen times since she had penned it last night. It had taken her some time to get her head around what her ex-husband, Jack, had said on the phone, but it boiled down to one thing in her mind, he was the bastard who had mown Michael down. As soon as he'd ended the call she knew she had to record what he had said while it was still fresh in her mind, and she'd sat in her car, in the shadowy play of the interior light, writing up the conversation verbatim. As she read it back now, she knew that on its own this was not sufficient evidence to prove that Jack had tried to kill Michael, but if she could find proof then she could send him to damnation. She picked up her mobile and dialled the number of her former Detective Sergeant, John Reid, back in her home town of Stirling – she needed assistance from someone in Scotland and he was as good and reliable as anyone she knew.

He answered almost immediately. 'Good Morning Dawn, or should I say Detective Superintendent Leggate?'

She caught the hint of friendly sarcasm in his husky Scottish brogue, and she could just picture him taking her call with one foot up on the corner of his desk, like he annoyingly always did, running a hand through his dark unruly hair; his appearance reminded her of Barry Newstead, but his skills as a detective reminded her of Hunter and that was why she needed his help.

'Morning John, how are things up there?'

'Not half as good as what's happening down where you are. I've seen you on television the last couple of nights – quite a celebrity you've become since you went and joined the Sassenachs.'

'Now, now, jealousy doesn't become you John Reid.'

He let out a hearty laugh. 'I'm guessing this is not a courtesy call boss, are you needing my help to solve things down there?'

'Funny you should say that.'

There was a pause as if her response had taken him aback. A second later he replied, 'Are there links with your investigation up here then?'

'Not with the case you've seen on the telly but there is something I need some help with.'

'What tells me this is something I'm going to find too tempting to resist.'

It was her turn to give a short laugh. Then, composing herself she said, 'What I'm going to ask you to do John is a little sensitive, but it is important and I need it done on the QT for the moment. Are you okay with that?'

'As long as I can quote you if it goes belly up?'

'It's not that dodgy. It's just a little enquiry I need doing.'

'Now where have I heard that before?'

She sniggered, 'Still the same John Reid – didn't nickname you *Mac the knife* for nothing.'

'Go on boss I'm listening.'

She told him about Michael's accident, the enquiries which were getting nowhere and then last night's phone call from her ex.'

He let out a whistle. 'I can see now why you said the word sensitive.'

'He's already embarrassed me once with his stalking and he was given a warning for that, so if I make this official, and it's nothing to do with him, it could blow up in my face and he could accuse me of harassing him. Michael's accident has been all over the news, and in the papers and on the internet so he could have got hold of the information that way…'

John Reid interrupted, 'But you don't think so?'

'No I don't. It was the way he said it. My instinct is that he tried to kill Michael because he's with me.'

'So what do you want me to do?'

'The last address I had for Jack was that bimbo's who he was shagging from work. But the car he had when we split up was a black Peugeot, which doesn't fit the description of the car that hit Michael. The car that knocked Michael down was a grey or silver saloon. What I'm asking you to do is to do a drive past his house and see if he owns a grey or silver car.'

'And if he does?'

'Then I'll reappraise what I need to do.'

'Consider it done.'

'Thank you John.'

'No problem. And it's good to hear from you again.'

'Good to hear your voice again.'

'Hey, and if you ever need a good DS'

'Got one, thank you. Far better.'

He burst out laughing, 'You can still cut a man down Dawn Leggate.' He paused and ended the call with, 'I'll get back to you as soon as I have anything.'

Her mood lifted, she stared at her phone for a few seconds before setting it down next to her journal. Now it was time to do her day job.

* * *

The human remains they had unearthed from Braithwaite's cellar were in a poor state. Doctor Anna Wilson had determined that the skeleton was that of a young woman aged between eighteen and twenty-five, and was between five foot three and five foot six inches in height. Death was as a result of strangulation. Buried with the body, crumpled, dirt-ridden, and damp, were a short yellow and black tartan skirt, a 1970s round collar, yellow blouse, and a red and black tank top, together with white bra and blue knickers. The fact that these were thrown in beside her meant that she had been buried naked. What was distinctive about the body was that her two upper front teeth were larger than her others, and had a gap between them, meaning they would have been visible when she smiled; this was something they were using as a key factor in the checks against missing persons. What they hadn't found was her shoes or any personal possessions. The possibility was that these had been taken as trophies.

That morning at briefing, Dawn Leggate was making it a priority to identify her. What she was also prioritising was the search for Terrence Arthur Braithwaite. The last sighting of him was in York city centre, where they lost him after he took a side road away from the busy outdoor market. The forensic team working at his home, and at the address of his latest victim Eric Wheelhouse, had very little to show for their examination. His neighbour's bungalow was in such a state that it would be the best part of a week before anything would be known. At Braithwaite's house, he had scrubbed down every flat surface with bleach and removed any documents with his name on them. There was nothing to indicate he had ever owned a computer or mobile phone and therefore the only way they had of tracing any contact he had with anyone was through his home phone records. They were still ploughing their way through CCTV evidence from his last sighting in York. By far the most significant thing they had uncovered was the two witness sightings they had of Braithwaite with blonde haired females – one with a young girl on the night he murdered Glynis Young, and the second on the night when he abducted and murdered Lesley Jane Warren. She was working on the assumption that these two females were one and the same person, though the team had no idea who she was.

Finishing the briefing, she put in a phone call to the Crime Scene Manager overseeing the forensic excavation of Braithwaite's 1970s home on Chapel Street. Duncan Wroe informed her that they had just unearthed the first signs of another body beneath the cellar, and she ended the call without any further questions, snatched up her coat and car keys and left the office to join him.

* * *

Hunter spent the morning at his father's gym, using the punch bag to get rid of some his frustration and then he did some sparring work with a couple of new protégés that had joined his dad's boxing stable. By the time he'd finished he was blowing hard and exhausted. Finishing off with sit-ups, he took a shower and then joined his dad in the office for a mug of tea. His dad asked him how things were going and he was about to answer when his mobile rang. It was Dawn Leggate. He signalled to his dad to give him a moment and answered the phone.

'Afternoon boss.'

'Afternoon Hunter, I'm the bearer of good news.'

'I'm reinstated?'

'Yes. You and Barry. I've just had the call from Professional Standards. It's like I said, I've got to give you both suitable words of advice, and you've got to go on some refresher training on informant handling, but the main thing is you're both back at work tomorrow. I want you in bright and early to catch up with where we're at, and then you and Grace have got some enquiries to do to see if we can find Braithwaite. You okay with that?'

'Sure boss, thanks.'

'You won't be thanking me when this job's over and I heap a pile of shite on you as punishment.'

Hunter punched the air as the call ended. It just felt as if the hod-load of bricks he had been carrying these past few days had been taken off his shoulders.

* * *

Dawn scooped up her most urgent paperwork and shoved it into her bag, her idea being that she would visit Michael in the hospital, and then go through it all back at home over a glass of wine and something to eat before going to bed. Zipping up her bag and slinging it over her shoulder, she gave her office the once over, turned off the light, closed the door and headed down the corridor to the MIT office to check all was quiet there. Entering, she was surprised to find Grace hunkered over her desk, a ream of papers scattered in front of her.

Grace turned her head at the sound of the doors opening, 'Evening boss.'

'I didn't expect you to still be here.'

'I'm just finishing off some paperwork. It's piled up these last few days.'

It suddenly dawned on her that Grace was picking up Hunter's workload as well as her own. She said, 'How're you coping without that partner of yours.'

'Okay. Bit of a strain though. Any sign that he'll be back soon?'

'Strange you should say that. I chatted with him earlier and gave him the good news. You'll be pleased to hear he'll be back in the morning. Professional standards have deemed that he's not in any way to blame for death of his informant and, though they are still investigating the allegation of assault against Braithwaite, given that he's now done a runner that's been put on the back burner. So, yes he's back.'

Grace smiled, 'That's good. In fact, now you've told me that I'm going to put this lot back in his tray for him to deal with.' She let out a laugh as she gathered up the loose papers.

Dawn let her bag slip down her arm and set it on Graces desk. Straight-faced she said, 'Can I ask you something Grace?'

Taking on a puzzled look Grace replied, 'Sure boss.'

'Terrence Braithwaite. Do you think I missed something? I'm not worried about him doing his disappearing act, but just going back to when we started doing his background checks and especially your conversation with Gordon Jennings – when he told you about the symbols and paintings in Braithwaite's old cellar. With hindsight I should have requested the excavation of his house sooner? At least that way we would have had him in custody and not on the run having murdered another innocent person.'

Grace seemed to think about the question for a few seconds before responding. 'To be honest boss we can all say that with hindsight we would have done things differently. You made a call which you thought was right at the time. We've got there in the end. And as you're asking I don't think detectives back then got it wrong. Think about the circumstances. Back then Braithwaite was seen as a rapist. As far as they were aware Glynis Young was killed after he was disturbed attacking her. And her body was dumped in the woods with no attempt to conceal it. The hallmarks of the rapes, the murder of Glynis Young and these murder victims are different. There was nothing at the time to suggest that he had killed before that incident with Glynis Young, and also, back then, there were no links to prostitutes or missing girls. The bodies we've now found in the cellar at his old house are because of our recent knowledge.' Shaking her head Grace added, 'You've not missed anything boss.'

Dawn picked her bag back up. 'Thank you for that Grace. You know, even with my years of experience, you get doubts whether you have got it right or not. I appreciate that.' Turning to leave she said, 'Now you dump all that work back on Hunter's desk and get yourself off to that family of yours.'

CHAPTER TWENTY
DAY FOURTEEN

'We're still waiting the outcome of DNA to confirm it but it looks like our first victim in the cellar is that of twenty-five-year-old Wendy Lomas from Harehills, in Leeds,' said Hunter glancing at the top of the print-out on his desk.

'You've got up to speed pretty quick,' interjected Dawn Leggate.

Hunter gave a half smile. 'I got in early boss.' He had been in since 7a.m. and the office where the HOLMES team were based had been his first port of call before he'd even put the kettle on. The digital facsimile of Wendy Lomas's Missing from Home report was displayed on the screen of one of the operators and Hunter had instantly asked for a copy to be printed off. In the quiet of the MIT room, before the team had started to drift in and congratulate him on his return, he had read the document carefully, and by the time he had finished he was in no doubt this was the woman forensics had found two days ago in Braithwaite's cellar. He continued, 'It's the HOLMES team we have to thank. They've done the work. The description of the clothing, though, and the victim's teeth made the identification easier.'

Dawn Leggate looked back at the incident board where photographs of the recent remains dug up from the cellar of 16 Chapel Street were affixed alongside those of Ann Marie Banks and Lesley Jane Warren as well as latest victim Eric Wheelhouse. 'So what do we know about her Hunter?'

'Wendy Lomas was reported missing on the twenty-eighth of October, nineteen-seventy, by her partner Thomas Whitehead. She had a son, Peter, who was then aged six and she was working as a prostitute.' He watched some of the team raise their eyebrows at his announcement. 'She hadn't been working the streets long – six months. Apparently her partner had got a badly broken leg playing Sunday morning football in the January of that year, which he wasn't insured for, and he was self-employed, so they went behind with their mortgage and were threatened with eviction. It seems that she told him she'd got a job working in a bar but in fact she went on the streets. Her partner had no idea. Thomas actually reported her missing in the early hours after she'd failed to come home, but because of the policy at that time and the fact that she was a prostitute, nothing was done to find her until he reported her missing a second time in the afternoon of the following day.'

'And by that time it was too late.' She spoke with an edge of frustration.

'To be fair boss she was probably dead by the time he reported her the first time.'

'Nevertheless, if things had been different back then – if we hadn't been so hung up about prostitutes – treating them like low-life – we might have prevented a lot of them being killed...' She stopped herself '...Sorry Hunter I'm digressing. Whinge over. Carry on.'

'According to the report Wendy used her car – a Ford Escort mk1 to pick up her punters. She used to park up near Leeds railway station and ply her trade around there, and in a couple of pubs nearby – mainly picking up businessmen, and then she'd drive to a cheap hotel on the edge of Leeds, do the business and then drop them back off. Police did check the hotel where she was a regular, and where she was also well known to the night porter, but she never used the hotel on the evening she disappeared, though her car was found abandoned in a side road near the railway station.'

'So what are we thinking? That Braithwaite and his mysterious female accomplice lured and abducted Wendy in Leeds or that for some reason she jumped on a train to Barnwell where she met Braithwaite and then ended up in his cellar – dead?'

'Well, we know that there's a direct train from Leeds to Barnwell, and we know from Gordon Jennings that during the Ripper era prostitutes came to Barnwell to do business here, but this is a decade before Peter Sutcliffe's reign. If you ask me I think what happened to Wendy was very similar to what happened to Ann Marie and Lesley – that more than likely she was picked up and lured back here, or abducted and killed somewhere and then her body was brought back here. My guess is that somewhere along the line, Braithwaite has a link to Leeds.'

Dawn eyed her team, 'Though it's not really relevant, I want to see if that is the case, okay?' She saw a few of her detectives nodding.

'Anything else Hunter?'

He shook his head. 'No. The rest of the report focuses on the extended search for her, and a media appeal, and of course her partner was interviewed a couple of times as a suspect – his alibi was that he was babysitting their son and he'd recently had a second op on his leg so his mobility wasn't good. I have tried to see if there is a contact number or an address, so I can speak with him, because he apparently moved a couple of years after her disappearance.'

She rubbed her hands. 'Okay, good job Hunter. Try and track Wendy's husband down and re-interview him. Good to have you back.' She pulled away her eyes and set them on Barry Newstead, slouched over his desk. 'And you too.'

Barry straightened and greeted her words with a weak smile.

Tugging back her gaze she set it on Grace, 'You had the task of going through his home phone records – anything enlightening?'

Grace separated a number of sheets she had in front of her, 'To be honest boss he didn't make many calls at all. There seems to be a regular once a month call to the Probation Service here, a regular call also to a pharmacist – he has a monthly med delivery, and there are a couple of calls from his solicitor in Sheffield. The only one on his list that is unusual is a number from Dunford Bridge, which is out in the sticks near Penistone. The number is from a phone box there, and he was rung three times from it – twice last year and once this year.'

Dawn displayed a puzzled frown. 'Are they long calls?'

Grace studied her print-out, running a finger down the telephone numbers. 'The first call in March last year lasted less than two minutes, the second in September, less than a minute, and one this year, five weeks ago, that lasted again less than a minute.'

Dawn looked around the room, 'And has anything cropped up about this Dunford Bridge place before in any of our other enquiries.' She watched her team share glances with each other before responding with a shake of the head or a shrug. Following the negative response she said, 'Okay, I want someone to run out there and give me a picture of what the place is like. And go back through records and see who he knows out that way. See if anyone from the Chapel estate moved out there. Is it where his female accomplice lives? There must be some relevance as to why Braithwaite should get a call from someone there, especially from a public phone.' She paused and then said, 'Terrence Arthur Braithwaite is our number one suspect for the murders of Eric Wheelhouse, Anne Marie Banks, Lesley Jane Warren and also for the two bodies we've uncovered in his old cellar. Doctor Wilson has still to do the post-mortem on the second body we found yesterday, but she has confirmed that it is female and that she was strangled like the other victims. Once I get more details I will be putting it out across the media along with his photograph, to see if we can flush him out. Make him panic. In the meantime, we will speak with his probation officer and see if he has links to Leeds and we'll give his solicitors a call and see who was dealing with his case and ask similar questions, including Dunford Bridge. I'm sure they'll bleat on about client confidentiality so we need to impress on them how vitally important it is that they don't impede our investigation – especially if they know where he is likely to be. And regarding the numbers he has telephoned, or been telephoned by, I want them flagging up and monitored. If any are activated, I want someone straight to the address. It's time to get Mister Braithwaite out of circulation for good and that goes for his accomplice as well.'

CHAPTER TWENTY-ONE

Limping along the lane, Terrence Arthur Braithwaite had his fleece collar up and head down to protect him from the elements. It was only a light rain that fell, but it was being picked up by such a fierce wind that it stung his face. When he had set off from the cottage an hour ago to explore his surroundings, the weather had been fine, but feeling the icy spits from rapidly gathering clouds, he was reminded how quickly conditions could change up here. He could already feel the damp beginning to seep through his clothes and, despite increasing his pace, he knew that he was not going to beat the rain, no matter how hard he tried. He cursed inwardly, for he knew he would have to suffer the cold and the wet for a good few hours even when he got back, for he dare not light a fire in daylight. That would bring attention to the cottage and thus to himself. And though there were no close neighbours, only a bunch of aged hippies squatting in a row of knocked-through terraced houses half a mile away, nevertheless, he couldn't afford any unwarranted visitors. To the public who passed the cottage and its outbuildings, it looked to be in the throes of long-term renovation work – which it was. Though, inside, it was a lot more habitable than it looked from the outside, and that was the reason why it made for the perfect hideaway.

Quarter of an hour later, tramping along the last of the bends in the narrow road, the weathered stone cottage, with its majestic backdrop of the Peak District, came into view. A muddy track quarter of a mile long, and a rusting, badly hanging gate were the only obstacles he had to endure before he unlocked the front door. He heaved a sigh of relief. He felt damp and thoroughly miserable, though thankfully the cold hadn't started to grab hold. A quick rub down with a towel and a change of clothing would see him good as new he told himself. But before taking that first step of his final stroll, he went through his ritual of looking all around; even scanning the cottage ahead. Only when satisfied the coast was clear did he step onto the dirt track. *You can never be too careful.*

Unlocking and opening the front door he got a nice surprise as he stepped inside; it was still warm, and he instantly put it down to the blazing fire he had made late last night; he had stopped feeding it logs at 4a.m. when he had finally fallen asleep on the sofa.

He pulled off his damp fleece and wet jeans, draped them over the clothes horse, changed quickly into a fisherman's jumper and fresh jeans and then lit the gas camping stove to make himself a hot drink. As he waited for the pan of water to heat up he drifted his gaze around the room. The two-foot thick walls that helped the building retain its heat in winter and keep it cool in summer were whitewashed. Much of it was yellowed and stained and in one corner, near the doorway that led into the kitchen, there was a damp patch; they had plans to get the place damp-proofed but that would have to be put on hold now it was his hidey-hole. The wooden sash windows were original and had thick black-out curtains drawn across to prevent anyone nosing inside and to stop the gas lamp and candlelight, that he needed at night, from being seen from outside. It left the room in constant gloom but he couldn't afford to take any chances even given the cottage's remoteness. That last thought brought about a flashback. He recalled his first sighting of this place. Its location could not have been better. It had the date 1725 above the door but his accomplice told him it had been built over the ruins of another farmhouse many hundreds of years older. The cellar beneath bore testament to that and was ideal for his plans. He had kitted it out to mirror the one back at Chapel Street, yet, unlike that one this one offered more privacy to pursue his craft. That thought prompted another – his accomplice. He wondered how long it would be before he put in an appearance. Seeking his support. Wanting reassurance. A crooked smile played on his lips. It had taken a long time grooming him to become so needy, so obedient, and some of that training had been brutal, but eventually he had seen the recklessness of his ways and changed. The same had to be said of his wife. Sheila had taken a long time to understand his needs – to adjust to his way of wanting things done, and it had been an uncomfortable journey, but in the end she had realised it was futile to resist.

CHAPTER TWENTY-TWO
DAY FIFTEEN

In upbeat mood, Dawn Leggate closed the front door behind her, kicked off her heels and made her way through to the kitchen where she set down her bag and switched on the kettle. She had just come away from the hospital. Michael had been wide awake when she entered the ward and had remained awake throughout her visit, managing a two-way conversation, even though some of it had been fragmented and at times gone off tangent. He knew he'd been involved in an accident but could recall nothing about it, and he had asked her how long he'd been unconscious and what had happened to him. She told him what she knew – that it was being treated as a hit and run and that an investigation was underway but that they hadn't caught who was responsible. She decided not to tell him about the phone call from her ex and that she now believed Jack had deliberately targeted him; she wanted to see what the outcome of her own enquiries were first before she told him that. She also mentioned the visits he'd had from his daughter and Hunter. He told her he hadn't been aware they'd been but he said how pleased he was and asked how they both were. When it came to talking about Hunter, she told him that he was doing well and working hard, but held back from telling him about the informant being gunned down and Hunter being suspended; she determined that was for another time. At the end of their hour Michael had become fidgety and she had seen him fighting to keep his eyes open. It had been her signal to say goodbye, and she kissed him and told him she loved him – for the first time in twelve days. She had left the ward brimming with happy tears. As she drove home she'd been able to take in the music playing on the radio, rather than worrying about her partner or thinking about the murder enquiry.

Making a coffee, she opened the fridge, not just for milk but seeking something decent by way of food. Since Michael's accident she had only gone through the motions of eating to sustain herself through the day, now she actually felt like she wanted to eat and, as she searched the shelves, she was so glad she'd stocked up with a good shop. She chose to make a salad, remembering she'd bought some fish which was in the freezer. While preparing her meal, she turned on the small TV, drunk her coffee and set the table. As she placed her knife and fork she couldn't help but wonder how long it would be before she was eating a meal with Michael again. This had been the most positive she had felt since the accident. Salad ready, she checked the timer on the cooker and, seeing she had another twenty minutes before the fish was cooked, turned down the sound of the TV and telephoned DS John Reid.

It didn't take him long to answer, 'Evening Dawn.'

'Good evening John I'm ringing to see if you have anything?'

'I was waiting for you to call – I have actually.'

'Oh, what's that?'

'Well it's not the news you wanted to hear I'm afraid.'

'Oh!'

'I did a few runs past the address you gave me, but there was no sign of anyone so I made a couple of enquiries with the neighbours, and one of them told me that for the past few months she'd only seen the woman who lived there and no man, so I checked what time she was generally in and went back this evening on my way home to check.'

'And you caught her?'

'Yes, she'd just come from the gym.' He paused and added, 'I can see now why he went for her…'

'John Reid, don't you dare.'

He made a soft chuckle, then said, 'On a serious note, we had a quite a decent chat about Jack. It took me a bit of time to get her to open up – she wanted to know why I was asking such personal questions – but as soon as I told her he was harassing a woman, she told me he'd hassled her after she'd ended their relationship and was more than happy to answer all my questions. I spent a good hour chatting with her and I don't want to pry about you two's relationship but I found some of what she told me quite disturbing. In fact, you might be on the right lines when you think he's responsible for what happened to Michael given what she's said.'

'Jack was always a bit deep, but we were okay. Well I thought we were initially. We had our ups and downs like any other married couple. It was mainly about me working late. He used to go into these sulks that lasted a few days, but I used to make it up to him when I had days off and he'd be fine again. Though, to be honest John, things did deteriorate towards the end, especially after my last promotion. That's when I found out about his affair.'

'She mentioned a bit about that. She said it started because she felt a bit sorry for him. He used to tell her that he felt constantly alone because you loved your job more than him.'

Dawn let off an exasperating sigh, 'The shit.'

'I know. Anyway, she says it started with him asking her if she'd go for a drink after work for a chat and that developed into the odd meal now and then. She said he used to go on about how lonely and neglected he felt, and one night she just invited him back to her house and that was it, as they say. It became a regular thing after that, even staying some weekends.'

'The bastard told me he was going away to conferences!'

'Well there you go. You know what he was up to now.' Pausing he continued, 'After a couple of months he was telling her he wanted to leave you, and asked her if he could move in and she agreed.'

'Bastard! I wouldn't mind but I never fucking neglected him.'

'If I wasn't one myself I'd say that's men for you.' He let out a shallow laugh again. 'Anyway the relationship ended almost three months ago. She decided it wasn't for her. She said he never wanted to do anything. I gathered from our conversation that she's a bit of a party girl and he'd rather stay in, and it just seemed to be one row after another so she called it a day and asked him to move out. She said he took it quite badly and that he began waiting outside the house for her for when she came home from work, begging for her to take him back, so she went to stay at a friend's for a week. Then, he started hassling her at work and she ended up making a complaint to the boss. He was warned, apparently, but continued and so he was fired. She said he turned up a couple of times shortly after he'd lost his job, threatening her, and she ended up calling the police, but the time they got there he'd driven off. I've spoken with the officers who took the call and they tell me they're still looking for him to give him a harassment warning but they don't know where he is. They can't locate him.'

'No idea?'

'None. Unless you can help?'

Thinking for a moment, she replied, 'His parents are still around. They live somewhere near Fort William, but to be honest, except for the odd phone call, he wasn't very close to them. I've got their address somewhere in my address book, which is still in one of the boxes in the garage here – I never unpacked it when I moved. I'll have a look through my stuff over the next couple of days. If you text me the officers' details, I'll give them a call. I also know he's got a couple of cousins near Aberdeen, but again, except for sending Christmas cards that was his only contact. Have you any idea about the car he's got.'

'The ex-girlfriend says that he bought a Volvo – he lost the company car after he was fired. I tried to get her to narrow it down, but she has no idea about the model – just says it's. Silver.'

'It was a silver saloon car that knocked Michael down.'

'I know.'

'Do you have a number by any chance?'

'Sorry Dawn. All she told me was that it wasn't brand new but neither was it old. We're looking at it probably being a couple of years old. If he's still got it. If he's got any sense he'll have dumped it.'

Sighing again she said, 'Thanks for this John.'

'Do you want me to do anything else?'

'No, you've done your bit and I'm very grateful. I'm going to let Traffic know about Jack's phone call to me the other night and also what you've just told me and let them circulate him as wanted. And, if in the mean time you get anything else, especially his car number, you'll give me a call? That'd be appreciated.'

'No problem Dawn. Hope it all comes good and you take care now.'

'And you John, thank you, I owe you one.'

Ending the call, Dawn clasped her phone two-handed and rested it against her chin, thinking through what she had just been told. Suddenly, out through the window above the sink, the rear security light blazed on and she targeted her gaze into the garden. She jumped when she caught sight of the figure standing in the middle of the lawn. It was Jack!

***

Within ten minutes, police officers were swarming all over the estate where Dawn lived. A police dog had picked up a scent of Jack but then lost it at the end of the cul-de-sac where there was a high wall and they were starting a fresh sweep from the other side.

Holding onto the work surface, Dawn was still shaking as she gave a description of her ex-husband to the concerned policewoman, who was repeating it over the airwaves to her colleagues. A full search was underway. Inside, Dawn was beating herself up. She had been useless. The moment she had seen it was Jack she had frozen. Under normal circumstances, had it been anyone else, she would have leapt into action and worried about the consequences later. But seeing it was Jack had rattled her completely – rooted her to the spot. She had eventually reacted, but it must have been the best part of ten seconds before she had dialled 999 and grabbed the biggest knife from the drawer. Now, as she tried to pull herself together, she was just glad that there had been a locked door and window between them. Goodness knows what would have happened had there not been. As she tried to dismiss the darkness engulfing her, a wave of nausea hit her.

CHAPTER TWENTY-THREE
DAY SIXTEEN

Shortly after 6a.m. Dawn gave up trying to force herself to sleep. She'd had a terrible night, flinching at the least little noise. She had been surprised at just how many different sounds there were around once the traffic outside had died down. Though, not all traffic – she was grateful for the security of the marked police car which drove past the house every hour; she'd got up once to watch it cruise by and not gone back to bed until she'd probed the shadows of every garden opposite. She had even got up once to double-check that the back door was locked. Jack's sudden appearance had made her a wreck. She couldn't believe he was doing this to her. How come she'd not spotted this trait in him all the time they were married. Had she neglected him?

Swinging her legs out of bed and pulling on her dressing gown she had just belted it around her when her mobile rang. She jumped. Heart-racing, she snatched it up from the bedside table and checked it wasn't a number she didn't recognise before answering. It wasn't. It was the Force Communications room. She wondered if they had caught Jack.

'Detective Superintendent Leggate.'

'Good morning Ma'am, communications here. Sorry to disturb you but we have you down as the on-call superintendent?'

The female call-handler's response wasn't what she expected. With all the drama going on in her life she had forgotten it was her turn on the call-out roster. She answered, 'Yes.'

'We've got a report of an abduction: a young woman dragged into a car near the woods off Doncaster Road.'

'Abduction?' she answered screwing up her face. 'That's a CID job. Have you contacted the District DI?'

'Yes ma'am, the DI is out there with CID Officers. He's the person who asked me to contact you. He says that he thinks it's linked to your investigation.'

CHAPTER TWENTY-FOUR

Dawn Leggate perched herself on the edge of Grace's desk and opened up morning briefing, 'Developments everyone! While some of you were tucked up in your warm and comfortable beds in the wee small hours, muggings here, was out on the streets dealing with an abduction.' She heard a couple of her team repeat the word 'abduction' and saw them exchange questioning glances. 'Abduction, yes. And what relevance does that have to our enquiry I can see you all asking yourselves?' She scoured the room, 'Well, eyes front, and I'll show and explain.' Adjusting her position, she aimed the remote she was holding at the large flat screen TV at the front of the room. Instantly a black and white, grainy, CCTV image appeared. The shot was frozen. Centre screen was a young, dark haired girl in tight black jeans and outdoor short jacket. She appeared to be in a large car park – a few cars were parked in clearly defined bays.

Dawn set the image to play.

The squads' eyes were glued to the TV. They watched footage of the girl, head down, slowly walking right towards the edge of the screen. Within seconds she had disappeared.

Dawn stopped play, back-tracked the CCTV to bring the girl back into view and then froze her image. Looking around her team, she pointed the remote at the TV and said, 'Our victim. Twenty-two-year-old, Becki Turner. What you have just seen is last night's footage of her leaving the Crown Hotel, where she works as a bar supervisor. At nine minutes past twelve she finished her shift and left the hotel to go to her home on Marshall Place where she lives with her husband, Mathew, and four-year-old daughter Amy. After she left the car park – you have just seen – she walked a short distance along the main road, crossed over towards the rugby ground and onto the old towpath. We know that because the bar manager saw her from the back door where he was having a smoke. Once she got onto the towpath her journey would be approximately quarter of a mile, upon which, she would emerge up onto the main Doncaster, Barnsley road, literally a few hundred yards from her home. It is here she was abducted. And we know that because it was witnessed.' Pausing again she studied the faces of some of her team. Then, she continued, 'At roughly twelve-thirty, a taxi driver was travelling along Doncaster Road, back to his office, when he spotted two people struggling with a young woman…' She jabbed the remote towards the TV… 'Becki. He said it looked like they were attempting to get her into the back of a dark coloured Ford Mondeo and so he pulled up to see what was going on. He saw that the two people struggling with Becki were a man and woman. The woman had her arm around Becki's neck, and one arm up her back, trying to force her into the car, while the man was holding open the back door, trying to grab her legs. The taxi driver shouted, and asked them, what was going on, to which the man turned around, and said, they were having trouble with their daughter. He asked if he should call the police and the man told him to fuck off. He said that he wasn't happy at all with what was happening and so he called us. The time of that call was logged as twelve-forty-two.'

'Why didn't he get out and help?' Tony Bullars question sounded like a snipe.

'Now, now Tony, we can't all be super heroes. He didn't just ignore it did he? He contacted us.' Waiting a moment, for her rejoinder to hit home, she continued, 'The response car attended, and got to the scene at twelve-fifty-one – nine minutes later – but there was no sign of the car or our abductors. They spoke to the taxi driver and got a description of the couple. Unfortunately, he hadn't taken the registration number of the Mondeo. A local search was carried out to track the car down, but to no avail. At that stage we had no idea who the girl was or if we had a genuine job. One hour later Becki Turner's husband rang in to say she hadn't arrived home. He had apparently tried ringing her mobile several times, and texted her without getting a response and so he'd rung the hotel. When the night porter told him what time she had left he rang us. It was at that stage CID got involved, and once they had got a full description of Becki's abductors' that's when they called me out.' Pausing again she eyed up her team. Their faces were full of concentration. She said, 'The description of the woman is not that good. The taxi driver didn't get a look at her face, and so he describes her as a heavily built woman, with blonde, collar length hair. She was wearing jeans. That's all he can remember. The man's description though is a lot better. He says he looked quite old, late sixties, maybe early seventies, clean shaven, and he was wearing a dark fleece jacket. He said that when he called out to them the man stepped towards him and he got the impression he had some kind of limp.' As she finished her sentence she caught her team trading excited looks. She said, 'I thought that would get a reaction. Now who does that remind you of?'

'Terrence Arthur Braithwaite.' Hunter responded.

'That was my response when I heard that description.' She aimed the remote at the TV and turned it off. 'I don't need to tell you how imperative it is that we track down Braithwaite. We really need to step up our game now. A young girl's life depends on it. We all know who we are up against. Braithwaite is a very dangerous man. A killer. But he hasn't disappeared. Last night's abduction proves that. I want everybody on this. Go back through your actions. I'm convinced there's something in them that will tell us where he and his female accomplice are hiding.' Taking a deep breath, she finished with, 'If it was Braithwaite involved in Becki Turner's abduction then it's probably a good thing the taxi driver didn't get out of the car. We could be dealing with another murder this morning.' She targeted her look at Tony Bullars to make a point.

He glanced away.

* * *

There was only Hunter and Grace in the office. Grace was checking back through Braithwaite's phone records and Hunter was catching up on the paperwork that had accumulated in his tray while he had been off. With a sigh he pushed back his chair. He needed a break.

'Fancy a brew?' he asked rising and stretching out his back.

Grace glanced up, nodded and returned to her list, highlighting another phone number that required checking.

Switching on the kettle, Hunter sauntered to the incident board while waiting for the water to boil. Hands on hips he scanned the board, reacquainting himself with the enquiry – following the spidery lines that connected photographs to timelines and information – digesting the updates. As he rested his gaze on the black and white photograph of 16 Chapel Street something caught his attention. In the front top right hand window of the terraced house it looked like there was someone looking out from behind the net curtains. He leaned in to get a closer look. There was someone there but the image was so small he couldn't pick out any of the person's features. He couldn't even make out if it was a male or female, though it looked like a young person. Turning around he said, 'This photograph of Braithwaite's house. When was it taken?'

Grace looked up, 'I think the boss said it was from around the time when he was on trial for the Glynis Young murder. Or it might have been just after he was convicted. Not quite sure. It was taken in nineteen-seventy-three that's for sure.'

'And who took it? Was it one of our shots?'

'No, I think the boss said she got it courtesy of the Chronicle. Why?'

'Just come and take a look at it will you.'

Grace left her desk and joined Hunter.

'Where am I looking?' she asked looking at the photo.

Hunter pointed at the front top right hand bedroom window, 'Is it me or is that someone behind the net curtains.'

Narrowing her eyes Grace stared at the spot where Hunter was pointing. After a couple of seconds, she said, 'There's definitely someone there, but I can't make them out properly.'

'Me neither,' he replied stepping back from the board. Returning to his desk he snatched up the phone. He had a reporter friend at The Barnwell Chronicle who could help. He quickly dialled her number.

CHAPTER TWENTY-FIVE
DAY EIGHTEEN

There was an A4 brown envelope waiting on his desk when he got in. In bold red letters across the top were the words PHOTOGRAPH PLEASE DO NOT BEND. He guessed what this was. The first thing he pulled out was the complimentary slip from his friend Zita Davies, the reporter at the Chronicle. The handwritten note read 'You make sure you ring me first.' He smiled, set it to one side and slid out the photograph. Zita hadn't let him down. It was a duplicate of the one on the incident board, but larger. Three times larger. And he could make out the image of the person who was standing behind the curtains in the bedroom. A cold shiver travelled down his spine. He was sure he recognised that face!

It was quarter of an hour before Grace walked in through the door. By that time Hunter was pacing around the room like someone tramping across hot coals.

'Where've you been?' he said as soon as she entered.

She threw him a puzzled look, glanced at the clock on the wall and then returned her gaze, 'What do you mean? This is my normal time. We can't all be in the office at the crack of dawn – some of us have to take our parental responsibilities seriously.'

He let out a laugh as she set down her handbag on her desk and began unbuttoning her coat. 'Listen, I've got something really interesting to show you.' He picked up the A4 black and white photo and thrust it towards her.

Heaving off her coat and dropping it onto her desk, Grace took the photo from his hand. 'What's so important you won't even give me time to take off my coat properly?'

Hunter targeted a finger at the photo. 'That was waiting for me this morning. It's a blown up copy of the one on the board. Remember the face behind the net curtains?'

Grace nodded.

'Well take another look it now the picture's bigger.'

Studying her face as she scrutinised the picture, Hunter waited with baited breath.

Raising her eyes from the photograph and fixing them on Hunter she said, 'I can see what looks like a young boy. I don't recognise him though. Should I know him?'

Hunter jabbed a finger, 'Take a look at the ears.'

She studied the photo for a couple of seconds before snapping up her head, 'It can't be?'

'You're seeing what I'm seeing aren't you?'

She nodded sharply, 'It surely can't be?'

'We'll soon know if it is!'

Plonking himself down on his chair he sought out the piece of paper with retired PC, Gordon Jennings' home telephone number written on it and, reading it off inside his head, dialled the number. It was a good ten seconds before the Scotsman answered.

'Gordon its Hunter Kerr, sorry have I woken you?'

There was a loud 'Grumph' Then he said, 'What time is it?'

'Half seven.'

Another 'Grumph,' followed by, 'There's only one half past seven in my life now and it's not in the morning.'

'Sorry Gordon, I wouldn't have rung you so early but it really is important.'

'I gather that. I'm awake now, fire away.'

'Gordon, did Terrence Braithwaite have a son?'

'No, why?'

'I'm looking at a photograph on my desk right now of 16 Chapel Street. It was photographed by The Chronicle during Braithwaite's trial in nineteen-seventy-three and behind the curtains of one of the bedrooms I can see a young boy looking down.'

There was a moment's silence before Gordon responded, 'Terrence Braithwaite didn't have a son, but Sheila, his wife, had a son with her first husband. Braithwaite brought him up. He doted on him by all accounts.'

Hunter took in a deep breath. 'Can you recall his name?'

There was another few seconds of quiet before the retired PC answered, 'It was an unusual name...'

'It wasn't Saville by any chance was it?' Hunter interjected.

'That's it! Saville. Saville Chambers. He kept his father's surname.'

'How old was he when Terry was arrested?'

'He was a teenager. Fourteen, fifteen – something like that. He looked younger than his age from what I remember. A quiet lad as well. A little bit withdrawn if you ask me.'

'Can you remember what happened to him?'

'I certainly can. After Braithwaite was arrested, and we found all that mumbo-jumbo in the cellar we contacted social services with a view to him being taken into care. Although we were locking Braithwaite up we weren't sure that leaving him with his mum was a good idea. We weren't exactly sure if she was involved in any way – you know – if she'd been protecting Terry.'

'So he went into care?'

'Not exactly. Sheila had a brother who had a smallholding somewhere up near Penistone. He and his wife took him in. As far as I know they brought him up.'

'Can you remember where that place was?'

There was a long pause and then he said, 'No sorry. I just know it was up near Penistone. I never went there.'

'It doesn't matter Gordon you've been a great help with what you've just told me.'

'I wish I'd have got the same words of gratitude back in the seventies.'

'Well I hope this detective's made up for the others. Keep your eyes on the news over the next few days – you might have just helped us clear the case up. Thank you.'

Setting down the phone a satisfied smile broke over Hunter's lips. He met Grace's inquiring look.

She said, 'I caught the name there. That's not who I think it is, is it?'

'I'm certain it is. The guy who introduced himself as Braithwaite's brief at Bridlington the other day is none other than his stepson.'

'Jesus! Would you believe it? You thinking what I'm thinking?'

'That he's involved. That he's an accomplice?'

Grace nodded.

'Well that would give us part of the jigsaw if we bear in mind what the witness Susan Braddock said about hearing two men's voices in the old chapel on the night Ann Marie was buried. I mean if Saville Chambers was fourteen, fifteen, in seventy-three, then he will have been twenty-five, twenty-six, in eighty-four. Though it doesn't answer who the woman might be.'

'Saville's girlfriend or wife maybe?'

Hunter shrugged his shoulders. 'The other thing that's just dawned on me – didn't you say that Braithwaite had a couple of calls from Dunford Bridge to his house phone?'

Grace drifted her gaze to her pending tray where she'd deposited Terrence Braithwaite's home phone call list. She pulled the few pages out and fanned them across her desk. The printouts provided details of the date, time, duration, and telephone number of each call made to Braithwaite's house phone. Running her finger down the columns of highlighted calls she stopped in several places before raising her eyes. 'There are three from the phone box at Dunford Bridge – two last year – one in March, and one in September, and one this year – the seventh of last month. None of the calls were for very long. Also, there are the calls which we originally thought were from his solicitors. Well they are from the solicitor's office but, knowing what we know now, what's betting they were from Saville Chambers. Three of those calls have been made since we found the bodies.'

'Okay that's great stuff,' he said vigorously rubbing his hands together. 'You and I, partner, have got some work to do. We need to find out where Saville Chambers lives and ideally where this smallholding is up at Dunford Bridge. It surely can't be that hard to find – there's only a dozen or so houses up there. It's my guess that's where we'll find Braithwaite.

CHAPTER TWENTY-SIX
DAY NINETEEN

Seven thirty a.m. Daylight was just breaking as the convoy of two CID cars, Crime Scene van and forensics van pulled into the street where Saville Chambers lived. Hunter and Grace – the arrest team – led the way. There were no bells and whistles, no high speed approach, just a gentle cruise into the tree-lined suburb.

Twenty yards from Chambers' 1950s, three-bedroom semi, Hunter eased off and edged towards the kerb, braking gently and turning off the engine. For a brief moment he looked out along the quiet road. Lots of houses had lights on in their bedroom windows, a sign the households were rising, but none of that activity had yet presented itself onto the streets. That wouldn't be long he told himself. Soon the curtains would be twitching and residents would be noseying from their driveways. He took in a slow but deep breath. He could feel his heart racing. Inside he was already buzzing from the adrenaline rush; this might be the day they caught their killer. Steadying his breathing, he glanced across at Grace. 'Ready?' he asked.

She met his gaze and dipped her head.

Gently pushing open their doors they got out and Hunter signalled to his back-up team of Tony Bullars and Mike Sampson, parked behind, to join them. As they got out of their car he gave them the thumbs-up sign, not saying a word. Then, each of them quietly closed their doors and began their soft-footed approach to the target house. The Forensics team stayed where they were; Hunter had already briefed them to wait on his call before they got out. Entering Saville Chambers' narrow driveway, Hunter spotted a dark blue Ford Mondeo parked down the side of the house. His heart leapt. He pointed it out and watched Grace, Tony and Mike's faces light up. Hunter gave them the thumbs up and they moved into action – Hunter and Grace taking the front while Tony and Mike slipped around to the back to block any escape.

Taking another deep breath, Hunter beat the front door loudly with the heel of his hand. He could hear the sound travel through into the hall. The noise was louder than he expected and he glanced upwards at the bedroom bay window. A light came on. Seconds later a voice shouted down the stairwell. 'Just a minute.' Hunter heard quick footsteps getting louder and a brief juggling with a key before the door opened.

Saville Chambers stood there, a striped dressing gown fastened around him, bleary-eyed and in need of a shave. As he looked from Hunter to Grace his face visibly paled. 'What on earth's this?' There was a nervous inflection in his voice.

'This Mr Chambers is your morning wake-up call.' Hunter replied.

For a couple of seconds, he stood with his mouth open. Then recovering, he said, 'I hope you've got a warrant?'

'Certainly have.' Hunter thrust a folded piece of paper towards his face and pushed him into the hallway.

Stumbling backwards, Saville Chambers seemed lost again for words. But once more it was only momentary. He said, 'This had better be good Sergeant Kerr.'

Grace stepped into the hall and closed the front door so that there was no escape for Chambers.

Hunter pressed in close to Chambers, deliberately invading his space and tapped the warrant on the bare upper part of his chest close to his throat.

Saville tried to step back but found himself hindered by the wall.

Hunter said, 'Is he here?'

Gulping Saville answered, 'Is who here?'

Hunter probed Chambers face, his eyes narrowing. Slowly he responded, 'Mr Chambers let me make myself very clear here. I am not in the mood to be fucked about. You did that at Bridlington Police station when you pretended to be Terry Braithwaite's solicitor, when in fact you are a solicitor's clerk, and I can tell you I'm pretty fucking annoyed about that, so don't wind me up any more than you've already done.'

Saville straightened, 'If you did your research you'll know that a solicitor's clerk can represent a suspect in a police station.'

'Oh I know that Mr Chambers, but on that occasion you were not there on behalf of your firm. We've spoken to them. They've had no official request to represent Terrence Braithwaite.' Hunter steadied the words leaving his mouth. He could feel himself getting tense and was doing his best to stay in control.

'You've spoken with my firm?' Saville nervously answered.

'We have. We know a lot about you Mr Chambers. Now I'll reiterate what I said a few seconds ago, I am not in the mood to be fucked about.' He paused and gave Saville a hardened stare. Then he said, 'Now where is your stepfather, Terrence Braithwaite?'

'I don't know what you're talking about. He's not here if you think he is. You can take a look if you don't believe me.'

Hunter pressed in closer until his nose was almost touching Saville's. 'We will take a look don't you worry. You, Mr Chambers, are in a heap of shit. We're already looking at a charge of assisting an offender. I am going to give you one minute to run things around in that stupid head of yours and give you the opportunity to make this right. If at the end of that minute you choose to carry on in this vein then you will suffer the consequences.' Hunter held off mentioning Becki Turner's abduction; that had been decided at the early briefing; although one of the descriptions fitted Terrence Braithwaite, there was nothing to suggest Chambers had been involved, although seeing the Ford Mondeo on Saville's driveway was making that a lot more promising now.

Saville made an attempt at moving sideways but Hunter slapped his hand against the wall to prevent him. He said, 'Thirty seconds!'

'You've no right to treat me like this. This is against the law.'

Hunter turned and exchanged looks with Grace. He said, 'Do you see me acting against the law here DC Marshall?'

Straight-faced she answered, 'Everything according to The Police and Criminal Evidence Act as far as I can see, Sergeant.'

Hunter turned back to Chambers, 'You heard that and now your time is up. What's it to be? Are you going to tell us where your stepfather is?'

'I don't know what you are talking about.'

Hunter stepped back and said loudly, 'Right, we take this place apart. Call in the others Grace.' Looking Chambers in the face he added, 'You are under arrest for assisting an offender.' He reached into the back of his waistband, pulled out his handcuffs and, grabbing hold of the solicitor's clerk's wrists, ratcheted them on and dragged him into the kitchen where he pushed him against a work surface. Looking him in the eyes he said, 'I don't want to hear one peep from you.'

As he finished speaking Hunter heard the front door opening and, turning, saw Tony Bullars and Mike Sampson trooping in. He called to them, 'Start upstairs and bring forensics in.'

'Forensics!' Saville cried.

Hunter turned around to face him, 'We are going to go through this house with a fine toothcomb. Did you not hear me when I said you'll suffer the consequences?'

For the next twenty minutes Hunter listened to the sounds of furniture being moved, cupboard doors and drawers being opened and closed, as the house was searched. He would like to have been with them but he knew his team would be doing a thorough job, whether he was there or not. From time to time he took a glimpse at his prisoner. He'd caught him squirming uncomfortably a few times and at one stage had seen him wiping sweat from his brow. He knew Chambers was getting worried; a sure sign that there was something here he hoped they wouldn't find.

Suddenly a call went up, 'Here!' It was Tony Bullars.

Hunter picked up the sound of hurried feet moving upstairs and wondered what they had found. Less than thirty seconds later Grace called down, 'Hunter you need to come up and see this.'

Hunter glanced at Chambers. His face was ashen. Grabbing him by the cuffs and hauling him up, he felt him wobble slightly. 'Upstairs, now.'

He led Chambers back along the hall and pulled him upstairs. On the landing he saw everyone congregated at the doorway of one of the rear bedrooms. Hunter left Chambers and walked to the doorway. Inside the bedroom Mike Sampson was standing beside a double wardrobe, both doors open. In his outstretched arms he was holding two blonde wigs. One was long and straight and the other was collar length with curls. He scrutinised the find for a few seconds and then switched his gaze to the open wardrobe. Inside, hanging from a rack, was an array of women's clothing. He shot his eyes back to the wigs held out in Mike's hands, then swivelled to meet Grace.

She said, 'You thinking what I'm thinking?'

Everyone's sight zeroed in on Saville Chambers.

CHAPTER TWENTY-SEVEN

In the interview room at Barnwell police station Hunter slipped off his jacket, draped it over a chair, undid the cuffs of his shirt, and slowly folded them back exposing his muscular forearms, all the time staring at Saville Chambers. It was mid-afternoon – seven hours since the solicitor's clerk had been arrested and placed in a cell, and though he was trying his best to hide his nervousness Hunter could read the signs, both in his face and his body language. Studying his prisoner's features as he seated himself opposite, Hunter knew he already had the advantage and couldn't help but issue a smile. Then, straightening his face he opened with, 'You've chosen not to have a solicitor Mr Chambers?'

Saville tried to respond but the words caught in his throat. Giving a slight cough, he answered, 'It seems pointless when I can represent myself.'

Hunter rolled his neck. 'Your choice, Mr Chambers. Now me, I'd be looking for all the help I could get right now.'

'And what's that supposed to mean? You shouldn't be talking to me in this manner.'

'I was only trying to give you some friendly advice. What's wrong with that?'

'Can we get on with this?'

At that point Grace walked into the room. She was carrying three brown paper exhibit bags.

Hunter watched Saville Chambers switch his gaze, casting his eyes on the bags as she set them down on the table.

Taking a seat, Grace switched on the recorder. Following a short buzz from the machine she spoke the formal preamble for recorded interviews and announced who she was. Hunter followed suit and, on finishing, invited Saville Chambers to give his name. He did so.

Hunter then said, 'Mr Chambers this morning you were arrested for assisting an offender. That offender being one Terrence Arthur Braithwaite. Can I confirm you understand why you were arrested?'

'Yes, but I think you'll find you have no proof of that. All I did was support him when you interviewed him at Bridlington Police station.'

Hunter held up a hand. 'I'll get around to that in a moment. First I want to talk through this morning. Following your arrest, we executed a warrant to search your home. You were present during that search – is that right?'

'Yes.'

'And during that search we found several items of women's clothing in the wardrobe in one of your rear bedrooms plus two blonde wigs. Is that right?'

Following a short pause and a loud gulp Saville answered, 'Yes.'

'Can you tell me who that clothing and those two wigs belong to?'

'No comment.'

'Are those items yours Mr Chambers?'

Saville blushed and said, 'No comment.'

'I'm not trying to trip you up or embarrass you Mr Chambers, but can I ask you – are you a cross-dresser?'

Flushing even further he answered, 'No comment.'

'It wouldn't be incriminating to admit that you wore women's clothing you know.'

Saville narrowed his eyes, 'You're enjoying this aren't you Sergeant Kerr?'

'Not at all, Mr Chambers. I'm simply trying to ascertain who the women's clothing in your wardrobe belongs to?'

'And I don't wish to answer that. Can we move on?'

'Of course, no problem.' Hunter momentary glanced at his hands, stretched out his fingers and interlocked them. Lifting his gaze, he said, 'The reason why I asked you that question is because following a thorough examination of each item of clothing we found among them three pieces of female clothing which are of particular interest to us.' Hunter picked up one of the exhibit bags Grace had bought in, and flipped it over to reveal a plastic window, allowing sight inside the bag. The contents were a single piece of black and white checked clothing. Hunter continued, 'I am showing the prisoner item TB 1, which is a pair of female checked trousers, size twelve. Mr Chambers these trousers are fashionably referred to as Oxford bags and I understand were very popular in the nineteen-seventies. Do you recognise them?'

Saville had lost the redness of his earlier blushing and now looked ashen. 'He stuttered, 'No comment.'

Hunter pulled across the other two exhibit bags and flipped these over revealing an item of pink clothing, and what appeared to be a folded woollen garment made up of large black and yellow squares. He said 'I am now showing Mr Chambers items TB2 and TB3, which is a female yellow cotton blouse, size twelve, and a black and yellow checked pullover, fashionably referred to as a tank top and also popular in the nineteen-seventies. Do you recognise these items Mr Chambers?'

'No comment.'

'As I say these items were found among the female clothing in the wardrobe at your home. Is there any reason why they should be hung up there?'

'No comment.'

'Fair enough Mr Chambers. I'll hold talking about them for now because I want to talk about something else. I want to talk to you about your home at sixteen Chapel Street. Is that okay?'

Saville threw a puzzled look, 'If you wish.'

'When did you go to live at that address?'

'From when I was born. It was my parent's home.'

'Those parents being?'

'Fred and Sheila.'

'I understand your dad died when you were young?'

'Yes, in an accident at work. He worked at the pit. He got crushed in a roof fall.'

'I'm sorry about that.'

'It was a long time ago. I was only eight.'

'Nevertheless, it's still sad when you lose a parent.'

Saville shrugged.

'And so you were brought up by your mum?'

'Yes.'

'Until Terrence Arthur Braithwaite came on the scene?'

Saville took a deep breath. 'Yes.'

'And what age were you when that happened.'

'I knew Terry before my dad died. He used to deliver our meat from the butchers.'

'How did you get on with him?'

'He was okay. He used to chat to my mum.'

Hunter nodded. 'And after your dad died, how long was it before your mum struck up a relationship with him, or you became aware that they were in a relationship?'

'I can't remember exactly. I was around nine – ten when he moved into our house.'

'And how did you feel about that.'

'Okay I suppose. I can't really remember.'

'And how did you get on with him?'

Saville again shrugged. 'Okay. He was all right.'

'Did you have a good relationship with him?'

'It was okay.'

'How did he treat you?'

Saville reddened. 'Look where is this line of questioning going?'

Hunter gestured with open hands, 'We all know what happened to Terry – what he was accused of and charged with. I mean the things he did made headline news. Not nice stuff at all, especially when you were so young and at an impressionable age. I'm only trying to find out what your relationship with him was as a young boy. Did he ever do anything that you were uncomfortable with, or act in a strange way that you didn't like?'

'I've said he was okay. Things were okay. Can we move on?'

Hunter drew back his hands and smiled. 'Of course. How long did Terrence Braithwaite live with you and your mother?'

Saville threw him a puzzled look. 'I don't understand. You know how long he lived with us. He was with us until the police arrested him.'

'What I'm getting at is, was there any period of time when he didn't live with you? Did Terry and your mum ever split up over anything?'

'No. There was only that time he went to prison for burglary.'

'Oh yes of course. What did you think about that?'

'I can't really remember.'

'Okay. And when he came out your mum married him, didn't she?'

'Yes.'

'What did you feel about that?'

'Nothing. It was her choice.'

'So she must have loved him?'

'I suppose so.'

'Did you ever see Terry abuse your mother?'

It was a couple of seconds before he replied, 'No.'

'You hesitated there. Any reason?'

'No,' he snapped. 'I-did-not-see-Terry-ever-abuse-my-mother. Satisfied?'

'If you say so.' Hunter paused before asking, 'How did your mother react when Terry was arrested for the murder of Glynis Young?'

'I don't know. I can't remember.'

'What did you think?'

'Nothing.'

'What? It didn't affect you? Your step-father being arrested for murder.'

'Can't remember how I felt.'

'It must have had some effect?'

'Look I've said I can't remember. Okay?'

Hunter studied Saville. After a couple of seconds, he said, 'Mr Chambers did you ever see Terrence Braithwaite do anything bad at your house. By that I mean hurt or kill anyone?'

'No! Definitely not.'

Although the response was immediate and emphatic Hunter caught that the words he spat out were fractured.'

'I tell you why I'm asking you that Mr Chambers, it's because, as you're aware, we've found a number of female bodies recently. One was in the old chapel and the other near the back garden of your old home, which is what we started to talk about when you and Terry were at Bridlington police station. Since then we have found two other bodies and it's those two I'm especially interested in because they were found in the cellar of your old house. Do you know anything about two female bodies buried beneath your cellar?'

'No.'

'I caught your answer there, but you don't seem surprised that two bodies were found in the cellar of your home. Is there something you want to tell me?'

'No. I'm not surprised because I've already heard on the news that you've found them.'

'Them? Mr Chambers. As far as I'm aware the news only broadcast that we found one body in the cellar.'

Saville coughed a couple of times before returning, 'I said *them* because you've just said you'd found two bodies. Look the cellar was off limits. Terry kept it padlocked. I never went down there.'

Hunter smiled. He had to give it to Saville Chambers – he was quick to pick up on the mistake he had just made. 'Okay, yes I suppose I did. Anyway we've spent a good few days trying to identify those bodies and we've learned that one of them is a woman called Wendy Lomas. Does that name mean anything to you?'

'No.'

'Wendy Lomas was reported missing on the twenty-eighth of October nineteen-seventy and I can tell you that since that date, thirty-nine years ago, nothing has been heard of her until we dug her body up from the cellar of your old home just over a week ago. Do you know anything about that?'

'No.'

'Mr Chambers how old were you in nineteen-seventy?'

He momentarily glanced up to the ceiling, then returning his eyes answered, 'Thirteen.'

'So it would be fair to say that at thirteen you would know if anything untoward was going on in your home? You're a bright enough man yes? So I'm guessing you would have been a bright young teenager?'

'It's a long time ago now, but yes.'

'And you definitely can't remember anything bad happening to any woman at your old home?'

'No.'

'Now you see I find that strange. I think when I was thirteen that if I'd seen and heard a lot of activity going on in my cellar I'd have been suspicious. Especially as you said earlier Terry used to keep it padlocked. Weren't you just a bit curious as to why that was?'

'No. I never gave it a second thought. As far as I was concerned there was nothing down there. The place was damp. You can believe me or not. That's your problem. I'm telling you I never saw anything happen to any woman at my old house and I never heard anything going on in the cellar. I don't know how she ended up being buried in the cellar. I can't help you.'

'Okay Mr Chambers, that's fine. But as you mentioned a couple of questions ago I said we'd found two bodies. Both of them in your cellar. And I've already said we managed to identify one of them as Wendy Lomas. We were able to do that because of the clothing on the body. It married up to her police Missing from Home report. But the second one we've had difficulty with because that body was buried naked. Had no clothing on it whatsoever.' Hunter took a few seconds out, focussing intently on Saville's eyes. Chambers shied away his gaze as Hunter continued, 'And then we found the clothing in your wardrobe. The three items of clothing I have just shown you.'

Saville Chambers' features swiftly took on a waxen appearance – a soft sheen of perspiration started to cover his skin.

Watching him for a few seconds Hunter said, 'Mr Chambers, you've gone white. Is something the matter? Has this line of questioning got to you?'

Saville tried to respond but for a moment the words wouldn't come out. Abruptly he blurted, 'No comment.'

Hunter raised his voice, 'On May the first, nineteen-seventy-two, twenty-three-year-old Barbara Mullins disappeared. She was last seen drinking in the Navigation Inn pub, not a stone's throw from your old house. Just over a week ago we found her body buried in the cellar of sixteen Chapel Street, and the clothing she was last wearing was found in your wardrobe this morning. Can you explain that?'

Shaking his head, he replied loudly, 'No comment.'

Hunter slowly pushed himself back in his seat. He rested his hands, palm flat on the table and with a steady voice said, 'Shall I tell you what I think Mr Chambers. I already know from the enquiries we have made that Terry has psychopathic tendencies. You'll have probably seen on the news that we're also now hunting him for the vicious murder of his disabled neighbour, which shows how dangerous he is. I think that he gradually manipulated and coerced you into doing his bidding. At first, probably just little things, like following women around in his van. It's my bet, from the women's clothing we've found, that he got you to dress as a girl when you were younger, and just for fun pulled a few of those women over and chatted to them while you sat there. A game between the pair of you. You not realising what was going on. But then there was Glynis Young, the girl he tried to rape and then killed at the lakes. That was when he took the game further.'

Saville Chambers started shaking his head.

Hunter continued, 'A witness has now come forward and told us that, on the night Glynis was killed, he saw what he thought was a young girl with long blonde hair sitting in the front passenger seat. My guess is that it was you in that van. Glynis was lulled into getting into the van because she thought she was getting into it with another girl. That she was safe. That's how Terry operated.'

'No!'

'And it's also my guess that when he escaped that day at your mother's funeral, which I think you helped him, by the way, that the pair of you did the same thing again with two prostitutes from Chapeltown. You dressing up, this time as a woman because you were older, and again they were lulled into getting into a van with the pair of you and brought back to Barnwell where they were killed and buried.'

Chambers shook his head more vigorously. 'No!'

'I'm right aren't I?'

Without warning Saville Chambers banged his hands on the table making Hunter and Grace jump. Eyes almost leaping from their sockets he shouted, 'You've no fucking idea what it was like living with Terry! He's fucking evil!'

* * *

Most of the team were sat at their desks, on their phones or working at their computers, when Hunter and Grace entered the office. All eyes rounded on them, faces etched with expectation.

Hunter held up his hands, 'Sorry guys we rattled him but not enough to get him to cough.'

A couple of them gave disappointed looks, not in an unkind way, but the majority exchanged glances of support.

DI Scaife stepped forward, 'Did you get anything?'

'Not really. Certainly nothing incriminating. He "no commented" about the women's clothing and then totally clammed up when we told him that we'd identified Barbara Mullins from the three items in his wardrobe.'

'You get any indication he might be involved?'

'Some reaction to our questions, especially when I asked him about the wigs and what we thought he and Terry had done, but not enough for court. I certainly gave him enough opportunity to put the blame squarely on Terry's shoulders but he didn't go for it.'

'Do you think he was a willing partner?'

'Again I relayed my thoughts and gave him the opportunity to respond with a satisfactory answer but he didn't. You could argue that maybe as a teenager he wasn't so much a willing participant – you know when Glynis Young was murdered, but then we have to also think about the girls that were buried in the cellar, which he completely denied knowledge of. And then there's Leslie Warren and Ann Marie Banks. When they were abducted and killed, Saville would have been in his mid-twenties. You can't really say Terry would have been able to manipulate him at that age.'

'What about last night's job – Becki Turner?'

'I didn't get round to that because of how he reacted. I'm going to ask him about her next. I'm going to give him an hour to calm down and then go in again.'

'Well they've searched his car but they haven't found anything belonging to her in it, so we don't know if it was his car involved last night or not.'

'What's happened to it?'

'They've recovered it on a low-loader and taken it to forensics. They're going to make a start on it this afternoon. If she was in that car we'll find out.'

'Good.'

'Going back to his interview, did you manage to talk to him about his uncle and aunt's place out at Dunford Bridge?'

'I had several goes at trying to get it out of him but as I say he clammed up. Refused to answer any more questions. Not even a 'no comment' out of him.' Hunter checked the DI's face. 'Have you got anything from the house?'

DI Scaife shook his head, 'We're still going through every item of women's clothing to see if there are any matches to the Missing from Home reports of our victims. We've found a woman's watch and a bracelet in a bedside drawer, which might be something, but other than that nothing. The house is clean. No sign that anyone was killed there. And no sign of Becki unfortunately. We've got his mobile though. Mike Sampson's gone through to Headquarters to see if the technicians can pull off any data, especially see where he's been with it. If he had it with him last night, or when he visited the smallholding belonging to his uncle and aunt, then we've got him and we should also get a location at Dunford Bridge.'

Hunter automatically crossed his fingers. 'Good stuff.' Then, looking around the room he asked, 'Where's the gaffer?'

'She's in her office with ACC Winterburn from Headquarters.'

'What, she's taking all the glory?' he said light heartedly with a smile.

'No, something's going on. The ACC turned up with two guys from Professional Standards. Not scheduled. They're talking behind closed doors. I went down five minutes ago and the door's still locked. They've been in there over half an hour.'

Hunter unexpectedly felt his chest tighten. The image of Shaggy being shot burst inside his head. Dawn Leggate told him that he was just going to get a bollocking. Was something else going on? The last thing he needed was to be suspended again. Swallowing hard he half turned, 'I'll go and see if she's free and bring her up to speed.'

* * *

Hunter caught the backs of the AAC and his Professional Standards entourage as they descended the back stairs. Feeling queasy and anxious he tramped along the corridor to Dawn Leggate's office. Her door was ajar and, snatching a mouthful of air, he rapped on it lightly and pushed it inwards. The Detective Superintendent was sitting behind her desk, her face full of concern.

Hunter could feel his mouth drying up and, forcing saliva up from his throat said, 'I've just seen the ACC with Professional

Standards on the stairs. The DI says they came to see you. It's not about me is it?'

Dawn ushered him in with her hand and pointed out a seat in front of her desk.

Hunter lowered himself slowly never taking his eyes off her.

With a firm mouth she answered, 'No, it's not about you Hunter. It's to do with me.'

Hunter studied her face and waited. He could see from her expression that she hadn't finished.

Bringing up her hands and clasping them under her chin she said, 'It's going to be out soon enough so you might as well be the first to know, Mike's accident was deliberate!'

Hunter frowned questioningly, 'Well we always thought that. Has someone been arrested?'

'Not yet they haven't, but they are going to be circulated as wanted within the next ten minutes.' She paused, took a deep breath and added, 'It was Jack!'

'Jack... Your ex?'

She nodded. 'They've found video footage of him pulling into a garage half an hour after the accident, examining the front of his Volvo. And they've tracked down a mobile technician who replaced his windscreen.'

'Bloody hell!'

'I can think of stronger words than that.'

'He tried to kill Mike?'

'It looks like it.'

'Good God! Has he always been like that – you know – having a violent streak?'

She shook her head, 'This isn't the Jack I know. I was married to him for eight years and, sure we had a few spats between us, and I've shared a few choice words with him since we split, but I never saw this coming. I mean trying to kill Mike. He's totally gone over the edge.'

'It's a heck of a way to try and get back at you.'

'Tell me about it.'

'I can understand the ACC coming to speak to you but why Professional Standards. You've not done anything wrong.'

'The IPCC will need to get involved. They're just trying to soften the blow for the Force. Work out a strategy.' In the air she finger-drew the word 'strategy' and issued a sarcastic half laugh. 'So what's next?'

'They're bringing in another SIO to support me, probably take over the enquiry, which pisses me off. And they've asked me not to go back home until Jack's arrested.' She paused, and said, 'Keep this to yourself for the next hour or so. I've got a few things to sort out and then I'll tell everyone at briefing.'

Hunter nodded and pushed himself up from his seat. He felt sorry for his boss yet, at the same time, selfishly relieved that it wasn't him back under the spotlight.

* * *

Hunter sat cradling his mug, half full of lukewarm tea. He had just set aside his journal; writing up that morning's interview with Saville Chambers, making notes along the way as he thought of different questions for the next one. He didn't think he had any involvement in the murder of Eric Wheelhouse but he was certain he was involved in the kidnapping of Becki Turner and so the challenge during the next round of questioning was to introduce Becki Turner's abduction and dupe Chambers into giving up the address at Dunford Bridge. He gazed across at Grace. She was on the phone, heavily in discussion, and it sounded as if it was still with the lawyer from CPS; he'd caught snippets while he'd been beavering away on his journal. He glanced over her head to where the wall clock was and saw that she had been on the phone for over twenty minutes. By the scowl on her face he could tell it wasn't going well.

Deciding he'd had enough of his tepid drink and would make a fresh brew, he pushed himself out of his chair, and was about step from behind his desk, when he caught her derisively mouth her thanks, slam down the phone, and mockingly add 'tosser', as she threw back her head, clenched her fists in the air and let out a growl.

'I gather from that it's not good news?'

She took a deep breath and muttered 'Count to ten Grace' and replied, 'It's not I'm afraid. Our solicitor says that the fact that he sat in on an interview and deceitfully supported Braithwaite under the guise of acting as his brief does not contribute towards a charge of assisting an offender. He also says that the fact that he refuses to disclose the address of the smallholding does not contribute towards the charge because we don't actually know for certain Braithwaite is holed up there.'

'What about him being an accessory to the murders?'

'That's even more frustrating! The fact that he has a wardrobe full of women's clothing, and two wigs, *and* we have the two statements that a young girl was seen in the van when Glynis Young was attacked, *and* that neighbour at Chapeltown saw a woman involved in putting a large bundle into the back of a van when Leslie Warren went missing, is merely circumstantial. As is the seventies clothing, despite them being exactly the same clothes the victim Barbara Mullins was last seen wearing, unless we can get a physical forensic link between victim and Saville, we've got to let him go.'

'So in other words, unless he admits his involvement he walks.'

'He walks!'

'Fuck!'

'My sentiments exactly.'

Hunter let out a frustrating sigh. 'We'd better get our thinking caps on and see how we're going to get Saville to cough.' He reached across and picked up Grace's mug, 'I'll make us a drink and then we'll sit down and plan the next interview.'

Hunter had just turned away from his desk when the office doors burst open and Mike Sampson walked in wearing a beaming smile. 'Got it!' he announced.

Everyone focussed on him.

He held up a clear plastic evidence bag. In it was a mobile phone. 'Saville Chambers phone is one of those with in-built GPS coordinates. The techies have tracked everywhere he's been with it since he took out the contract two years ago and guess where one of those places is?'

Hunter responded first. 'Becki Turner's abduction?'

Mike nodded, 'Places him on Doncaster Road at twelve-twenty last night and follows the route he took afterwards in the early hours.'

'The smallholding at Dunford Bridge?'

'Absolutely.'

'He took Becki Turner up to Dunford Bridge?'

'It certainly looks like it.'

Hunter punched the air, 'Yes.'

'Fucking big fat yes.'

'Now where's that district map? – we've got a girl to find and a serial killer to bring in. Saville Chambers can wait.'

CHAPTER TWENTY-EIGHT

Terrence Arthur Braithwaite silently lifted the latch and gently eased open the door that led down to the cellar, cautious not to make any noise. For a moment he stood in the doorway, listening. The light behind him picked out the first few stone steps, after that everything was in shadow, but that didn't trouble him because, even in the dark, he was familiar with the way ahead.

And it would be more frightening this way, he thought.

Being extra careful not to drag his limping leg, he made his way down, little by little, taking in shallow breaths and exhaling gradually. At the bottom he stopped again and listened. Not a murmur. Cracking a smile, he set off again, feeling his way along the cold lime-washed wall to where it ended and opened out into the main cellar. Here it was pitch black so he couldn't see her, but he could hear her because of her laboured breathing; the tape he had sealed across her mouth was forcing her to breathe through her nose. And he could smell her – she'd pissed herself.

Raising his torch, aiming it in her direction, he flicked it on. The bright light made a direct hit upon her face, making her jump, almost toppling the chair she was tied to over. The terror in her eyes was a sight to behold. It was just the effect he wanted.

He had time with this one, he told himself. No need for a quick kill. This time he could saviour every moment.

Lowering the beam from her eyes, but leaving it so that he could still see the fear in her face, he stepped towards her.

She tried to scream but the gag muzzled her cries.

Standing before her he noticed the blood – most of it dry – around her wrists and ankles where the barbed wire restraints had dug into her skin when she'd struggled. He reached out to touch her hair. She tried to pull her head away so he grabbed a handful of locks and yanked her forward.

She let out a muffled yell.

Closing in on her, she flinched, closing her eyes. He could feel her trembling as he pressed his face nearer. He began licking her cheek. Her tremble became a shake and she started to cry.

'There' he said quietly, releasing his grip on her hair and stroking it. 'You and I are going to have so much fun, aren't we?'

Her response was a long stifled howl.

He let out a laugh, straightened, switched off his torch so that she was faced with the dark again, and made his way back up to the kitchen.

CHAPTER TWENTY-NINE
DAY TWENTY

The arrest and search team travelled up to the outer reaches and the bleakest section of the policing district in darkness; daybreak was a good hour away – they wanted the element of surprise.

The convoy swung off the A628 Woodhead road to Manchester onto a thin tarmac stretch that was not only signposted Dunford Bridge but also the Trans Pennine Trail. It also informed them that their target destination lay only two miles away.

Sitting with the Task Force in the back of their van, Hunter felt an unbelievable electric buzz running through his body. The surge had started yesterday, as soon as Mike Sampson had revealed where Saville Chambers' remote smallholding was located. Since then everything he had done to pull the operation together had been as if he was under the influence of a speed enhancing drug; it was a remarkable sensation that he loved. Even when he got home last night he hadn't managed to come down and had hardly slept a wink. Yet he felt surprisingly fresh.

That morning Hunter had got into work a good hour before briefing; which had started at six a.m. with each officer on the team being given a copy of the operation order. Quickly drawing breath he rattled through each section meticulously and set out the objective – the arrest of Terrence Arthur Braithwaite – with clipped precision. Then, in two transit vans, the team, consisting of himself, Grace, Tony Bullars, Mike Sampson, Carol Ragen and Barry Newstead, plus a dozen Task Force personnel, had hit the road at quarter to seven.

They were in their final run-up.

Hunter tapped the driver on the shoulder. 'Slow down here, we're almost there,' he instructed..

Slowing for the bend ahead, the driver gently swept it around the curve and started to edge towards the grass verge. Another hundred yards along, mounting the nearside set of wheels up onto the grass, he stopped.

The van behind did likewise.

As quietly as possible everyone got out. While Hunter and his squad checked they had their forensic gloves and torches, the Task Force officers put on their final pieces of kit – their protective vests, gloves and helmets – and then Hunter drew then together into a circle.

Except for the sound of the wind, which was freezing, the area was quiet. Hunter wasn't surprised given the isolated location. From the fly-past photographs taken by the Force helicopter he knew that, except for a small cluster of distant cottages and a couple of farms, the area around here was predominantly farmland. Saville Chambers' place was about three hundred yards away, protected by a perimeter of centuries-old, waist high stone walls and a metal gate.

For a second time that morning Hunter confirmed that everyone understood the plan and, on receiving a round of nods, said, 'Let's go.'

With quick-steps the team marched until they came to the metal gate. Although the gate was old and rusted the padlock and chain on it was new. The bolt croppers they were carrying put paid to it on their first bite and two officers eased the gate open. The path to the long stone cottage and set of outbuildings was springy soft and partly overgrown; it was quite apparent it hadn't been used much to travel down.

Task Force took the lead, fanning out, treading slowly towards the building. It lay in darkness – there was no sign of life inside.

Hanging back with his colleagues, Hunter could feel his heart banging against his chest as his eyes picked out the silhouettes of the dark-clad officers taking up their positions. Four officers – two either side of the building – disappeared to the rear of the cottage, the remaining eight lined up either side of the front door. Against the stonework, he could just make out the outlines of the officers and he watched as one to the left of the door raised his right arm. He held it there momentary, his helmet turning in the direction of the one holding the battering ram. Then, with a swift downwards swipe of his padded-gloved hand he yelled 'Police!' and a split-second later the battering ram smashed the ancient wooden door at lock-level, crashing it inwards with ease. Almost choreographed, the officers piled in one after the other and Hunter caught flashes of intense white beams dancing around the interior of the cottage. Less than ten seconds later a figure appeared in the doorway.

'Here's here,' shouted a voice.

Hunter recognised it as the Sergeant's and began moving in.

When Hunter got inside, the first thing he saw was Task Force circling Terrence Braithwaite, who was sat on a sofa in T-shirt and underpants, in front of an ember glowing fire. One of the officers was playing his thousand-candle Dragonlight on his face and Braithwaite was trying to shield his eyes from the blinding light. In the halo created, Hunter saw that his hair was bedraggled, and he gathered by the clump of loose bedding lying around him that he had been asleep on the sofa prior to the bust. He smiled to himself. Everything had come together.

Hunter stepped from behind the sofa to face his prisoner. The officer lowered the beam of his powerful torch and Hunter said, 'Good morning Mr Braithwaite. We meet again.' Although Terrence Braithwaite was looking directly at him he could see from his expression that he was struggling to see him. He said, 'It's Detective Sergeant Kerr, Mr Braithwaite. We met at Bridlington and you and I have some business to finish.'

Braithwaite dropped his chin and muttered, 'Fuck off.'

'So glad to hear you're pleased to see me. Now it just gives me the pleasure of saying, I am arresting you on suspicion of murder.' Cautioning him, Hunter bent forward and clamped his hand around the wizened flesh and muscle of Braithwaite's upper arm. He tried to shake free and Hunter tightened the hold, 'Now I'm sure you're not going to be that foolish are you,' he said and hauled him forward.

Braithwaite tumbled off the settee onto his knees letting out a moan.

With his free hand Hunter slipped the handcuffs out of his waistband and clicked then around Braithwaite's wrists. 'There now, that was painless wasn't it? Now I want you stay here while we search this place and then we're going back to the station for a nice little chat.' Hunter pressed him backwards onto the sofa. Turning, he said to Barry, 'Keep an eye on him while we turn the place over will you?'

Barry signalled a salute and replied sardonically, 'Aye, aye Sergeant.'

Shaking his head, Hunter glowered at Barry, then beckoning to the others, he instructed them to begin their search.

Although Hunter knew that the building was old, as curtains were whipped open to give them better light to work in, he saw on closer inspection, just how aged it was; the whitewashed walls were flaking in most places, as were the ceilings, and in a couple of corners there was evidence of damp. *This place needed some work.*

After giving each room the once over, he broke up the team and allocated them a room apiece. Hunter went upstairs with Grace and Tony Bullars. It only had two bedrooms, each of which had one small window which let in minimal light in the early dawn and torches were required, especially for the corners. As Hunter looked around the first bedroom and noted the amount of cobwebs covering the painted stone walls he could see that it hadn't been used for years, probably even decades. In this one there was a Victorian brass bed which had a mattress, but it was so stained and covered in dust that no one in their right mind would have slept on it, he told himself. As he pulled on his latex gloves and ran his eyes over the room one more time he wasn't relishing the prospect of this search.

Ten minutes later, job done, but nothing found, he left Grace and Tony to the second bedroom and nipped downstairs to see how the other teams were getting on and check on his prisoner. Braithwaite was still sat on the sofa. They had released his cuffs to enable him to pull on a jumper and a pair of jeans and one of the blankets he had used as bedding was draped around his shoulders. He raised his eyes as Hunter entered and offered up a smug grin. Hunter met his gaze and held a locked stare, expecting him to shy away but he never flinched. Hunter gathered by that reaction that Braithwaite was pretty confident they weren't going to find anything incriminating here. For a moment he wanted to physically wipe the grin off his face but then he checked himself and broke away his gaze, fixing it on one of the Task Force who was rummaging through a cupboard set in the wall. The man turned his head.

'Anything?' Hunter asked.

Tight-lipped the man shook his head and went back to his search. Hunter decided to go through to the back where the kitchen was and had just set off when a call came from there.

'Got something!'

Hunter rushed through the doorway. Two officers were standing next to a large oak dresser that they had heaved away from the wall.

'Here,' one of the officers said, casting his head into the space between the dresser and the wall.

Hunter walked past them and stepped into the gap. He immediately saw what the officer was indicating – a smaller than normal door set into the plaster. His heart lurched. Carefully lifting the latch and pulling it open, he found himself looking at a sloping ceiling and a set of worn stone steps that descended below ground level. He couldn't see anything beyond the fifth step, but he knew there were more. Taking out his powerful mini torch he switched it on. The intense beam lit up the staircase giving him a view all the way to the bottom – a distance of just over two metres – where he was faced by a white-washed stone wall. Taking a breath and holding it, trying to contain his excitement, he listened for a few seconds and, hearing nothing, began a slow descent. As he approached the wall he had to duck his head to avoid hitting the ceiling, and stooping, he could see that a flagstone path branched away right. He took it. The atmosphere was noticeably colder and smelled damp and he shuddered, the torch shaking in his hand, causing bright dancing light to play on the walls and ceiling, creating a spooky effect. He steadied, re-focussed, and followed the line of the wall. He had only gone a couple of metres when the path shifted left and, turning the corner, he found himself in a cavern of a room. At first, the cone of light hit the far wall picking out nothing but white space but, feeling a buzz of nervous electricity surge through him, he started to arc the torch around. He had only moved the torch a metre when he came across a number of painted symbols – an upside down cross, a five-star pentacle and the mark of the beast, which he recognised as antichrist daubs – and he remembered what Gordon Jennings had told them about the symbols he had seen in Braithwaite's cellar in Chapel Street. He continued sweeping the torch. A few seconds later it brushed past a huddled image that made him jump. He instantly swung it back and stopped his beam on the shape. Head resting on chest, dark hair covering her face, he recognised Becki Turner from the clothes she was wearing. Her arms and legs were bound to a metal chair she was hunched on and looked bloodied. Hunter's heart missed a beat and he let out a loud gasp. As he did so, Becki flinched, lifting her head. Duct tape covered her eyes and mouth. Hunter's blood coursed so swiftly through his body that he could hear it rushing between his ears. He'd found Becki Turner – and she was alive.

From above a distant call came, 'Have you found anything?'

Hunter couldn't hold back, 'You bet I have! I need an ambulance here straight away.'

A pair of metal snips took care of the barbed wire restraints and DC Carol Ragen bathed and bound Becki Turner's wounds using the task force first aid kit. To say the ordeal she had gone through, Becki was in surprisingly good spirits and, with tears of joy, she was able to tell them everything that had happened to her. Grace took notes knowing it would be many more hours before Becki would be fit and able enough to give a formal statement. She wasn't worried about getting a full account from her right now – the priority was getting her proper medical treatment and getting her examined by a Force Medical Examiner. Everything else could wait.

* * *

In the detention suite at Barnwell Police Station, Hunter gently closed the interview room door as he stepped out into the corridor. Holding onto the handle a second he exchanged glances with Grace and broke into a smile. Neither of them said anything as they climbed the stairs, taking the back route up to the MIT office. The eyes of the entire team were on them as they entered the office. Both of them wore a deadpan look as they set their eyes on the expectant faces of their colleagues.

'Well?' probed Detective Superintendent Dawn Leggate stepping forward, 'How did it go with Saville Chambers?'

Hunter glanced quickly at Grace then, returning his eyes to his team, he couldn't hold out any longer and burst into a jubilant grin, 'He's coughed.'

The cheer that went up deafened him.

It was a good few minutes before the room quietened. Dawn Leggate made three loud calls for 'order' before the team started returning to their seats. Finally, scouring the room ensuring everyone had settled to listen she demanded of Hunter, 'Come on then tell us what he said?'

Hunter plonked himself on the edge of his desk and, setting aside his interview notes, responded, 'He realised it was on top of him as soon as I told him we had Terry and found Becki alive. The first thing he asked me was, "has he said anything?" I told him he hadn't, but he didn't need to now that we'd got Becki back – that she'd been able to tell us everything. After that he just broke down.' Pausing, Hunter's mouth tightened, 'When I say he broke down, it wasn't quite as simple as that. It took him a bit of time to get over the embarrassment about the wearing of women's clothing, but once we got over that the rest was easy. His confession was a bit sad really – not that I feel sorry for him – but the first thing told us was about was how Terry had caught him trying on his mum's stuff when he was ten years' old and threatened to tell her and all his mates unless he did something for him. He agreed to, not realising what he was getting himself into, and he said that one-day Terry came home with that long blonde wig and some girl's clothes and told him to try them on. Apparently Terry had chosen clothes that made him look like a very young girl. Then he made him go out dressed like that and they cruised around the area in his van. According to him, Terry made him do that a few times, and he said no one gave them a second look, and then one-day Terry drove across to Leeds, where he told him that he knew someone from his first prison spell for burglary. They went to this pub – he can't remember the name – Terry made him stay in the van while he went inside. He said that Terry was in there about an hour, and then came out alone and said he had some business to do, and he took him somewhere near the railway station. While they were driving down this street Terry told him that this was where prostitutes hung out and that he was going to have a bit of fun. He pulled up to one of the girls and started chatting to her while Saville sat in the front of the van. Saville says the woman never gave him a second glance and didn't realise he was actually a young boy, and so when Terry asked her to get in, she did. Terry then drove to this industrial estate, just outside the city and told the woman to get in the back. He made him get out and stand outside. He said he watched Terry have sex with her, and then he strangled her as soon as he finished – killed her in the back of the van while he was watching. He couldn't believe what he'd seen. He said he was terrified, and Terry told him that the police wouldn't believe him if he said what had happened, because he would tell them he was involved and he would also go to prison. He said Terry drove back to Barnwell with the girl's body covered up in the back of the van. They returned through the back-roads and they had to pull over because he was physically sick. He said Terry parked the van in an old garage on the estate until later that night, and when his mum went to bingo, Terry brought the body into the house wrapped up in an old blanket and told him to help him bury her in the cellar.' Pausing again, Hunter glanced at the faces of the MIT squad. They were hanging onto every word. He continued, 'That girl was Wendy Lomas. Terry apparently showed him a newspaper with her photograph in it and asked him how he felt about "doing someone?" A couple of months after that Terry drove him to Leeds, again dressed up as a girl, and they picked up a second girl – Barbara Mullins. He said Terry had sex with her and strangled her exactly like he'd done Wendy. They did the same again with her body. He said Terry made him help him bury Barbara in the cellar when his mum went out again, but this time Terry stripped the body and told him to put the girl's clothes on and stood there until he dressed in them.' Hunter saw a few of the team shaking their heads in disbelief. He continued, 'After that there was Glynis Young. Saville said that by this time Terry made him dress up as a girl nearly every time his mum went to bingo and they'd go for a drive around the area. He said that when they saw Glynis she was crying and Terry pulled over and asked her what was the matter, and she said she'd just fallen out with her boyfriend. Terry asked if she wanted a lift and at first she said no but then he pointed to Saville and said "look I've got my daughter in with me, I'm not going to bite you" and that's when she got in.' Hunter observed his colleagues for a moment, 'We all know the rest. Apparently when the police came he told Saville that he wouldn't tell on him, and of course he never did. He said that he and his mum used to go and visit Terry in prison, and that when his mum died he broke the news to him, and that's when Terry asked him to help him escape when he came out for the funeral. Saville's also admitted he was with Terry when they killed Ann Marie Banks and he watched him kill Lesley Jane Warren at the flat in Chapeltown, and helped him bring her body back and bury her. Again he was dressed in women's clothing, which fits with what our neighbour witness said.' Hunter took a deep breath, 'He also said that Terry took stuff off the bodies – bits of jewellery and a couple of purses and a few other things. Terry told him to hide them. We've found those items in the cellar at Dunford Bridge, so it ties everything up quite nicely. And, as you also know, we found Eric Wheelhouses ears. The sick bastard had kept those as trophies as well. It's certainly sealed Terry Braithwaite's fate. This time he'll not be coming out. He'll die in prison.'

* * *

At the bar, in the back room of the George and Dragon pub, Barry Newstead hooked an arm around Hunter's shoulders and man-hugged him. 'Good job me old mucker. Five murders detected and two serial killers locked up. Not bad for a beginner. I'll make a detective of you yet.'

Hunter broke into a grin and wriggled himself free from Barry's clutches, 'Coming from you I'll take that as a compliment.'

'It is, bearing in mind how you performed on that first job we worked on, remember?'

'You won't ever let me ever forget it, will you?'

Barry started chuckling. 'It still makes me laugh every time I think about it. Those two paramedic's faces were a picture.'

'I was so embarrassed afterwards.'

'That was a classic faux pas I'll never forget. In fact, if I'm still around for your retirement it'll be something I put into my speech. There was our female victim, lying on the floor, stabbed at least a dozen times by her husband. I'm there, putting on the cuffs and locking him up, and there you are drawing around her outline with yellow chalk. Just as I'm asking you what on earth you're doing, those two paramedics come rushing in, and you reply, "I'm just drawing around her body for evidence," The paramedics just stopped in their tracks and looked at you as though you were out of your mind, and I had to say, "but she's not dead. She's still alive!" Your face! You didn't know where to put yourself. It was a good job she was unconscious at the time. Seeing you doing that might have given her a heart attack, and seen her off good and proper.' Barry started to laugh again.

'All right, all right. You've had your fun. I was a naïve detective back then. I thought it was like I saw in the movies. I didn't know you didn't draw around bodies.'

'Certainly not round live ones.' Once more he guffawed. Then, straightening his face, he added, 'And now I have to say, credit where credit's due. That was a good result today. You've more than redeemed yourself over the years. Especially with this one. The case will make headline news tomorrow, and you're not going to get a look in, you know that?'

Hunter shrugged, 'That's not what we sign up for though, is it? At least I've the satisfaction of knowing what my contribution was. You know what it's like – you've had the same happen to you over the years. You just get on with it don't you? We didn't join this job for praise, just to make a difference.'

'You sound like an advert,' he smirked. Barry slugged the last of his beer, set down his empty glass and raised a hand to catch the bar man's attention. Turning, he asked Hunter, 'Want a top up?'

Hunter eyed his glass. It was still half full. 'No thanks mate, better not, this is my second. The last thing I need is to get breathalysed. I've had enough of being suspended to last me a lifetime.'

Barry handed his glass over to the waiting barman and took out a fiver. When the barman stepped away to pull his pint, Barry indicated over his shoulder to a trestle-seat where Dawn Leggate was sitting, chatting with Grace and Carol Ragen. 'What about what's happened in the gaffer's life eh? I mean Mike almost getting killed by a hit and run driver, and then discovering it was her ex that did it, that must be a real shocker. What with this enquiry, and all that going on, I don't know how she's functioned some days, especially the ACC and Professional Standards getting involved. That is really some weight to carry around on your shoulders. I only hope we catch him soon for her sake.'

Hunter agreed with a nod. He wanted to look back over his shoulder, to where the other three were sat, but knew that Dawn was savvy enough to guess that they were discussing her and so resisted. He said, 'I have to say I have the deepest admiration for her. Things are not going to be easy for her, the position she's in. There're a lot of jealous bosses out there who will try and make capital of this. It's probably scuppered her chances of the next rank. I feel sorry for her. She's a very good gaffer. I thought after Mike no one would replace him but we couldn't have wished to get a better boss.'

'I have to agree,' replied Barry, accepting his freshly filled glass from the barman and handing over his money. He'd swallowed a good quarter of the beer by the time the man returned with his change. Wiping the froth from his moustache he added, 'Anyway the good thing is, we know who we're after. Jack can't stay on the run for ever. The Mounties always get their man,' he chuckled.

The MIT squad all finished their drinks at roughly the same time. Hunter was the first to say he had enough and everyone agreed that it was time for home.

Pulling on his overcoat, Hunter checked his watch. nine-fifteen p.m. He suddenly realised how hungry he was. The last time he'd eaten was seven hours ago and that had only been a ham salad sandwich. He decided he'd grab some supper on the way home and eat it while watching the news. He pulled out his car keys from his coat pocket and was the first to step out of the side door into the pub car park. As he aimed the fob at his Audi, he became conscious of Barry and the girls following him out. He was about to turn and wish them goodnight when a pair of headlights flashed on, catching him in full beam, instantly blinding him. At the same time as a myriad of bright dots and flashes exploded into his field of vision, he heard the loud revving of an engine, followed by a squeal of tyres. His instinct told him it was coming directly for him, and, although he couldn't see a damn thing, he flung himself sideways, shouldering the wall.

* * *

Barry stood in the side doorway zipping up his coat, keeping his eye on Hunter making his way to his car. As Dawn, Grace and Carol appeared behind him, he stepped into the car park and waited for them to join him. Then, the four of them began their stroll to their cars. In the instant he saw Hunter's car indicators flash on he saw a set of headlights blaze into life at the back of the car park and caught the screech of tyres as it raced out of its parking spot. It took him just one second to realise the speeding car was heading towards them, especially that it was zeroing in on Dawn, who was a good few yards away. Barry instantly leapt into action, launching himself towards his boss, and just as the car was about to plough into her, he threw himself sideways, catching her with his bulk, bundling her aside. The car's offside thumped his thighs and mid-section, smashing into him with such force that it rocketed him upwards, and spiralled him backwards, flinging him to the tarmac with a sickening crunch.

* * *

The collision with the wall knocked all the wind out of Hunter, but his actions saved him from a worse fate – the speeding car missed him by as little as two feet. As it flew past he could just make out that only one person was in it, though he couldn't make out who the driver was.

Following its path, preparing to note its registration, he heard a loud bang, and simultaneously saw a human shape being tossed into the air. At the same time, he saw the car veer out of control, and a split-second later watched it smash head-on into the corner of an outbuilding opposite the pub side-entrance. Pushing himself away from the wall, he sprinted towards the driver's side and yanked open the door, throwing it back against its hinges. The airbag had detonated and the driver's face and chest were resting against the cushion. The man was letting out a light moan. Reaching inside, Hunter grabbed hold of the driver's jacket collar and, with a swift heave, dragged him sideways out of his seat, slinging him heavily towards the ground. The dark haired man let out a sharp yell as he hit the floor, followed by another as Hunter fell on top of him. In a flash Hunter was grabbing at his arm, ramming it up his back, at the same time pressing his face into the tarmac. The man let out a loud squeal and, with eyes bulging, started screaming, 'This is your fault. I told you this wasn't finished.'

Hunter was trying to make sense of it all and then Dawn appeared at his side. He glanced up at her while trying to strengthen the arm-lock on his struggling prisoner. He could see her face was horror-struck and she yelled, 'Jack!' it all fitted into place. Before he could say anything, Grace was beside him, coming to his assistance. She had her handcuffs out of her bag and was searching out Jack Leggate's wrist. Hunter twisted one hand outwards and she clamped on the first cuff. Then she grabbed his other arm and completed the task. As soon as the restraints were in place Jack stopped wriggling.

Positioning one knee in the middle of his back Hunter switched his gaze to where he had seen someone hit by Jack's car. What he saw made his stomach churn. Carol Ragen was kneeling beside Barry, a look of astonishment on her face. Although the car park was only bathed in weak light from the pub's windows, Hunter could see how misshapen and still his friend lay. A dark pool surrounded his head and his eyes were closed. A strange sensation overcame him. It was the same feeling as when he'd seen Shaggy lying on the road after he'd been shot. The word 'no' was repeatedly screaming inside his head. Pushing himself off from Jack he ran to his friend's side and dropped to his knees. His eyes scrambled the full length of Barry's crumpled torso, before settling on his chest. He concentrated hard on the sternum section, seeking out Barry's breathing, but there appeared to be no movement. He pressed an ear to his chest, willing to hear or feel something, but there was nothing. He glanced up and shouted, 'Get an ambulance! For fuck's sake get an ambulance!'

* * *

Outside the Intensive Care theatre, Hunter wandered aimlessly back and forth along the corridor, waiting for news. A team were working on his buddy in theatre two; they had been doing so for over half an hour. He kept returning to the theatre door, pressing an ear to it, listening to the frantic activity going on behind, trying to visualise what was happening. Although he couldn't pick out anything that was being said, he knew it didn't sound good – that his friend's life was in danger. He was about to return to the door again when the ICU entrance doors crashed open and in stumbled

Sue Siddons – Barry's partner – followed by Grace and Carol Ragen. Sue was wearing a sweatshirt and jeans and by her lack of make-up he guessed she'd come straight from her bed. Her face wore a look of horror. She made a bee-line for him.

'They've said Barry's been knocked down!'

Hunter was about to respond when theatre two's doors opened and out stepped a slim man in green scrubs pulling down his face-mask. The expression he bore did not look as though he was the bearer of good news.

Sue reached Hunter's side and she grabbed his arm. Hunter's gaze leapt from the surgeon, to her and then back.

The man directed his gaze at Sue and in a calm voice, he said, 'Mrs Newstead?'

Shaking her head Sue replied, 'We're not married – I'm Barry's partner.'

'It's not good news I'm afraid!' the man said softly 'When Barry was bought in he had suffered very serious injuries. He had a lot of internal bleeding. We operated to try and stem it, but there were complications and he had a cardiac arrest.' He paused and took a deep breath. 'We did our best to save him, but I'm sorry to tell you that he died a few moments ago.'

Sue let out a howl that was almost animal-like.

Hunter felt her legs buckle and he snapped his arms around her to stop her falling. Holding onto her, grabbing her even tighter, he felt her head press against his neck. She started to tremble and then she sobbed. He could feel his chest tighten, at the same time his eyes started to well up. He tried to hold himself together, but Sue's sobbing overwhelmed him and he couldn't stop himself from weeping. Within seconds both were inconsolable.

AFTERWORD

I would like to thank the following people, who collectively, have helped turn an idea into a published novel.

First up, Kevin Ware. I first met Kevin in the cells at Barnsley, when I was a Detective Sergeant and he was a drugs support worker providing care and services to drug abusers. After our first meeting it would be fair to say that, thereafter, Kevin became a port of call whenever I dealt with anyone who had a drug habit. Upon my retirement, I bumped into Kevin at the gym and we talked about my writing. I told him about the 'Beast' character I was developing and he told me about his time working at Rampton hospital. The up-shot was that Kevin helped me 'flesh out' Terrence Arthur Braithwaite.

Next up, forensic anthropologist, Dr Anna Williams. Anna came to a three-day crime writing event I organised and I took the opportunity to probe her about her fascinating job. Anna gratefully helped me with the excavation and examination of my corpses.

I cannot thank enough, fellow writers Lesley Merrin and Sam Swanney, and my wife Liz, who read my first draft, and kindly pointed out what worked and what didn't. Their help was invaluable.

Finally, there is Wills, my cover designer. Even though he takes no notice of my ideas, he comes up with some terrific images. Thanks also go to Susan Hunt, my proof reader and editor, and I cannot finish without giving special thanks to Darren Laws, CEO of Caffeine Nights. Not just because he is my publisher, but because he goes that extra mile. He always responds to every phone call, text and e-mail and is the nicest guy to do business with.

Michael Fowler